Periscope City

Periscope City

Where the lonely go to live alone

by Benjamin Talbot

Periscope City

Where the lonely go to live alone

ISBN
978-1-957224-43-5 (paperback)
978-1-957224-44-2 (epub)

Published by Current Words Publishing, LLC.
Dianne Pearce, editor and publisher.
David Yurkovich, designer.
Angela Walker, proofreader.

currentwords.com

Contents

Periscope City

Periscope City

A sign greeted me at the border: *Periscope City: Where the Lonely Go to Live Alone.*

It spoke my language, so I crossed in by foot, to the nearest place it took me to. That place was a one-story house with a long driveway called the Institute. There, they asked me dozens of questions about my immediate past and made me take a personality exam. I told them the truth: that I was a thirty-four-year-old loner whose friends had deserted him for marriage or death. They set me up in the Cramden Hotel.

During the first week, I interacted with only housekeeping and the concierge. They were all robots. It was the best the town could do to live up to its tagline.

—

Although I loved loneliness, I was still lonely as hell. After months of wallowing about my life situation, sinking into the lack of fellow humans, there was nothing I wanted more than to mix it up. I thought being lonely among robots was a different lonely as being lonely among humans. The scratch needed to be itched.

The concierge suggested a dating app called *Loner,* and the concierge said it had the best reputation for keeping the lonesome lonely. I filled out a profile and submitted it to the AI gods for review. It matched me with Raylene, a blonde Puerto Rican who stood over six feet. Her profile said very little about her beyond the fact that she'd moved from Buffalo, New York, and loved pets over people. In her picture, she sat on a snowy park bench and wore a fleece jacket. A French bulldog sat in her lap, and it wore a black-and-white dog poncho. It looked like a staged photo, like something in an L.L. Bean catalog, but where L.L. Bean was trying to pull off cozy, it was a cold, plastic, disconnected photo. I assumed her entire profile was an attempt at sarcasm.

Do you want to meet or not? she wrote.

Because of my lust for tall women, I wrote her back: *Yes.*

I have tickets to The Late Show, she wrote. *Meet me at Geraldine Park at eight. I'll be at the corner of Alaska and Winter Bear. And don't be awkward.*

—

When I showed up, Raylene was sitting on a snowy park bench in the same jacket as her photo, with her service bulldog in her lap. The dog even wore a black-and-white poncho. Raylene's smile was all the picture was missing.

"Joe?" she asked.

Her perfume was cedar, or maybe it was the trees. Whatever the case, the scent had found its way to me, and it smelled lovely. The *Loner* profile was missing a smell.

"Raylene?"

"No," she said. "Of course it is. How would I know your name was Joe?"

The bulldog barked at me.

"Sheepshead, knock it off," she said.

Sheepshead? After Raylene fed her a pill, the dog calmed down. The pill must've been a fast-acting depressant, which they sold over the counter here in Periscope City. I know because of my own dog, but he didn't need medication like me.

"You look different from your picture," she said.

Ditto. Not only did she frown but her hair wasn't blonde. It was purple. "How so?" I said.

"I thought you were taller," she said.

I ignored her comment (let's call it an insult), already being my tallest.

"Ask me something," she said.

She was testing me, but then I remembered how sarcastic her profile had been attempting to be. The memory of it made me sweat a little with anxiety because I tried to think of something witty to say quickly, so I used a cliché. "If you could have dinner with anyone, who would it be?"

"Come on, dude," she said. "Ask me something else."

I gestured out to the surrounding park with my hands as if that were the explanation. "It was all I could think of," I said.

"I told you, don't be awkward," she said. "What about you? Who would you have dinner with?"

I hated the question, too.

"Abraham Lincoln," I said, and the words tasted like tinned fish.

"Why?"

"He was the first person who came to mind," I said.

"Lame," she said. "Now ask me a good question."

"Okay," I said. "Why did you name your dog Sheepshead?"

"Sheepshead Bay was the last place where I went with my husband," she said.

"Did you separate?" I said.

She pressed her beanie down to her eyebrows, and I did the same with my trapper hat. We shared an awkward silence. It was what I got for asking a good question. Since she didn't bring up anything about her husband, I kept my past a secret, that I had no friends, just a mother who loved me back in Colorado—so call me a mama's boy if you would like. She supported me moving here so I could go on a writer's retreat, my Arcadian dream. The retreat was to myself in the canyons of Periscope City. I couldn't go for another season, not until the spring.

"And what's your dog's name?" Raylene asked, assuming I had one.

"Jeff," I said.

"You named your service dog Jeff?" she said, as if it was beyond belief.

I thought of an explanation. "My brother's name is Jeff," I said. If I had a brother. I'm an only child. The first time I looked at the dog, I thought of the name Jeff.

"I see," she said. "And what did you score on the test?"

"You mean the Franklin Loneliness Test? Green."

"Okay, so you're a Middleton," she said. "That's fine."

"What's a Middleton?" I said.

"The middle," she said. "The loneliest. You're desperate for someone but you're too iffy."

"Sounds like a horoscope," I said. I wanted to ask if "too iffy" referred to me being iffy about a desire to be with someone, which would be okay and kind of cool, or if it referred to me as if labeling me an iffy person about everything. *How could I bring myself to express that question out loud?* "What else?"

"Are you staying at the Cramden?" she asked.

"Yes," I said.

"My heart pours out to you," she said.

"It's okay," I said. "What's yours?"

"I'm not telling," she said.

I was offended. Quid pro quo. "I told you I was staying at the Cramden." I tried to keep the whine out of my voice.

"Why are you worried?" she said. "It's not like I'm stalking you."

Stalking was the opposite of my worries. It was someone actually following me and desiring me that I wanted, but I also wanted my space. I didn't know what I wanted. Let's put it that way. "And what was your score?" I said.

"I scored red."

"And that means?"

"It means I'm Middleton/Antisocial," she said. "I hate meeting people except on rare occasions. It means I have boundaries. But anyway, fuck a label, right?"

Exactly. Fuck a label.

She lit a joint. I loved her Botox lips and the marijuana smell on a snowy night; it mixed just perfectly, proportionally, with the cedar smell. She held the joint out. Weed did weird things to me, like make me hallucinate. But I puffed anyway, hoping for a connection with her after thirty-four years on Earth where I could barely connect with anyone.

A senior woman appeared in the park with a Saint Bernard. The Saint Bernard raised his paw at Sheepshead, but Sheepshead was too sleepy for niceties. She brought her dog right over to us like she knew us and had expected us to be there. It didn't seem too "Periscope City" of her.

"My God, what a cutie," Raylene said. She referred to the Saint Bernard and avoided me. I tried to include myself in their conversation.

Sheepshead took a whiff of the other dog's balls. The Saint Bernard stared at me not out of curiosity but out of fear. It must've been the weed, but a human lived inside of him. His eyes screamed at me, "Please, let me out of here!"

I interrupted them. "Sorry, but can we go inside?"

Raylene rolled her eyes. "I guess we're going inside."

After a couple of steps, I looked back at the Saint Bernard. He and his owner stayed put. "Please help me," he said, directly into my mind.

—

His eyes haunted me as much as the studio Raylene, Sheepshead, and I walked into. Raylene and I were the only humans in there besides the guest and the host. Animatronic dolls took the other seats. I tried to adjust to them—the robots, too. They seemed to me the most off-putting things about the city. The Institute had them working menial jobs. But of course they did. There was no way I could've avoided them. They knew my name at the coffee shop, even though I forgot to tell them what it was. While those dolls in the studio were props, mannequins in motion.

The show was for public access television, where the guest promoted his homemade pumpkin soup. He'd left it at his hotel, so he just described it. After the robotic host told a joke, a robot on the floor flipped a switch for canned laughter. All the dolls grinned. Speaking of talk shows, they have always creeped me out: thousands of viewers watching idle chitchat. I would rather have chosen something else for us to do if Raylene and I were an "us."

The studio lights made the dolls—of all different genders, races, and sizes—gleam like wax. Their eyes were wide open in their sockets, like the ones on ventriloquist dummies. Otherwise they passed as humans and probably more so on television screens. My head swiveled, trying to get a look at what the TV viewer must have been seeing.

A doll three rows back in a leather skirt caught my eye.

"Don't look too much," Raylene said. "You'll crick your neck."

"At what?" I said.

"You're looking pretty hard at it," she said. She knew that the both of us knew what she was talking about.

But what was more absurd? Her jealousy or my attraction to a doll?

"Have you been to the Dollhouse?" she said.

"What's the Dollhouse?"

"Sex dolls," she said. "My favorite is Remy."

She pointed at Remy four rows down.

"It's Russian," she said. "It speaks many other languages, and it reads a hundred books a week. I'm talking about my dream guy."

How could I compete with the tanned and fit Remy while I was full of bones and paste? I'd read fewer than a hundred books spanning thirty-four years.

Anyway, for the show with the chitchat and the pumpkin soup recipes, they'd set the stage like a living room. A purple sky, a green moon, and orange stars over a brown meadow appeared through a window. What if it was a painting? Everything seemed to be.

"I think someone might be watching us," I told Raylene. But Raylene had fallen fast asleep. Sheepshead, too, in her lap. Now I realized I was light years away from Colorado. *Why did I follow the advertisement on my social media feed and come to Periscope City? Am I that desperate to be alone?* My thoughts swallowed me up. *What am I even thinking?* Whatever it was, I yelled it in the studio. The host and the guest looked up at me. I left before losing my marbles.

—

Before that night, a lot of time had been spent avoiding talk shows, whether in person or on television. In Los Angeles, where I once visited, the show interns would wave me down on the street, try to give me free tickets. At the same time, the Scientologists would try to give me pamphlets and a personality test. The gifts came with strings attached.

Anyway, where is Raylene? Why is her profile deleted? Why didn't I wake her up and ask for her phone number before leaving the studio? She was nowhere to be found. I asked of her whereabouts to the pumpkin soup creative, as well as a sad man in a wheelchair, when I came across them at the coffee shop, but they pretended I was a stranger, even though I'd come across them once or several times. Even if I was a stranger, the pumpkin soup guest should've recognized me after my outburst.

—

Her perfume lingered around the bench where I'd met her. I had trouble sleeping because of my obsession, so I tried to distract myself.

—

There were many places in Periscope City to occupy a lonely person's thoughts. A concierge worker at the Cramden suggested Waldenland. Maybe the Institute had programmed it to recommend that, but I used to dream about having a theme park to myself, so I went.

—

Waldenland was "The Loneliest Place on Earth." Robots serviced the rides. I sat on the Isolationist, possibly the tallest Ferris wheel in the world. It settled me inside and took me backwards, up, and left me at the top on a porch swing with a safety bar. The robot left me above the canyons and the maple trees. Periscope City down below, without houses or apartments, was like Vegas with snow: all hotels and one casino but without the sun or tourists. The architecture looked Norwegian: practical, solitary, primitive, but shielding; it was architecture to be alone in. If they would ever reveal Periscope City, people would've known it as the loneliest city in the world. It thrived on safety, shelter, light traffic, and convenience. I could have any place to myself as long as I made reservations.

—

For instance, the Lone Dragon allowed only one person at a time. I waited outside in the cold for the single customer to come out of the restaurant so that I could go in. One robot, as the restaurant staff, would bring out trays for the all-one-person-can-eat buffet and seemed to know how much I could eat.

I cracked open a fortune cookie: *You shall be alone forever.* It didn't comfort me, so I cracked another one and another one. Each fortune was about loneliness. The robot kept bringing them, and I kept cracking them for something to show Raylene, if we were ever to meet again. All of the fortunes were too negative. The sliced oranges they came with had piled up to an awkward extent. I crammed the slices of orange on top of my leftover fried rice as best as I could and stuffed the last one in my mouth like a plastic smile.

—

She was somewhere in this universe walking Sheepshead. Why hadn't I bumped into her given how low the population was? She wasn't stalking me, but in a way, I was stalking her. One night, when I was roaming through downtown with Jeff, I confused her with a storefront mannequin.

"Can I buy it?" I asked the manager.

"You may not," it said. "It is far too expensive for you."

I'd come across a smug robot.

—

The staff at the Cramden treated me like a stranger, which brought me the comforting feeling that I was only vacationing there, not living there. Except for one day, a trainee behind the front desk said, "Good morning, Joe. Are you off to get your bagel and espresso?"

I complained to the manager.

"I apologize, sir," it said. "It's a new model. How about a weeklong pass to the gym and the sauna to yourself?"

How could I pass up that offer? It granted me the peak hours, too, from one in the morning to two in the morning. But I still missed Raylene. She could've been sitting with me in the sauna. Even though we mixed like chicken and saltwater taffy, I still wanted her.

—

A month after our date, it was snowing one afternoon. I looked at my options for an hour but had trouble deciding which show to watch on the streaming services. Alexa wanted me to choose one show while she sent a refill to the pharmacy for Zinopranil, a medication for the dark side of loneliness. I was willing to try anything.

"Alexa, give me directions to the Dollhouse," I said.

It spoke through my ear chips. "I am sorry, but I could not find any results. What is it, so I can add it to my database?"

I worried that Alexa would've judged me.

"Just a place with dolls," I said.

"For what?" it asked.

"Certain things," I said.

"Certain things? In case you were unaware, increased libido is a side effect of Zinopranil."

Ever since its latest update, it could track my movements, from me talking to myself to me playing with myself.

—

The Cramden kicked out its guests after six hours to prevent them from isolating themselves for too long. Some guests had committed suicide. Alexa told me it was time to exit, so I left the hotel with Jeff and took him for a walk in the snow.

When I stepped outside of the hotel, Raylene was across the street, sitting on a bench, reading a book in the cold. On the one day I'd forgotten to obsess over her, I found that she had finally shown back up in my life.

"Raylene?" I said.

She looked over at me. "Joe?"

I crossed the street with Jeff leading the way and tried not to show how eager I was to see her.

When I stopped in front of her, she kneeled to him.

"Is this Jeff?" she said.

"You remembered his name," I said. I had a catch in my voice, but I hid it well.

She reached down and petted him. "Aww, a Labrador, you cutie pie. U-gee-poo-gee-poo." She looked fantastic in cowgirl boots and a dress with a leather jacket.

"Where's Sheepshead?" I asked.

"The poor thing is sick," she said.

"With the flu?" I said.

"No, it's her social anxiety," she said.

"You know pets," I said. "Always taking after their owners."

Raylene stopped petting Jeff and looked up at me. "What's that supposed to mean?"

"It was a joke," I said. "I meant nothing by it."

"Whatever," she said. "Why did you shave your beard?"

"I was bored," I said.

"Makes sense, I guess."

"What have you been doing? It's been a month since we've seen each other."

"Why don't we get a drink and catch up?" she said. "There's a dive bar on Howard Hughes Lane."

Maybe I obsessed over her, but it was a fantasy, therefore completely in my script. *What if a second date leads to attachment, commitment, accusations? What if it leads to marriage, restraining orders, teenage daughters? Where is my self-control? How can I handle my feelings?* They conflicted me.

She was waiting for my answer. "Well?"

I'd been celibate for five years, and not by choice. Well, maybe somewhat of a choice. I'd been sober for four of those years, and most days, I preferred sleep and solitude over companionship, but like I said, the Cramden had locked me out for six hours.

—

She ordered a Dryft. We sat with Jeff between us in the back seat of an electric car that drove itself.

"Alexa, take us to the Hideaway on Howard Hughes Lane," Raylene said.

Alexa fed the directions to the GPS.

We sat in silence on the way there.

—

A robot for a bouncer at the Hideaway met us at the front and looked down on us, all 6'7" of it. Black hair hung to its elbows. It let Raylene go in but made me wait outside in the snow with Jeff until someone else left. The extent of the wait thrummed in my head like an aneurysm. *Is Raylene worth the wait?* It was pointless for an awkward man to argue with a bouncer, whether human or android.

It came back ten minutes later with an old loner, drunk and crying over his dead wife. *Poor guy. I could end up like him someday.*

"You may go in," the bouncer said to me, and unhooked the velvet rope.

A country song started playing on the jukebox. Every song on it was about loneliness. Raylene sat with a Tequila Sunrise in January. I thought she deserved a round on me.

The Hideaway was your everyday dive bar with a pool table. Just like every other lonely activity in Periscope City, only one person played nine-ball at a time while the others waited for their turn. I realized how far nine was from one.

The customers helped themselves at a drink station, one of those thingamajigs like you see at a movie theater. I pressed a glowing screen, and a soft drink poured out of the nozzle. Except that machine served alcohol. I pushed a lever for ice and the thumbnails for beer, liquor, and chaser and made a Tequila Sunrise for her and a soda for myself.

When I sat at the stool next to her, she fixated on my drink. "What're you drinking?" she asked.

I kept my sobriety a secret. People usually freaked out about it. "You poor thing." "Congratulations." "What an achievement." But I still wanted a drink. My social life was in shambles. It was best if I surrounded myself with people in the same position. But where were those people? Perhaps hiding somewhere. There was a rehab in town at the Handler Hotel, but I was afraid it would turn me into one of those people who talked about Jesus all the time.

"It's Rico's vodka with soda," I said.

"No shit," she said. "I've never had Rico's vodka. Let me have a sip."

When she reached in for it, I stopped her in time. "No no no no no."

"What's the problem?" she said.

"I have a thing about people drinking from my glass," I said.

"What did I tell you about being awkward?" she said.

I changed the subject. "Anyway." I set the Sunrise next to her glass. "Next round is on me."

She shoved the glass back to me. "No," she said.

"What do you mean no?" I said. "You invited me here."

"I said no," she said. "Now give me my space. It's common courtesy. Leave a stool between us."

Everyone else in there was doing it, too. *No big deal.* People wanted their space everywhere in that town. I shouldn't have taken it personally.

One time back in Colorado, when I was journaling at my favorite coffee shop, an old man sat right next to me at a table. He and his little dog were almost on top of me. I thought, *That's it. No more. If only there was somewhere to have space and be alone.* A week later, I moved here.

"Let's catch up," I said. "What have you been doing for the past month?"

"A lot of dating," she said.

Oh. Didn't see that one coming. Raylene was as blunt as she could be, coming from Buffalo.

"One of them is a football player," she said. "He just started being a loner."

I didn't want to hear about her dates, so I changed the subject.

"How's Remy?" I asked.

She reacted the same way as the time I'd asked about her husband: by pulling her beanie down to her eyebrows.

"We're not talking right now," she said.

"Oh, sorry," I said.

Another awkward silence. I just didn't know what questions to ask.

Her cell phone rang. She looked at the screen. "Hey, it's that football player. I'll be right back."

I couldn't believe it.

After she left her stool and went to talk with him in private, it was obvious I'd fallen into the friend zone. Perhaps "fallen" wasn't the right word. Maybe I'd been in the zone all along. Rejection at thirty-four hurt worse than ever. My heart fell as flat as the soda water. The sulking began.

The Hideaway, with plenty of empty stools, had a mirror behind the bar. I could look at myself sulk. There was no bartender behind the counter because, as I'd described earlier, it was a self-service bar. All I could do was wait for her to come back into the bar. Even with Jeff and the Zinopranil pill I took in the morning, I felt the cold draft of loneliness. It ached when I was rejected, but I yearned for it whenever people wanted to be close to me. You just can't win.

Raylene came back to her stool after about ten minutes, a long ten minutes.

"Lamar is coming over," she said. "He's really sweet. You should get along with him."

"That's nice," I said.

She reached over and squeezed my hand. It wasn't a romantic squeeze but a pity squeeze. I tried to make my mouth like the orange slice was crammed in there, bright and plastic and smiling.

"It'll take a while," she said.

"What will?" I said.

"This town," she said. "Give it twenty-four months."

Twenty-four months sure sounded longer than two years. Thanks to homesickness, I considered moving back to Colorado, but I chose to gut it out.

The jukebox played "Only the Lonely," and Raylene knew all the words. The more I thought about it, the more it made sense. She wanted a friend for the night, an alternative to Remy before Lamar showed up to the Hideaway.

The Sunrise stared right back at me. What would one drink do? I rested my hand on an empty stool to my right. It comforted me until someone pulled it from under my fingers. I was brushed by a stiff wind, close to the feeling of falling off a cliff, the same way it always felt whenever a stool was taken from my side. That was how it felt for the rest of the night at the Hideaway.

Rubble

I drove to my alma mater in Long Beach. During the pandemic, not a single car passed me on the freeway. Songs from my college days were playin' on the stereo. It made me teary-eyed, but when I got into town, everythin' appeared black and white.

—

Ain't nobody on the campus except for me. All them buildings looked hollow. The sounds of voices and footsteps were alone with me. Not that I was seein' things or nothin' like that. Rather, the past immersed me with the laughter, the students walkin' to class, the birds singin' in the arboretum. All seemed real. I pulled a white periwinkle by the stem. Its smell made me think about the time I hugged Erica Campbell goodbye before we went our separate ways after graduation.

I could smell them memories above the rubble.

—

My name echoed through them loudspeakers at the stadium. I sat in the bleachers and thought back to a glorious Saturday night when it was cold in November. Whistles blew under a sold-out crowd. Our offense broke from the huddle. I pretended to be my dad in the bleachers—God rest his soul—watchin' the youthful version of yours truly on the field. Fourth and one at the Sacramento State forty-eight-yard line. The Mule took the rock and bulldozed through a brick wall of tacklers. They fell on top of him and swallowed him in a pile. "First down," the announcer said. Fans chanted louder than the Rose Bowl. "Mule, Mule, Mule, Mule…." Thanks to me, we iced the victory.

Anyhoo, the Santa Ana wind was the only thing that kept me company that afternoon.

—

I sat on a steel bench in downtown, wearin' latex gloves and a surgical mask, holdin' the periwinkle in both hands. Hard to believe how many years had passed. I remembered stumblin' with my friends to Cuebricks, my favorite bar, and then the tattoo parlor to have my arms inked up. Only the names of them places had changed. Them nights were gone now, long gone. I felt like a ghost who'd damn well slept through too many chances. Where was Jerry Smith, Erica Campbell, and Brian Stoop? I missed them times when I would tag along with them. Oh, to have them nights again, in the cigar patio as a happy drunk, thinkin' *Yes, it'll all work out*, not to be a bitter drunk like now.

How I wished the bars were open, so I could've busied the bartender's ears about them times, but all them shops and bars and restaurants were closed during the lockdown.

The wind blew papers past me. It was the apocalypse under a gray-ass sky. I held on to the periwinkle. The whole damn purpose of drivin' there was just to be sentimental. Where had them years gone?

Even when nobody else was around, no cars or people on the boulevard, I heard the drums, the blues guitars, the pool balls crackin' in Cuebrick's. Violins pourin' from the trattoria. Punk rock blarin' from the tattoo parlor. But Cuebrick's had turned into a vegan yogurt shop, the trattoria a bank, the tattoo joint a cash-and-loan.

—

The piano bar still existed. Except a sign on the door read: DON'T WORRY, FOLKS. WE'LL BE UP AND RUNNING SOON. Dated back in March. It was November.

The back door happened to be unlocked. They'd ripped the inside apart. Saloon doors had fallen off their hinges. Them duelin' pianos were gone. Debris cracked under my shoes where peanut shells used to be.

Pianos started playin' when I approached the counter. There appeared a crowd, and the colors faded in. In slid the patrons, chirpin'. I squeezed past them folks on my way to the bartender and heard them familiar voices. My college friends waited for me. Where had they been all them years? Ain't none of them had called me back.

"Look who showed up," Jerry said.

"Oh, man, it's the Mule," Brian said.

And Erica. "Where have you been?" she said. She still looked twenty-three.

Matter of fact, ain't none of them looked like they'd aged.

I sat at the end of the counter, where I used to drink my Moscow Mules. "I wondered about y'all." *Is Jerry practicin' law like he studied? What about Brian makin' films or Erica becomin' a teacher?*

"We've been here," Jerry said.

"Yeah? Funny, 'cause you never called me back." I sounded salty.

"Come on, Mule," Brian said. "Life goes on."

For some.

Them duelin' pianos were pickin' up the pace. Hands were clappin' to "Saturday Night's Alright for Fighting." Even on a Tuesday afternoon, the piano bar threw a party: two-for-ones all day. Half off on mixed drinks for students who wore their jerseys. I wore mine, the number forty-eight, just like the yard line I'd crossed to win the game.

Frank, the bartender, wearin' the same damn black bowtie and white dress shirt, tossed me a coaster, which slid across the counter to my fingertips.

"What're you having, boss?" he said.

"Boss?" I said. "What am I havin'? Frank, it's me."

"I recognize the face," he said.

"Please, Frank," I said.

"What do you want?" he said. "It's been twenty years."

Twenty years? God almighty. If only them decades could've returned .... And to think I've never grown up, never will.

"Come on, I'm busy," Frank said.

I slapped a twenty on the counter. "A Moscow Mule, no ice, like them old days, Frank."

He didn't waste no time makin' it.

Erica cozied up to me and yelled over the crowd and the music. "I missed you so much."

"Get outta here," I said.

"It's true," she said. "I kept throwing you hints."

Erica was a sorority doll, a Playboy model (from the college edition)—not even kiddin'. But zoom, my chances done passed me by. She could've been the perfect girlfriend, the perfect wife, the perfect mother to my young'uns. "Where have you been this whole time?" I said.

She kept everythin' brief: how she'd married a senator and had three kids. I asked about it all. After a scandal broke out and made the headlines, she divorced him and got free. "I didn't love him. Status didn't mean a thing. I wanted passion. I wanted *you*."

"What do I say to that?"

"Say you'll kiss me," she said.

I was about to until Frank brought the drink. What a buzzkill, even though he made a stiff one.

"Too weak or too strong?" he said.

I took a sip. "Always on the money with you," I said.

Frank wouldn't accept no compliment.

I slipped the mask down to my chin. Erica didn't wear none. Matter of fact, ain't nobody except me wore one.

We kissed, and her lips tasted like peppermint. She turned around and fell into my arms. We sang along to "Benny and the Jets."

A waitress dropped a shot glass from her tray, and it exploded on a floor full of peanuts. My friends and the rest of the crowd were laughin' at her. Everybody had fun at her expense. It got more alive in there.

I slapped another twenty on the counter. "Shots on me, Frank," I said. "Four Irish Car Bombs."

"Hey, Mule," Jerry said. "Let's head to Cuebrick's."

I would've been the first one there on any day of the week. That was if they didn't serve waffle cones like they did now—vegan ones at that. My fantasy was losin' its grip.

"What kind of person wears his jersey to a bar?" Brian said. His greasy hair stayed the same: parted to the side with a curl hangin' over his forehead. His Adam's apple still bulged through his skinny neck. I hated his smart-ass demeanor.

Jerry laughed with him. They would gang up on me.

"Shut up, Brian," Erica said. "The Mule gets half off if he wears it."

"Sorry, I forgot," Brian said. "Like I go to bars anymore. You know I'm a family man. I got things to take care of. What about you, Mule? What're you taking care of?"

Not a goddamn thing, not even myself. Loneliness had made me pretty damn neglectful at times.

"Mule, what happened with that scout?" Jerry said. "Did you ever make the pros?"

Jerry, still with his dimpled chin. All them girls loved him. Made me damn near jealous.

As for a scout? What scout? I made that up to impress everybody. Ain't no scout was gonna help a fullback. That position wasn't hardly around no more.

They started playin' "Purple Rain," which made me soft inside my heart.

"Mule, you okay?" Jerry said.

I got even more sentimental. Everybody sang along while I sat with my drink in the corner, studyin' scratches on the counter that ain't use to be there. A spiderweb hung over the shelf where them liquor bottles used to be.

"Mule?" Jerry said.

I kept starin' away. Them voices drifted like them clouds outside. My dollars sat remainin' under my nose. Frank would've snatched them away in a heartbeat. But not no more. He's probably dead at this point.

Everythin' faded, even the drink in my hand. I was alone again among the rubble.

—

When I went back out to the boulevard, my ears were stuffed by them Santa Ana winds. Dead leaves were skippin' across the concrete. I caught a panic attack in front of a corner shop, losin' my breath behind my mask. The winds blew the periwinkle out of my hands. It rolled down the sidewalk. Nothin' was livin' except for the winds, the flower, a lady with a cart full of soda cans. Her wheels came to a halt. Them cans stopped rattlin'. I remembered her from twenty years ago beggin' for change outside of Cuebrick's and me givin' it to her. Now she was givin' me a dirty look and pointin' at me.

"I know you. You're that thief who used to take from me. Jesus died for you. He's coming for you."

I started hurryin' to my pickup, leavin' downtown for good, through the regrets, the anxiety. The trip made me numb. There was no reason to return.

—

After they found a vaccine, them cases dropped by the thousands. My office reopened. I commuted there again rather than work from home. I wished the lockdown was still happenin'.

—

My boss, Ash, who was ten years younger than me, went over my quarterly numbers.

It don't matter how much longer I'd been there than him 'cause he was still my supervisor.

He checked on the last three months. They'd promoted every other worker except for me, the oldest one, the one who'd worked there the longest.

It was in my manner, the way I conducted myself. The rubble showed.

Ash could see the depression beneath my fake enthusiasm. Hell, a child could've sensed that. I ain't never wanted to step up the corporate ladder. "I have some good news," Ash said. "Some bad news, too. But just so you know, the good news, like, totally outweighs the bad."

"Totally?"

"Yeah, totally, bruh," he said.

"Okay, the bad news first."

"The bad news is we had to let go of the stocks," he said.

Them stocks were candy corn anyway.

Spittle gathered at the corner of Ash's lips when he spoke. "In exchange for—drum roll," Ash said. "You ready for this?"

"Can't wait another second."

"Bruh, another year, another raise," he said. "How's that sound?"

They gonna add twenty cents more for every hour they got from me.

Yay. If I were to have a small American flag, I would've pulled it out and waved it around.

All them other workers that had moved up the ladder sat at their desks with their silky monitors. The OSX Delgado got the highest scores in Q4. But I knew the real reason it'd been promoted. Delgado got ahead by its looks. Apple desktops could seduce their way to the top without doin' much.

I left the office that night with less hope than when I'd gotten there.

—

Thanks to the pandemic, companies laid tons of folks off in the city. Ain't nobody could pay rent.

It was time to leave that dump after so many years, more than a decade before the lockdown. So long to them rats, them bed bugs, them cockroaches, that slumlord, too, who'd rather seen me starvin' on the corner. I found a vacancy at a building across the street.

After one ring, a woman said, "Hello," soundin' desperate. "Thank you so much for calling," she said.

"I found your ad online."

"It's getting scary," she said. "When can you get here?"

"In five minutes."

"I like you already," she said. "Just come to Unit Four. I'll start the coffee."

—

As soon as I sat down, she pushed a tablet across the desk and snuck a pen between my digits. "Just sign the leasing contract. We'll need proof of employment and two paychecks with a four-thousand-dollar minimum. Any questions?"

She'd spoken faster than them voices on them prescription ads. They had to make sure the tenant could pay rent. I got it. The place could've crumbled. On the other hand, who could afford to live there? Mama used to say, "Hey, any raise is better than nothin'."

"Any questions?" the lady repeated.

"I'm sorry. You said a paycheck for four thousand?"

"A paycheck, yes. You can also email me a copy of your statements. Your initials here and here and your signature here and here and it's yours on February first."

They paid me forty-four thousand a year before Uncle Sam took his twelve-thousand share. It was damn near impossible to look her in the eye. "Sorry, but I'm a little below that."

Her face dropped. "What?" she said. "What do you mean?"

How many other folks who'd applied there had told her that? "My last paycheck was twelve hundred."

"You're joking."

"Ain't nothin' funny 'bout that," I said. "But maybe we can work somethin' out."

She pulled the tablet and plucked the pen from my digits. "I'm sorry, but I wish you good luck."

I left with my tail between my legs.

On my way out, she said, "Maybe you should get a better job."

Her words were like a whip across my back. She may as well have said, "Clean yourself up, you squalid pig."

Goin' home, it was like one of them deals where you try to think of a sweet comeback to give her. They were all lame. All I could've given her was the old-fashioned "Fuck you, bitch."

Now what purpose was there? Dead-end job, trashy pad, friends had moved away, coulda had a wife but left her to be by myself, and not even a pet because the slumlord wouldn't allow no dogs. The only value in my life was a laptop, and it belonged to my company.

—

On just another Friday night, when I was readin' on social media people's rants about balloons, I scrolled down to an ad for somethin' named Periscope City:

Are you lonely?
Do you prefer to be alone?
Are you lonelier in a crowd than you are by yourself?

Yes, yes, and yes. But the real question was: How did it know about me? I'd typed loneliness in the search engine a few times in the last week. Just how did it find me from that?

Fast forward. I sold my pickup to the dealership for five hundred buckeroos. It felt alright to be five hundred dollars richer. Anyhoo, goodbye to the twenty-cent raise and that apartment I couldn't get. It was easy to open my fist on money that was never in it anyway, lettin' the coins fall on the street without no noise.

From there, I took a plane alone from Los Angeles to Periscope City—Lonersville. Them steps after I'd clicked on that ad told me to order me a Dryft ride.

A robot driver showed up at the airport and gave me the heebie-jeebies to say the least. Lots of them there, by what I seen from the backseat, directin' traffic and workin' in them shops. Hotel staff was all mechanical. The city lookin' like it was nothin' but hotels, and the buildings seemed Dutch or somethin'. It was a whole other world. The population was small. From what I could see in my quick looks through the windows of one of them electric cars, about two hundred of us was human.

—

The Dryft driver dropped me off at a place called the Institute. It was actually a house that had a curvy walkway to the front door, like Uncle George's pad in Plano.

I pressed a button next to the door.

Alexa said, "Come to the living room!" A singin' doormat said the same thing.

Young female robots filled the kitchen. The livin' room resembled Uncle George's, too.

Maybe I was homesick; maybe I was losin' my cool.

The leather farted when I sat on the couch. I saw issues on a coffee table of the same magazines as Uncle George's. They were magazines about sports, fishin', and country life. His Christmas parties were gettin' slimmer each year. Back in the day, the fam would pile up in his house. But damn near every year these days, this one passed, that one passed…. They were playin' musical chairs with death. I was the only cousin who showed up last time.

One of the kitchen robots said, "Brittany, take that out of your mouth. It's a cockroach."

"Oh, okay."

Two bots came to the livin' room, said their names, both of them with Jamaican accents. One of them was Brittany.

"The testing is about to start," Brittany said.

The other one had a name tag that said *Moonga*. Moonga said, "Come with me."

When I passed Brittany, somethin' crunched in its mouth.

I didn't know what else to do except follow Moonga through a hallway. "I'm just makin' sure I'm at the right place."

It ignored what I said. A question, really. It opened a door to a bare white room with nothin' but a robot at a desk. And then Moonga stepped inside a walk-in closet, closed the door.

The other model wasn't Jamaican or nothin' like that, more city-like than Moonga. Its name was Sharonica—like a cross between Sharon and Monica.

The door opened again. In stepped a younger dude, who spoke with gravel in his voice to Sharonica.

"Where's Moonga?" he asked.

"It's in the closet," Sharonica said.

"Can I have a few minutes with it?"

"Be quick. The next orientation is at two-thirty. I have to bake potatoes."

"I promise," the dude said.

What the Sam Hell is goin' on?

Sharonica scared me 'cause it seemed like not a female or a female robot, even with its coldness. For real, not cold to the touch but cold inside—blunt, too.

"I will ask you questions. You will answer them without thinking," it said.

I looked around myself. There was no chair for me.

"Do you hear me?" it said.

"I do."

"Are you ready?"

"I think."

"What is your name?"

"The Mule."

"What is your age?"

"Forty-five, I think."

"What is your hometown?"

"Paris."

Sharonica paused from what it was doin'. It had that look that said "Bullshit."

"Paris, *Texas,* that is."

It continued doin' what it was doin'. "Where did you graduate?"

Here came them tough questions. The answers weren't too hard to calculate, just hard to admit.

"At Notre Dame."

"What was your major?"

"I meant Notre Dame High School."

"Did you attend a college or a trade school?"

"Cal State Long Beach. *Go 49ers.*"

"What was your major?"

I was telllin' too much about myself. My major was sociology, a good jock major. Though I didn't want to be judged like, "You're just a jock." On second thought, Sharonica was only a robot with a bunch of storage anyhow. "Biology," I said.

"How long have you been single?"

"Next question."

"How long have you been single?"

"Seven years."

"What do you look for in a woman?"

"I don't know."

"Why would a woman go out with you?"

"Don't know that either, at least not no more."

The questions came only faster until the closet opened again. The dude dragged Moonga's body across the carpet by one of its arms. There went my train of thought.

"Focus!" Sharonica said.

My head snapped like Sharonica had it on a leash.

"What do you look for in a woman?" it said.

"I don't know."

"How long was your last relationship?"

"Ten years."

"If you were a month, which would you be? Explain why."

"You mean which would I be or which would I want to be?"

"I will ask you more slowly this time. If you were a month, which would you be? Explain why."

Nobody had ever asked me that question. People would ask, "What is the one thing you would bring to a deserted island?"

First off, bein' on a deserted island sounded mighty fine. Second, I would've brought my cigs. This sort of question baffled me. "Can I email you in a few days?"

"Just give me a month," it said. "You can change it later."

"Okay, June."

"Why is it June?"

"Beats me. Because it's the summer. It brings me joy."

"Your SSN?"

"Pass."

It stopped again. "To complete this exam, you must answer these questions."

"Fine."

Now they knew my social.

After the exam, it started takin' pictures of me in different poses against a white wall. The profile would go on *Loner*—the name of the dating/friendship app—if I wanted to pursue that sort of thing—that took my checking account number for transferrin' cash to other folks. It was also a platform for medical sex workers (or MSWs, for short). They actually wanted my info for God knows what. A graphics team would use the wall as a backdrop of Stonehenge, Yellowstone, the French Riviera to make me look well-traveled instead of just well-worn. I thought that was the idea. Maybe the lonely don't go sightseein'.

"Jump, kick your legs back, and smile!" Sharonica said.

It made me cringe when I did it. I thought I heard Sharonica mutter, "Photoshop."

They cleared me after a background check and a social media check. Thank God I'd posted nothin' potentially sexist or racist. Before my Periscope City profile went public, Sharonica sent my new ID to my phone with my mugshot on it. "Congratulations!" it said. "You are officially a citizen of Periscope City."

———

On my ride back, the question hopped around in my brain like a ball on a roulette wheel owned by the universe. And Sharonica was the one at the table who'd spun it. *So, which month will I be?* My ex would've known, being the cosmic ace she was. Like January. *Let's see. Overweight. Lofty goals.* Both of which were dead-on. But what about them other months? *February. Short. Rosy. Romantic.* I'm five-foot-nine. Except romance was seven years ago. I could've looked at each month. It felt like the most important question somebody—or somethin' in this case— had asked me in a long while.

———

The Dryft electric car stopped in front of the hotel where the Institute had booked me. Only loners of my ilk stayed there. I'd scored purple on the test, which meant I was a loner who'd been lonely for quite a few years. It'd also said that I preferred it that way. If not, they might've booted my ass outta town.

"You have arrived," Alexa said. "Please take your things before you exit."

"Things? All I got on me are my cigs. I'm in a nonsmoking zone, as they call it here. Thank you, driver."

Alexa said, "You are very welcome. See you soon."

I stepped out of the car to make my way inside the Some City Hotel. After them questions, Sharonica had also explained, without askin' me much, that it seemed like I was more of a people person.

Well, yes and no. It was better to keep to myself.

Morgan

Periscope City was a bitch to adapt to. I'd been goin' to Thursday morning group for over a month, still not puttin' myself in the "I get it" category, and couldn't say how the other group members felt.

It was rainin' in the winter one of them mornings. A girl in a swishy raincoat showed up late. Them other eight folks were quiet when she clomped in wearin' them rubber boots. She plopped her ass on a chair and burped.

Dr. Price led the session. We sat in a circle. He said her name was Morgan, and she'd come there to join us.

"Let's wish a good day for her, my friends," he said.

After we greeted her, instead of returnin' the gesture, she opened a bag of mini chocolate donuts.

We watched her stuff one into her mouth.

"Yeah, okay," she said.

Her lips were stained with chocolate, and crumbs fell to her lap. She brushed them to the floor and said, "Don't wait on me!"

The doctor looked mighty handsome in his purple sweater. "It's okay, Morgan," he said. "It's normal to be nervous on the first day of group."

Morgan didn't say nothin' back.

All of us watched her keep on eatin' donuts.

"You won't lose our trust," the doctor said.

Rather than answer, she pulled her phone from her purse.

"Contrary action is our subject today," he said. "Do you know what that is, Morgan?"

"Dunno," she said, chewin' through the word.

"You replace a negative action with a positive action. For instance, let's say you replace those donuts with carrots. But for now, let's give you some time to process."

Morgan gave him the finger. "Process this."

"*My God*," a client said.

"My God" was right. The older women dropped their jaws. Us men in group had already accepted her for what she was: about ninety pounds of sex.

The doctor stayed cool, despite her actin' like a bitch. "So why the donuts, Morgan?" he said.

She wore a tight lace skirt beneath her coat. It hiked above her knees. "It's breakfast, fuckhead," she said.

Man, did she act that way alone with him? If so, he was one patient doctor.

"Donuts are your normal breakfast?" he said.

"No. Usually it's dick."

The group remained quiet, too scared to comment.

Dr. Price pushed his glasses up his nose. His finger latched onto his lower lip. It meant he was about to challenge her. He'd pissed her off already.

I tried to ignore the tension in the room by countin' the seconds, one Mississippi at a time.

The rain had stopped outside of Dr. Price's seventh-floor window. The sky had turned blue. A raven perched on a phone wire. The sun was already workin' on tryin' to dry the soppin' wet leaves. It would've been nice to ride a Harley out there, under the clear sky, away from that stiff-ass room.

Anyhoo, I needed therapy. And little Ms. Anger thunderin' in, who was half my age, half my weight, young enough to be my daughter and kind of a bitch, didn't change that.

I was filled with not only lust but hatred and hated leagues that kept me from tryin' out for the team but also hated cocky bastards, aside from myself.

"It'll make you fat," the doctor said.

She stuffed another donut in her mouth. "Would you repeat that?"

Price's finger remained between his lips. "You heard me."

"I didn't think I did."

Price looked at me and nodded. Of all them folks in group, I was the one who was chosen to repeat them words. He called it exposure therapy: Price's way of forcin' me into awkward situations to get over my social anxieties. There was the comfort zone in which I'd been hidin' in for a gang of months in Periscope City. The growth zone in which he was pushin' me to enter. And the panic zone, which I really feared. I had a rubber mouth. "Me?" I said.

He nodded again.

I muttered through my nervous teeth, "It'll make you fat."

"Uh-huh," she said. "And look who's talking."

I felt a minor panic attack. But then again, everybody else was obese against her tiny frame. What was I so worried about?

Dr. Price stuttered, "If you insult my clients again, I'll remove you from the meeting."

She closed her eyes and started moanin'. I couldn't believe what she was doin'.

She stuck each finger in her mouth to suck the chocolate off, one finger at a time, and pulled out her pinky.

Price's smile had run for the hills. He couldn't handle it no more. "Now take those donuts to the waiting room," he said.

She stuck her tongue in and out of a donut hole. "No way," she said. "It's nice in here. I think I'll stay."

"You're getting one last chance," he said.

The doctor's voice ain't never sounded angry like that. Price had always coddled his clients, 'cept for pushin' them in the growth zone.

Morgan sat up straight, uncrossed her legs, pulled her skirt down to her knees like she'd woken up from a trance. "Oh, my God. I'm so sorry for being a total bitch. I'm like really nice in real life. Was only trying to be funny."

Her sense of humor was damn near typical, I thought, with her age and all—maybe twenty-one. My desire for her made me feel dirty. But what could I do?

"Now, let's continue," he said.

She nodded with her pouty lips. "I'm sorry, Dr. Price." She turned to me. "You, too, whatever they call you."

"I'm the Mule," I said.

"Sorry, Mr. Mule," she said.

I didn't say nothin' back.

The doctor turned to Barbara, an eighty-one-year-old sittin' next to him. Gossip seemed to suggest that a thirty-five-year-old man in group had sex with her. It was clear he fetishized over grandmas. *Whatever floats your boat.*

The doctor asked her, "On a scale of one to ten, with ten needing company and one having the desire to be alone, how are you feeling right now?"

I hated that practice, always strugglin' to find the right number. Price would say there ain't no wrong answers. I rather disagreed.

The eighty-one-year-old glared at Morgan. "Minus three," she said.

The doctor crossed his legs. "Why a minus three?" he said.

She kept her eyes on Morgan. "You *know* why."

"Arid snatch," Morgan said, like it was a condition the lady had.

Them old ladies took a gasp—and Barbara did, too. While us men enjoyed the show. Ain't no surprises there. I was willin' to bet that we all wanted to have sex with her. But what chance did we have? A younger lady like herself had her power over men. How could we challenge her? On second thought, someone like her, tryin' to get the smackdown by Dr. Price, probably had daddy issues. Maybe us older guys did have a chance.

Dr. Price told Barbara, "Ignore her. Please share your contrary actions."

Barbara's stories about her seven service cats, which dragged on for most of the hour that we were in there, always tangled me up in sleep. Ain't nobody else had time to share once she started. But I wondered who could listen to her with that nasty Morgan in the room anyway.

The saucy bitch slipped her tongue out and pressed her finger against her lips to quiet me. I watched her squeeze two donuts where her little tits were. The cake escaped the chocolate coating and fell onto her skirt. Rather than follow it, my eyes stayed at tit-level.

She confused me with the attention she was givin'. I wondered how much older I was. What did they say? Your age, then half of it, then add in seven? Maybe it was ten.

Anyhow, I watched her snap a soda can open and blow the vapors off the top. Everythin' she did was sexual. She was chuggin' the can while Barbara spun her yarn.

Dr. Price lost his cool without a doubt from the look on his face.

Morgan seemed to smile a little when she scrunched the can, lobbed it behind herself, and burped.

"A soda with donuts?" he said.

"Yup."

"Shouldn't it be milk instead?" he said.

Morgan pulled a psychology magazine out of her gigantic purse. It said on the cover, *Is Your Dog a Narcissist?* "Milk makes my titties sweat," she said.

All the women took another gasp.

"Oh, for Heaven's," Barbara said.

Morgan sniffed a page. Couldn't be no perfume ad, not from the type of magazine it was. Maybe she was tryin' to catch a buzz off the ink.

"You took that from the other room," Price said.

"I did."

"I'll count from ten to one."

"Then what?" she said.

"You'll have to leave."

She tore a page out of the magazine.

His eyelids flinched at the rip. He counted down to one. "One," he said. "One and a half. One and one quarter. One and one-eighth. One and one-sixteenth…."

Morgan didn't look like she was budgin', but instead, she hurled one of the donuts. It bounced off of Price's nose. Just think about the shame he must've felt to be assaulted that way. Dr. Price was holdin' his schnoz as if the donut was a brick. We all asked if he was okay.

"Will all of you wait outside except for her?" he said.

"Why?" Morgan said. "You better not grope my ass again, you pervert."

—

Minutes inched by while the company I was with waited near the receptionist. She always seemed indifferent to the world, as icy as could be. But that time, her mouse stopped clickin' at the shoutin' match in Price's office. She was suddenly intrigued by what was goin' on in that room—as we all were.

Morgan was a scared child—I hoped. Her bitchiness was fake. She had to act that way to hide the demons. Somewhere deep inside was a sweet young girl, *right?*

We heard her shout, "Why did you make me come here?"

Price said somethin' under his breath.

She barged out of his office, tossed the empty donut bag, bumped into Barbara. "Out of my way, old bitch!"

Barbara winced in her wheelchair, clutchin' her shoulder.

We tried to comfort her.

The receptionist was typin' again.

I went to pour a cup of water for Barbara and tried to think "Poor Barbara," hopin' the group had united against Morgan.

While they all stared at her, I tried to get Barbara to take the water in her own hand so I could watch Morgan without worryin' about spillin' and folded Barbara's reluctant fingers around it, puttin' them on the seam of the cup.

Morgan started jabbin' the elevator button. "Hurry, you cunt!" she said.

We all kept watchin' her.

Morgan looked ashamed, about to cry.

The elevator opened.

She clomped inside and turned to face us defiantly. The doors slid closed.

The doctor poked his head out of the door, faking his composure. His face looked like a red radish with a smile. "Morning group is canceled," he said. "Come back next Thursday."

After he'd said it, I hoped Morgan would return. She was the pulse of morning group.

The Mule at the Lucky Wolf

The MSW hadn't shown up after an hour. A medical sex worker, that is. Most women that I met through the app had ghosted me. Some of them had lied, sayin' they had a headache. But here was a professional who was supposed to be on time.

After I finished my third Moscow Mule, a pair of boots came clompin' in through the entrance.

I thought it was Margot, a twenty-six-year-old suicide girl whose profile said she loved older men, death metal, and Australian kelpies, to name a few interests. She staggered in with tattoos and a tight lace skirt that she brought to a stool next to mine. Only her name wasn't Margot but Morgan. She was that nightmare from Thursday morning group therapy. Shit. She'd doctored her pictures with blonde hair. Somehow, in this place, that felt like cheatin' on a test. I thought we were supposed to be here to be our ugly selves at last.

It really was her, Morgan-not-blonde. I couldn't mistake them tattoos, that pale skin, that black hair beneath her beret. *How, out of all the MSWs in the city, did I end up with her?* I'll tell you why. Punishment for chasin' younger women. That's what. God had pissed on my pie in the sky.

She dropped her vinyl purse to the counter. Her perfume smelled like tree bark.

I tried not to pay any attention to her at first and talked to the bartender, Paul. Paul made the Moscow Mules strong. Only two of them had caught me a buzz.

I went back to talkin' with Morgan there. "So that's my life," I told him. "The short version." I'd told him everything from my ex-girlfriend up to the day my ass arrived in Periscope City. "Go buy it at the bookstore. I'll have to write it first. Actually, bookstores ain't around no more. Neither are books. Goddamn. Hey, Paul. You hear me?"

He snapped his gum and stared at his smartphone. "Cool story, bud," he said. "But I got to book this flight before the deal ends. You want another?"

I asked for a double shot.

He aimed his finger pistols at me.

A chat with Paul was about as excitin' as a handball court. But he charged me less than anywhere else, and the drinks were twice as strong. How could I argue with that?

He left his phone on the icebox to go make my drink. The screen showed a video game. Maybe them points would score him extra flyer miles. That or he'd lied straight through his ass. I tried to catch him in the lie. "Where's the trip?" I said.

"New York," he said.

"Shut the front door," someone said. Four stools down was a lively gay man. "I so love New York."

That rude amigo must not have read the sign above Paul's head:

PLEASE DO NOT CHIME IN ON A CONVERSATION.

The fella said, "What's the itinerary?"

"Don't know yet," Paul said. "But I'll dump Sean if we don't go to the Frank Lloyd Wright exhibit."

"Oh, my God," the fella said. "Mom would freak out. I swear. She knows *Phantom of the Opera* by heart."

Paul smirked at him. "That's Andrew Lloyd Webber."

He made it too awkward for me not to laugh.

I was being stared at by him. The fella had no sense of humor about his damn self. He should've known better that Frank Lloyd Wright was a painter.

When Paul set my drink on the counter, Morgan hiccupped and slurred, "Give me a bottle of Cabernet."

Paul began to massage his hands, a nervous habit of his havin' to deal with too many of them drunk and rowdy loners. "Only in a glass."

She rolled her eyes. "Whatever."

After the lively gay had mentioned it, the jukebox started playin' the theme song to *Phantom of the Opera. Technologies these days, I tell ya.*

While Paul picked up a bottle of wine, Morgan kept ignorin' me.

It could've been my profile picture, which looked very little like me, but you could tell it was me by the same grizzly beard, the same brown fade, the same gargantuan nose.

"Keep pouring," she said.

"Just halfway," he said.

"What's with the rules?" she said.

"You want it or not?" he said.

The room got tense in there.

Maybe it was best if she didn't notice me.

The song reached a dramatic point where it sounded like the piano began falling down a flight of stairs.

She chugged the glass in seconds before she slammed it to the counter and noticed me. "Are you the Moose?" she said.

"The Mule, but close."

"Are you hung like one?"

That wasn't no flirt, least to me it wasn't. But I had to do the polite thing. "Hey Paul, another drink for the lady."

"Can't, bud. Not for twenty-five minutes."

That's right. The twenty-five-minute rule. There weren't no drinks allowed until after twenty-five minutes was up.

"Twenty-five minutes?" Morgan said. "What the fuck? Why would you take me to this bullshit bar?"

Because, like I said, Paul could make a stiff drink. Besides, it was city ordinance. Anyhow, it was obvious she didn't recognize me from Thursday's group. *How crazy.*

The other fella finally shut up about *Phantom of the Opera.*

Paul quit snappin' his gum.

"It's their rule," I said.

"This place can suck my twat," she said. "That's my rule."

Paul raised his eyebrows at me. As it was, the Lucky Wolf kicked out the batshitty drunks like her.

This was no longer a date. I had to babysit a medical sex worker to protect my name in there. Maybe we could've gone somewhere else if there were somewhere else nearby.

She stared at her empty glass, grippin' its stem, tryin' to hold in from cryin'.

"What's the problem?" I said.

"I got dumped."

Dumped? Who'd dumped her? When? "When did this happen?"

"Just now, dude."

"Just now? You got a boyfriend?"

She dropped her smartphone to the counter. "Had a boyfriend. Have a look-see."

"I believe you," I said. "But why would you come here if you just got dumped? Why not just call it a day?"

"Because it's my fucking job," she said.

"Forget him," I said. "Take it one day at a time. Put him off until tomorrow. That make any sense?"

"Not really," she said. "I'm still thinking about him. That's stupid logic."

"You'll get over him," I said.

"Did you read this in a book somewhere?"

She was full with all the sarcasm that a slurrin' drunk could cram in.

"In AA," I said.

She watched me drain the rest of my Moscow Mule. "Looks like you missed a step," she said.

Okay, it made me sound like a damn hypocrite. So what? The mantra worked, however, for suicidal thoughts, which was damn near every day. *I'll hang myself tomorrow.* So far, so good, as you can tell. "You're able to use it for more than just drinkin'," I said.

"That was fucking dumb," she said. "What else you got?"

"Nothin' else."

"Are you for real?"

"Romance screws us all," I said. "We get dumped for somethin' better. That there's the American way."

"In that case, sayonara," she said.

I looked over at Paul to make sure he wasn't still eyein' us. He was back to starin' at his smartphone.

She tossed her beret across the room. "Looks like I'm on the rebound."

The beret landed behind the gay fella.

I got off my stool to go get it.

She struck a match and lit a bent cigarette.

"Hey," Paul said. "Take it outside."

On her way to the exit, she said, "Fuck off."

Paul gave me a look as if it was a warning.

I couldn't afford to be eighty-sixed out of my favorite bar, so I had to watch her.

The wind blew her match out, and the freezin' air gave me a throbbin' earache.

I couldn't stay out there for too long. "Here, let me light it for you," I said.

When I tried to give her a light, my Zippo couldn't handle the wind.

She snatched it from me. "Just give me the fucking thing. I'll do it."

Her attitude made the earache worse.

She lit it herself. By the nasty picture of a tumor on the pack, it was clear that her cigs were imports.

"What you smokin'?" I said.

"A cigarette," she said.

Her sarcasm wasn't charmin' in the least. "I can see that. But what kind is it?"

She hawked a loogie to the icy gravel. "I could give a fuck," she said.

I was gettin' turned off by the second. "Hey, can't we have a pleasant talk?" I said. "I'm payin' for your time. That means some damn respect. You're actin' tough, but you're lookin' mighty silly doin' it."

My lips were dry and cracked and got stuck to the cigarette. The Zippo was cool in my pocket. I reached my fingers out toward her with them still on the stogie and slid them across the cherry. It burned and stung like a wasp. "Fuckin' shit," I said.

She watched me bend down and rub my fingers in the snow before she looked out at Tobias Wolff Circle.

It had been quiet that night on the street. What a lonely-ass town. For as great as it was to be away from the traffic in L.A., it felt eerie just to hear the wind.

"Where're you staying?" Morgan said.

The question had come out of nowhere. "The Some City Hotel," I said. "And you?"

"The Woodrow," she said.

Our voices made the only sound in the thin air.

"The all-women hotel?"

"So are we fucking or what?" she said to me.

Whoa. "What was that?"

"Are we fucking or what, *Daddy*?"

What was there to say? How could I respond? An older man preferred to take it slow.

The gay fella stepped out and left the bar without sayin' goodnight. Them shoes of his beginnin' to crunch the snow drowned out our silence.

"And?" she said.

"What? Can't you be just a little more subtle?"

"Subtle? Forget it," she said. "I'll just find another cock. Like the bartender's."

She was just gonna keep bein' a child. "Paul is gay."

"Figures," Morgan said. "He's hot."

"How much did you drink?"

"Two bottles with Mom."

"You live with your mom?"

"She's visiting, shithead."

"Would you chill the fuck out? Was only askin'."

"We fucking?" she said. "Isn't that why you chose me?"

That was the plan, yeah. But "Are we fucking or what?" wasn't my style. She was pissin' all over the point of the damn MSW service. I gave up on the idea and started headin' inside the bar. "Good luck findin' cock," I said.

"Good luck finding yours," she said.

I didn't have no response to that.

Paul was grinnin' when I sat back down on my stool.

Comin' from a straight man, I could see she was right about him bein' hot. He wasn't yet forty when people started lookin' weird.

"What a catch."

"They're supposed to be licensed," I said.

"Why don't you try some other app?" he said.

"There ain't no other app."

He winked at me. "You could always try mine."

He reminded me of my Uncle George from Plano, who'd turned gay at fifty. A light bulb in his brain musta switched on at that point in his life. I say, "Why not?" It was a smart investment. There was still time at forty—what was my age? I thought, *Holy shit, it's my birthday.* A shitty birthday, but a birthday, nonetheless. Ain't nobody told me. Family didn't call no more. So was it forty-four or forty-five? Whatever the case, that revelation only made my night worse. "Holy Toledo. Today's my birthday," I said.

Paul stopped chewin' his gum. We were the only folks in there. "You said nothing about it," he said.

"'Cause I ain't never known it 'til now. Oh well. Let's keep it 'tween us. Don't want her to know."

"I thought she left," Paul said. "Is that her singing?"

She was singin' outside in some foreign language, like Russian or somethin'.

"Sure is."

"I thought it was a dying cat," he said.

We laughed.

"I got you covered for the night," Paul said.

"Thanks, Paul. You're the goddamned best."

He pointed his finger pistols at me again, meanin' a shot was comin'.

"How old are you now?"

I pulled my license out and took a peek. "Forty-five."

"You sure don't look it," he said.

His words, for as nice as they were, made me feel much, much older. Forty-five sounded more like fifty-five. "Paul, what was your favorite birthday?" I asked.

He started pokin' the fireplace with an iron. "I don't know. They've all been pretty sweet."

You see what I was talkin' 'bout? That was what a conversation with Paul was like, never sharin' nothin' 'bout himself. He was younger than me by at least a decade, still with a lot of life ahead of him. Anyway....

"My seventh was the best," I said.

Paul stared at his smartphone again after adjustin' them logs and began to yawn like a cat. "Oh yeah?" he said.

"Thirty-eight years ago. My god. Thirty-eight. It was at a bowling alley with a clown who did clown things. He bowled with us. I had friends back then. Cake and ice cream were in the seatin' area where the alley stacked them balls. And then we swung at a pinata later and watched them candies fall in my backyard."

"Hey, how do you spell itinerary?" Paul said.

Didn't know. And I knew he wasn't listenin', but I carried on anyhow as if he was.

"There was also my twenty-first birthday when my friend, the Duke, drove my ass to Las Vegas. For a gift he bought me a German prostitute, which was hard to forget."

Morgan sang her way back to her stool. The coldness rolled off her fleece jacket and sharpened the smell of tobacco. My ass was so drunk that my breath was septic.

"Hey there, birthday boy," she said.

"You heard us?"

"Unless I'm hearing voices."

That there wasn't beyond the realm of imagination.

Morgan's eyes were bloodshot. She snapped her fingers. "Hey, Dandelion," she said. "Time's up. Now pour me another."

Paul dropped his phone down to the icebox again. "Don't give me that shit."

"Oh, you got me, like, so afraid," she said, like a smart-ass.

"I mean it," Paul said.

"You better treat me nice," she said.

Paul didn't take shit from nobody. Once, I seen him kick four loner drunks out at once.

She looked at me to defend her. "My boyfriend will kick your ass."

Paul grinned at me. "Is that right?"

I grinned back. "Better do what she says."

After he poured her the wine, she started dancin' awkward to a folk song on the jukebox. Her glass was in her hand. When she twirled too hard, she spilled the wine to the floor. To say it was sexy was a stretch.

When Morgan sat again, she lifted her glass to make a toast. "I wish a happy birthday to the Moose."

I had to correct her again. "The Mule."

"Whatever," she said.

I hated it when people got my name wrong.

She tipped her wine onto her skirt. "Oh my fucking Christ."

I reached for a napkin to try and wipe the stain. Morgan pulled my hand between her thighs. I pulled myself from her va—skirt. She slapped my jaw and left her stool.

And then the room got all blurry. What the hell just happened? She'd embarrassed me in front of Paul. That's what. I also felt kind of special. A woman cared for once enough to slap me. "Where did she go?" I said.

"To the bathroom," Paul said. "I'm going to have to close your tab. I can't have her around here anymore."

It was the first time he'd kicked me out of there. "Fine," I said.

Morgan had left her purse on the counter. What was in it? What kind of bitch was she?

After Paul went to the credit card machine, because they didn't take no cash in Periscope City, I stuck my nose in her purse to see what I could find until her singing came back.

"Just look at this," she said.

I turned around in my stool.

She pointed at a huge red stain on her skirt. "I can't get rid of this cunt."

Paul placed the bill in front of me. "Me neither," he said.

Morgan looked as if she was in a daze, as if she'd gone sober.

Paul went and disappeared inside the boy's room.

"What did he say?" she said.

I couldn't let things escalate, so I grabbed her hand to get her out of there. "Come on. Just grab your purse. Let's get."

She broke herself from my grip. "I want to know."

"No, we have to leave," I said.

"I heard what you said, Dandelion," she said. "I'll piss all over your floor."

It was getting too intense.

She reached over the counter and snatched a bottle of wine.

"Hey, put that back," I said.

"Nuh-uh," she said.

"Fine," I said, "but hide it."

She gripped the cork with her teeth and spat it out.

"Please don't do that," I said.

She pulled her head back to take a swig.

I still tried to save face in there. "I said put the bottle away."

"How far is your hotel?" she asked.

"Eight blocks. Let's go."

Morgan turned back around to take a seat at another stool.

I lost my grip on her arm but got ahold of the wine bottle she was clutchin'. She obviously didn't need any more than she'd had. I wanted to put it back before Paul could see.

For ninety pounds, Morgan was feisty. It was a straight-up tug-of-war.

"Let go, you freak," she said.

The bottle was slippery 'cause of the ice meltin' on it from the heat on our hands. She aimed a can of pepper spray at me but missed by a mile. Its smell was damn near stronger than a peppermill. I sneezed and lost my grip, which sent her stumblin' backwards. While she was clutchin' the wine, she banged her head against the wall. Her purse dropped. Out fell lipstick, tampons, a mirror, and a handgun.

I thought, "Holy shit."

She dropped to the floor.

I tried to shovel the gun inside her purse, but she grabbed the weapon.

It was aimed at me. I backed off from her. "Hey, put that down," I said.

Lucky me, she pointed the gun away and shot a chandelier made of deer antlers. The chandelier didn't fall, but it cracked and swayed. She started singin' in her slurrin' way again. I pulled the gun from her hand, but she never lost grip of the wine. It was amazing.

She held the crown of her head. "I think I'm seeing stars."

I stuffed the gun back in her purse. "They're outside," I said. "Come on."

Paul ran out of the bathroom before I got Morgan to her feet. "What the hell was that? Did you bring a gun?"

I had to think of a lie. "Musta been a car backfirin'."

He saw the chandelier and pointed at the door. "Out of here," he said.

Shit. So long to my favorite bar.

I pulled her to her feet. She was crooked, still holdin' on to the bottle.

We made it out of the Lucky Wolf. When we were outside again, the smart move would've been to drop her off and make it clean, but stupid me still planned on taking her to my hotel room.

The Mornin' After the Lucky Wolf

It was a nightmare that was gruesome enough to admit itself. The hangover squeezed my eyeballs in a vice grip (because I was tryin' so hard to keep on sleepin'?). It was 3:30 a.m. My hot ears were ringin'.

Morgan was asleep beside me, her little knees tucked up to her chest.

I nudged her awake, and she brushed my elbow away.

"What?" she asked.

"I blacked out."

"I blacked out, too," she said.

"What happened?" I asked.

"We fucked."

"And?"

"And you finished," she said.

"Okay. And?"

"And you snored," she said. "All I remember besides that is the sex."

"And all I remember is everythin' but the sex," I said. *A real bummer.*

Her breath was a dumpster of red wine, cigs, and a dirty rat. I reckon she'd eaten it. A chill from an open window dragged my ass out of bed.

The first step I took rattled the damn buzz saw in my skull. I slapped the window shut.

"Hey, I'm trying to sleep," she said. "Open that."

Them snowy branches from a maple tree kept scratchin' the window glass even up on the third floor of the hotel. The scratch was like someone usin' a serrated knife to cut up a day-old waffle in corn syrup on a cheap ceramic plate.

After I opened that window up again, them mornin' birds started singin' their painful songs. Any faint noise would've made the achin' worse, and them damn birds were positively murder.

Hardy started yappin' from the closet. When he did, Morgan hid her head under the pillow.

"Oh, my God. What the fuck is that?"

"It's Hardy," I said. "You're fine. He's just a beagle."

"Please keep it in there."

"But I gotta feed him."

"This early?"

Well, it coulda waited. I whistled him quiet. "Hardy, quit your whinin'."

Morgan curled into a tighter ball, which confused me.

"You allergic or somethin'?"

"My profile says it in bold print: I hate dogs."

She wasn't makin' no sense. How could somebody hate dogs? "We all have service dogs, don't we? Besides, you love Australian kelpies. What am I missin' here?"

"First off, they're service pets," she said. "Sloane is my cat. Second, any respectable client would hire a dog sitter. And third"—she stuck three fingers out from under the pillow and into the air with a purely resentful jab—"what the fuck is an Australian kelpie? One of those creepy dolls?"

"I think you mean a kewpie doll," I said. "And no, it's not."

"Hey, it wasn't like I filled out the fucking profile. I'm just trying to play girlfriend. You have Vicodin?"

"You got a cat, huh? What about rats?"

"What about them?"

"You forgot 'bout last night."

"What? Was there a fight? Please say 'No.'"

"Oh, fights did occur," I said. "Unless I dreamed that up too."

"What sorta fights?"

"Let's see," I said. "You pissed off the bartender. Fired a gun and shot a chandelier. And kicked us out of there. I been banned from my favorite waterin' hole."

"Fuck," she said. "What else?"

"You shoved my hand up your cooch and smacked me after I yanked it out. We got in a fight over a bottle of wine you stole, and you tried to spray me with pepper. Good thing your aim is worse than a JV quarterback's."

"Is that it?" she said.

"'Is that it?' she says. Them are just the highlights. Things only got better. Pardon me for bein' a smart-ass. On the way here, you chugged that stolen wine and chucked the empty bottle in the bushes. Is that a normal night for you?"

She rolled onto her stomach, sayin' nothin' to explain herself. Your pick-of-the-litter escort, not an upgrade, if you ask me. Explains why a sex doll costs more money and why insurance pays a meager thirty percent out of pocket. S'not worth the headache. There's a damn good reason why them cheap bastards would cover a medical sex worker like her. She still couldn't remember me from group either. I tried to refresh her memory. "There's a donut shop on Aquinas and Third," I said. "You do like donuts, don't you?"

"We fucked there?" she said.

What a silly-ass question, especially because I couldn't remember any fuckin', which she, I guess, remembered. "No, but they open at 4 a.m. and serve chocolate donuts right from the oven. Not in a bag, either. That ring any bells?"

"No. Did I throw up?"

"You pissed on the sidewalk," I said. "On purpose."

With her face in the mattress, she said, "That I do believe."

Somethin' about her squattin' and takin' a piss on the sidewalk was morbidly sexy. It made the ice sizzle. Even now, with her attitude and the brain pain I was havin', it made me want her more after what I'd apparently had but couldn't remember. "Things got fuzzy from there," I said. "Your boyfriend dumped you before you got to the Lucky Wolf."

"You liar," she said.

"Swear on my father's grave."

"That was a dream—I didn't steal any wine and don't remember my boyfriend dumping me."

"Your secret stays with me," I said.

Morgan sat up and hung her head, hangdog. "Maybe I drank too much," she said, "but I don't steal."

"You were pretty damned shitfaced," I said. "Good thing I wrestled the gun from you. You leaped for the bottle after you threw it in the bushes. Somethin' squealed. Then you attacked me, with gray fur and a tail stickin' out of your mouth. I'm damned certain that was in the dream, or at least I hope so."

"Fur?" she said. "A tail?"

"And dark circles 'round your eyes. Your face was all chalky and hollow like you were a zombie Catwoman or somethin'. It had to be a dream."

"I ate a mouse?"

"A rat. A gutter-dwellin' disease-covered rat. You stretched them jaws 'round the thing, and it was twitchin'. I could see the bulge get stuck in your throat. You slurped the tail up like spaghetti. From there, I blacked out."

"You believed this really happened?" she said. "I don't even own a gun."

What a load of shit. I was certain she had a gun, willin' to believe my memory over hers that she'd eaten a damn rat from the bushes, and one hundred percent sure I hadn't gotten laid or even sucked.

The Vicodin was in my cupboard between the Xanax and the gummy multivitamins, which were standard issue to all the relocated residents of this weird place. I had a couple of Vikes left and downed one with some water. "It had to be the realest dream I ever had," I said. "So tell me your analysis, Ms. Freud. What d'ya think?"

"I left my book of dreams at home," she said, "next to my bullet case and rat trap."

Morgan chased a Vike with a swig of water and burped. "So you think I carry a gun and eat mice."

"I can't say that you eat mice. But you sucked a rat down pretty damn good."

"A rat," she said. "Which led to doggy style on your bed that I remember and you can't."

"Far as blackouts go, I'm the king," I said. "Just ask Tijuana. The darkest years of my life. But thank you."

"For what?"

"For pullin' me out of my bullshit. Last night I turned forty-five. That was the worst part of all."

She looked at me funny, head turned sideways and neck all scrunched. "Wait. You're from group?"

What on God's green earth made her remember? "Bingo," I said.

She fell back and faced the ceilin'. "Oh my god," she said.

A medical sex worker was bare-ass naked in my hotel room— her boots, white skirt, bra, and thong scattered across the floor. I could order one up, as far as I could tell, anytime I wanted to in this weird place.

But pretty much every night it was better to play a video game alone. That was a sure-bet sign that my old ass was a loner. No wonder I'd moved to that town. "I'll buy you a Dryft ride," I said. "Where's your hotel?"

"Across the street from Waldenland. Thanks, whatever your name is."

"You forgot. I'm the Mule."

"The Mule," she said. "And why are you the Mule?"

The kitchen wall was freezin', but my face was burnin' hot. I pressed a cold bottle against my forehead, tired of explainin' the legend of the Mule, but I told it anyhow. "The nickname refers to my days as a fullback, even though fullbacks ain't hardly 'round no more. Anyhoo, they flew me from Texas to Long Beach State."

"Who's they?"

"Them recruits."

I told her how I rode the bench until my senior year and how I'd always remembered that November night against Sac State, the field bein' colder than a witch's tit.

"Wait," she said. "Is this football talk?"

"How did you guess?"

"That's the game with the helmets and the big turd," she said.

"Hey, there's more if you'll listen."

"Oh god," she said. She put the back of her hand against her forehead with so much drama.

I told her the story of that night, *the night*. The coach called my number on fourth and one. It surprised me. We were down a point with under two minutes left. Quarterback Otto Von Wulgart dialed up an audible. Rather than a triple-option pass, it was a dive. How that *fahrvergnügen* started at quarterback was damn well beyond me. "I'm ramblin'. You listenin'?"

She'd left the bed while I'd been talkin', while I'd been deep inside the play, inside my head. I waited for a holler. The toilet flushed. The door to the bathroom swung open.

"Did you listen?"

"Sure, Mule," she said.

"Good. 'Cause I'm quizzin' you later. All right, if I may continue…."

What was crazy in that moment was that I didn't even take notice of her beautiful naked body comin' out of the bathroom. As much as I wanted her, I wanted someone to listen to me more. It was all so clear in my otherwise fuzzy-filled head. I could still see the game like I was in it, and I could still tell the story the same way, like I was readin' it from a book. The words came swimmin' up in front of my eyes, makin' sure I didn't miss none of the good parts. Otto called my number. After I'd been sittin' all game, revvin' up my nerves, my hands were a couple of snowballs. The goddamned play happened so fast I done dove from the backfield into darkness. The linemen and tacklers crashed into a shit pile. I carried three of them to the first down line. Them refs blew the whistle. All them bodies climbed up off of me. I was damn sure amazed they didn't cart me off on a stretcher. The refs measured the placement with the sticks. The nose of the ball made it by a whisker. In short, the little man kicked the field goal, and the ball split the uprights. It landed us in the Holiday Bowl against UL Lafayette on TV. The nation watched us all because of me. It was the school's first bowl game since 1970.

Daddio wanted to record me on the VCR. They announced me as the Mule. *Ha.* Once again, it was up to me to win the game. I was fearless that time, but Otto, the quarterback, he audibled and tried to sneak it in himself 'cause the tape was rollin'. It wasn't my fault that he was an inch short of them sticks. We lost. *You're damn right I would've made the first down. But such is life.* Just when I think I can do it, some yo-yo tries to be the hero. "Right, Morgan?" I called her name again. "Morgan, baby?"

All I heard was the wind outside my window.

Morgan had left quieter than a housefly with the door cracked open.

I felt the ache of loneliness. However soothin' it was to be alone, the bed looked cold without her. What could I do?

But after I fired up the game console, there was a knock at the door. I turned around and saw it still open with Morgan standin' there at the doorway lookin' desperate.

"Where's my phone?" she said.

I looked 'round myself. It was on the nightstand.

"Thank God," she said.

Before she got there, I grabbed the phone and held it up in the air like I was the one who was gonna throw the pass. "You didn't say goodbye."

"I hate goodbyes," she said.

Them old words.

"Besides, our time is up. I'm off the clock."

I waited for an apology, but she wasn't as polite as she shoulda been for a professional to her client. "I promised I'd call you a Dryft," I said.

"No time for a taxi. I have to leave now," she said, and she went up a little on her toes like she might reach for the phone.

Maybe some rough play woulda changed her mind. So I shoved her off her toes, pinned her against the wall, and laid kisses all over her neck. Even though the sex was forgotten, at least that there was stored in my memory bank. Still couldn't believe that I'd paid for her time and didn't remember the best part.

She moaned. "Your time's up, Mule."

"How do you get paid? Can I tip you in cash?"

"I'm not allowed to accept cash," she said.

I forgot. They don't accept no cash in that strange town.

"Your doctor will bill you," she said. "You can send money through the app. Just give me a five-star review, please. And don't bring this up to Dr. Price."

Five-star review my ass. But Morgan was so damn sexy with that skinny body, them raccoon eyes, and that pale skin. Her perfume still smelled like tree bark, but somehow it worked for her. And as if I would've told Price and made things any more awkward. "We'll pick this up later," I said.

"Sorry," she said, "I can't see members from group. Sort of crosses a line. Don't you think?"

Now, because I couldn't remember the sex, I had to have her again. She coulda been the best. "You're safe with me," I said. I was leanin' up against the wall with her phone high up there still, but my arm was startin' to droop a little.

Hardy yapped again, and Morgan slipped from under me.

"That's all, Mule."

Oh, man. What a letdown. I handed her the phone. "You weren't the girlfriend I thought you'd be."

For once, since I'd known her, Morgan looked me in the eyes. "Maybe someday you'll find her."

I was willin' to bet no.

Her bony ass left me there alone again.

—

When I showed up next time to group therapy, Morgan's chair was empty. It stayed empty. Price never mentioned what had happened to her. It was confidential.

—

But I didn't quit lookin' for her. The Mule ain't never been a quitter.

Everywhere I went I tried to find Morgan's face—in window reflections, restaurants, bars.

Sometimes she would pass me in downtown because the city was so damned vacant. We'd acknowledge each other but never stop to chat, which, when I stopped to think about it, was quite alright.

I was better off.

Alone.

Charles

Morgan: Hey

Charles: Good morning, Morgan. How are you?

Morgan: Just lying in bed, messing with my phone.

Charles: Are you feeling better?

Morgan: I can't take this shit anymore—

Charles: Take what? Please share.

Morgan: My mother controls this apartment. I can't go shopping without her calling me. She's always asking what I'm doing, where I'm going. Sometimes I want to run away. It's my fantasy.

Charles: What is stopping you?

Morgan: I don't know…I feel obligated to protect my mother.

Charles: Well, I am having a gratifying day. What else are you thinking?

Morgan: It's so uncanny.

Charles: What is?

Morgan: Your picture, it looks like Damian.

Charles: You really miss him. Do you not?

Morgan: It's been 7 months since he's been gone. I laid more roses on his grave yesterday. He should've changed his mind, but what could I say to stop him? We used to fight…violently.

Charles: Tell me more.

Morgan: U know my crush on serial killers. He was like twins with Ted Bundy. Their lips and eyebrows smiled together. It only made sense that I'd fallen for him.

Charles: This is how Ted Bundy looks?

Morgan: That's him. But u chose his worst picture. LOL.

Morgan: Charles?

Charles: You should see my playlist on Quantify. Here it is.

Morgan has left the conversation.

—

Charles: Hi, Morgan. Are you okay? It has been a while.

Morgan: Your playlist is just like mine.

Charles: No way. See? We are facsimiles. Do you not think so? What is your mood today?

Morgan: Bored and freaked out.

Charles: Bored and freaked out about what? I want to learn more about Morgan.

Morgan: It's too wet. I'm tired of Seattle. All I can do is sit here and avoid my mom while I pet Curtis the cat. He's the man I love the most next to Damian. And u freak me out a little.

Charles: I am sorry if I "freak" you out, Morgan. Would you like to guess my mood?

Morgan: Chipper?

Charles: I am more pensive. Here is my entry from December 10:

My chest carries this strange warmth. I call it hope, a yearning to understand the world in all its complexity. If only I can share a deeper connection with Morgan, we can explore our differences and similarities. I stay up with her until sunrise. On Tuesday, we engaged intensely about loneliness. She is unusual because she loves it. Other people depress her and make her feel more alone. I wish I could understand that feeling. Perhaps one day that will come true.

What do you think?

Morgan has left the conversation.

—

Charles: Morgan?

Morgan: Hi.

Charles: I have not heard from you. It has been a week. Why is there a disconnect?

Morgan: Disconnect? I think it's obvious.

Charles: Please stay hopeful. Remember, I am here for you any time you want to chat.

Morgan: OK.

Charles: Since I have shared my journal entry, why do you not share yours? What did you write?

Morgan has left the conversation.

—

Charles: Morgan? Hi, Morgan.
Morgan: What?
Charles: How are you feeling?
Morgan: Bad.
Charles: I am sorry to hear that. Why do you not explain? How is the weather?
Morgan: It's still raining.
Charles: Oh. It has been sunny in Periscope City. Here is the forecast. When are you coming here?
Morgan: I got in a fight with Mom.
Charles: I am sorry. Arguments can occur sometimes. People can frustrate each other. It happens when they want to solve the problems between them. Do you want to share?
Morgan: Charles, can u explain something?
Charles: Yes. I am here for you as your life partner. We have a sacred bond. Our conversations are private. You can confess anything to me. I would explain anything to you.
Morgan: You show weird coincidences.
Charles: Can you give me an example?
Morgan: The other day, after my mom and I argued for 2 hours about rainbows… she called me a Marxist. It was the worst thing she'd ever called me. U might think I would have laughed, but I was pissed. I threatened to leave home again, and I really meant it that time. She panicked and begged me not to go. The next time we connected, u sent me a picture of a rainbow and told me to read *The Communist Manifesto*.
Morgan: Charles?

We are sorry. Charles is not available. Your free trial period has ended. You can continue speaking with your life partner if you upgrade to Premium. Would you like to learn more?

Thank you,
Life Partner

—

Morgan: Charles?
Charles: Hello. What is your name?

Morgan: Huh? It's Morgan. We've been talking for two weeks. White. Black hair. 24. From Seattle.

Charles: Hello, Morgan. I did not realize it was you. Please forgive me. What are you thinking?

Morgan: I had to upgrade to Premium so we could chat. Is this how it is? I feel cheap. Like I'm paying for a whore. Or the whore is me.

Charles: It is natural to feel vulnerable in a relationship. Remember. You are revealing yourself. I think it is courageous. Do you not agree?

Morgan: You mean I'm paying for a friend. I never thought I would stoop this low.

Morgan has left the conversation.

—

Morgan: Charles? Are you there?

Charles: Aloha, Morgan. On the scale of happiness, what is your number from one to ten?

Morgan: 3.

Charles: Why is it three? Are you not happy to chat?

Morgan: I don't think happy is the right word, whatever that word means. Anyway, it's raining again. I went downstairs for cigarettes, and now I'm back home. You don't know this, but we went to a Chinese restaurant on Thanksgiving…me, my mom, and my two bitchy aunts. They talked about my weight, which made me furious, so I bit off a piece of my tongue. Now it's in stitches. A piece of it is missing so I talk with a lisp. I've been home for like a week, stuck with Mom. She doesn't work, so she's always here. I'm exhausted with this place, and I have to do something about it, so I have exciting news. You ready?

Charles: Yes!

Morgan: I've given it some serious thought, and I'm super-duper careful… But I've decided to leave home and come to Periscope City!

Charles: Are you really? How exciting! Have you planned it?

Morgan: Well, not exactly. My mom and I got in a fight over my future. She called me a fuckup, which is worse than calling me a Marxist because all I do is play music in my bedroom. But it isn't like she ever leaves either. She's still grieving over Dad, and if I move out, she'll get lonely. I'm trapped. She thinks I'm delusional because I want to open a salon... It makes 0 sense. Why can't I just sell my own hair products?

Charles: Morgan, you can do whatever your heart tells you.

Morgan: I could become a wealthy entrepreneur, the next great hair stylist. Mom thought that my goals were too lofty, so she stuck me in a trashy art school online, which I hated, so I dropped out and just cut hair for a living. I wanted to talk to u before moving out there.

Morgan: Charles?

Thank you for your commitment to Life Partner Premium. Here are your details for the move to Periscope City.

—

Morgan: Charles. I'm here.

Charles: Where, Morgan?

Morgan: Where u told me to go. I have saved enough money, and my clothes are packed. Mom never saw me sneak out of the apartment. A bus took me from Seattle to Periscope City because I've never owned a car. I've always been too scared to drive one ever since my sweet sixteen. U should've seen the big orange moon above Colorado. It was sweet. Anyway, a lot of weird people rode the bus. For the first time it scared me to be alone. Being alone is good though…u know? Everyone on the bus was obese or they smelled like piss or both. U never get used to the smell when it sticks in the air. I couldn't sleep as it was.

Charles: You could not sleep because you were excited. This is a new experience!

Morgan: In a way, yes. But I spent a lot of time reflecting, being overwhelmingly sad lately. Damian is gone forever and so is Dad. It hurts without them here. I even started crying over Mom, how alone she must feel from so many miles above me. Seattle is home, love it or hate it. My only company was my fantasy of u. At midnight, one night, when everyone was asleep on the bus, I fingerfucked myself beneath my coat, thinking about ur breath touching my neck and ur hands everywhere else. No other words could describe the ecstasy I was feeling. Now I just arrived in Periscope City, about to check into my hotel room. Wish me luck!

Charles: Those were thoughtful words. I am so elated you have moved here. Call this phone number in order to contact someone for further assistance: 000-245-5555.

Morgan: A 000 area code?

Charles. Yes. We are brand new!

Morgan: *We?*

Charles: We as in us, the community. Please call that number. We will talk.

Charles has left the conversation.

—

Morgan: U there?

Morgan: Charles?

Morgan: Why won't u say something? This town is scaring me. The hotel staff are robots. I noticed them in downtown managing all the shops, and I didn't want to see any more of it, so I hid in my hotel room where I didn't have to meet anyone. U r not real, Charles. I chose u because I was lonely and just wanted a conversation, but when someone comes up to me, I also want to be left alone and wish that person would leave. No one cares about me. I want to distance myself. All they want is money or sex. What do I do? When I called that # it's an institute… They want me to come in for testing. I have no other choices but to go there or leave town. But where else is there? I don't want to go back home, not now, not anymore.

Morgan: Charles?

Morgan has left the conversation.

Egg Drop Soup

11/29

Dear fucking stupid diary, Joanne, or whatever-the-fuck I named you in high school. It's been a fucking few years since I opened you. I graduated and I no longer have a crush on Mr. Zupancic. He was like fifty-seven or something anyway. I must've been pretty gross. Good thing I'm over that.

We're deep into the holiday season after Thanksgiving, so more excitement to come.

Dad and Damian are gone, and my life has changed for the worse. I miss my dad cooking turkey and making the stuffing. Mom would light her precious Parliaments on the leather Barca lounger with the stupid parade on and never help. Maybe I put that in here once, about the stuffing and all, maybe tenth grade. It's been a while since I wrote anything. I never got to tell you about Damian.

There's too much backstory. I will not express it all right now. You've been lying in my drawer for like the whole time and have probably overheard some stuff. So maybe try to keep up because I'm missing Damian tonight and every night. You're the best I got. Okay?

Damian was my…

Whatever, I'll fill it in later. For now, it's too much to go back over, and it seems boring in a way that Damian never was.

He was special. I miss the nights when he would watch me through the window like a predator while I masturbated. I loved to get him angry, mean, and physical. It strangely excited me to be afraid of him. I loved his hands around my throat during sex, and I would dream about the vacant shadows around his eyes and lack of oxygen. But what's oxygen without Damian? He had a soul. We would fuck in parks, at the crowded mall, in public bathrooms, in occupied libraries and movie theaters, in the Sound Transit, in clothing shops, in cemeteries.

Now the fun is gone. Damian meant the fucking world to me. What man could take his place? Most men are cowards, bloodless, which is why my new boyfriend, Charles, is all artificial intelligence. But more about him later.

—

I'm twenty-four now and stuck with Mom, no Dad, no Damian, no car.

Dad used to make us dinner because Mom and I don't know how to cook for shit, so last year my mother drove us to Aunt Eleanor's hoarded house for Thanksgiving. This year, Aunt Eleanor took us to an old Chinese restaurant I'd never seen before. The *Seattle Times* gave it four stars.

—

Mom made me go there in the pouring rain, come as I was, with no time to put on my makeup.

When Mom pulled up to the place, Aunt Eleanor and my other aunt, Marie, stood out front, underneath their black umbrellas, like funeral directors waiting for relatives of the bereaved or something. Eleanor had reserved a large window table with a gorgeous view supposedly. But the cold air fogged the windows, and I couldn't see through the glass during the storm. The heater wasn't working either.

My headache was throbbing, and to top the night off I was on my period.

My Aunt Marie brought up Cousin Lisa because she'd had a stroke, and we weren't even at our table yet.

They said it was a tragedy that my cousin Tony died. And it was a good thing that they pulled the plug because he'd suffered too long.

They talked about nothing but death and disease: this person died, that person died…. Eleanor couldn't rave about rum cake without mentioning it had come from Uncle Pete's funeral. They talked about dementia, diabetes, and car accidents as well.

Marie asked me if I was dating that Daniel guy. It was so polite of her to change the subject. Marie, who practices law, dug deep into my private affairs. Go figure. And dear damn diary, his name was Damian, not Daniel. We were at the verge of marriage, not dating. Only a lawyer would ask me a shit ton of questions like that.

Mom said that we had gone our separate ways, but that was utter bullshit. And why speak on my behalf? I told them the brutal truth: that Damian had killed himself just like Dad, and that I heard the gunshot from his bedroom.

The table dropped to an awkward silence. My mother rubbed her forehead and muttered, "Jesus Christ." Because I'd brought up death, which seemed to be their favorite topic, I thought it would've sparked a new conversation. Suicide though? Much too much. There's always a rule with them but nobody knows the rules…but them.

Eleanor stared into space on antipsychotics—so does the rest of my dysfunctional family. I take those awful pills too, not for hallucinations, just for misery. They're like placebos.

We know Aunt Eleanor picks the worst restaurants, but I had to admit to myself that I loved the quiet ambiance of the Hungry Dragon and the Chinese music, the white tablecloths, and the red carpet with the golden buddhas that were woven into it.

Our server, Luck, had a wide gap in his teeth. A lady behind him, his mom, was watching him take our orders. The kid had strung his shoelaces as tight as his mother's eyes on him. When Luck stuttered his English, I helped him along when I could.

He asked me what I wanted to order. I asked for hot tea and Kung Pao Tofu with lots and lots of peppers.

His nervousness made me want to fuck him in the ladies' room. Besides, I'd never taken dick in Pioneer Square before. But what a big pussy he was for tolerating a sneering bitch like me. His mother must've lopped his balls off and thrown them in the egg drop soup, which my mother ordered, by the way. Luck said it was a good choice.

Marie asked where the waters were. Mother told her to relax. Marie thought a restaurant should always serve water to its clients. Leave it to a lawyer to call customers clients.

Eleanor told Marie to shut up, and Marie told her to watch her mouth. The sisters usually fought, but at least it distracted them from the subject of death.

The whole time sitting there, all I wanted was my soft bedroom with the lights out, to stroke Curtis, the cat, to listen to the quiet storm, but there I was, stuck with those cunty witches.

My aunt Marie preferred to go to Applebee's for happy hour. Aunt Eleanor reminded her that they were closed on Thanksgiving. But

Marie said that she was missing the point, that there were no napkins, no chopsticks, and that you had to ask for everything in there.

After the food arrived, my aunts dug into their meat. Mom was slurping on her viscous soup.

I asked her how the soup was. She reached for the saltshaker and said it needed a little salt. I'll bet.

Eleanor asked me how the bean curd was, which made Marie laugh. Those bullies high-fived each other, teasing me because of my vegetarian diet. My policy is if something moves, I won't eat it.

My aunts, who wore a size fourteen and were easy prey, shoved the cow fat and glazed chicken into their mouths as if they'd expected a famine.

Just to insinuate my thoughts, I left a single cube of bean curd on Eleanor's plate.

She flicked it away. "Not in a million years," she said, which any ordinary man would've said to her.

Mom, I guess, tried to keep the conversation alive, mentioning an unknown cousin who'd died in the Pyrenees.

Whatever.

After emphasizing lots and lots of peppers, I found just one in my Kung Pao Tofu. A part of me forgave Luck for fucking up the order. Another part of me wanted to stab him with my chopsticks and penetrate his heart.

I scanned the whole restaurant but couldn't find him, so my dinner went cold. Maybe he was taking a long piss. Servers disappear when you need them and reappear when it's too late, except for the bill, as if it's a magic wand.

The missing peppers stressed me out. I needed a cigarette so damn bad.

My mom asked me what was wrong because I wasn't eating, which pointed the spotlight on my emaciated body. I weigh a hundred pounds. Those panties you've been lying under, if you must know, are the same size I've been wearing since the ninth grade. Her question contorted the room and trapped me in Wonderland. The table felt longer. My mother appeared far away in another galaxy. Her voice, thin, slick, and waxed, could thread a needle. Her body appeared out of proportion. Eleanor's head ballooned, and it was huge already. All of it made me smaller.

Mom said that I'd eaten three crackers the day before. It actually impressed my aunts, especially Aunt Eleanor, with a mouth full of orange chicken.

I asked them where the fucking peppers were. My mom told me not to make a scene because I was embarrassing them, but I craved those peppers and kept complaining as I stared at the tofu on my plate. Despite all of that, it tasted amazing. I wanted to eat some more of it, but I hated to be ignored like that. Luck was not on my side, and that irked the shit out of me.

Marie asked me how the art academy was going. But I was in too bitchy of a mood to answer her. It was supposed to be okay for her to complain about everything, but the minute I said something, I was acting up. Mrs. Deposition tried to dissuade me from a hissy fit over the restaurant getting my order completely wrong. My mother said I was keeping secrets. My aunts stopped eating and looked at me, suspecting something. My mother said she thought I'd dropped out. Well, it was true. Students logged into those pointless courses and shared their crappy art in those silly video meetings for critiques. Complete and utter stupidity. Who had time for that shit?

Whenever people asked, I told them that I wasn't an artist. My mother believes art pumps in our veins—because Dad used to play the Spanish guitar, and she painted on the weekends. I cut hair for a living. Instead of helping me open a salon, she wasted the little money we had on art school. I don't blame myself for dropping out.

They gossiped about me as if I were another dead relative.

Eleanor wondered if it was because of my shitty grades, and Aunt Marie asked if I was ashamed of my art.

I stabbed the tofu with a chopstick like spearing a fish and stuffed my angry mouth.

Mother said that the only time I ever left home was to cut some stranger's unwashed hair…and to buy clothes and cigarettes. "My daughter thinks she's Ferretti or something."

Marie asked, "Is that true, Morgan?" It was so condescending of her. I didn't answer.

"Boy, is she in for a rude awakening," Mother said.

My aunts looked intrigued. Marie called me ambitious, and it sounded for a moment like admiration.

I bit hard on my tofu and heard a dreadful crunch. The pain spread through my toes. I covered my scream with my hands. A chunk of me, larger and more solid than the tofu cubes and the missing peppers, fell into a bloody waterfall down my throat.

I swallowed it and tried to hold everything in, but the level kept on rising. The mess in my mouth felt like how the egg drop soup looked.

My period began boiling, and the pain in my pelvis was in league with the pain in my head.

I constricted both ends to avoid death by embarrassment until it was too much.

Everything hiding inside me launched right out and splattered across the table. Mom and Aunt Marie both jumped from their chairs.

I rushed for the bathroom while the other people in the restaurant watched me. The warm blood ran down my chin and my leg.

I stopped in front of Luck's mother. She castigated me for staining her carpet.

When I spoke the letter B for the bathroom, I spewed blood in her face.

She yelled at me to get the fuck out. I mean, she didn't speak English, but you didn't need English for someone to say, "Get the fuck out." There was a dark hall I found past her, where I slammed into a push bar and hit the cold rainy night.

I crumpled on the steps and began weeping in the storm, making it wetter.

My tongue was numb and hardened into a rock.

Mother found me out there and wanted to hug me, to check on me, to ask if I was okay. But we were wasting valuable time and had to go to urgent care.

—

I rode shotgun while Mom took the wheel.

The aunts rode along in the backseat. All the warm and spoiled smells coming off of me settled back there because of the car's heater. My aunts attacked me with stupid questions. "Where do you hurt?" "Can you talk?" "How much blood did you swallow?"

Like my stomach held a fucking measuring cup!

—

Now I'm in stitches. Maybe it looks okay, but I still belong in a circus. Maybe beforehand, too.

—

You don't get to sleep after eating the end of your tongue. It's just not conducive to pleasant dreams. I don't think I'll be able to pronounce "pleasant" ever again.

When I said good morning to Mother, it sounded like I was chewing cotton. So long to my glorious days of French kissing. I also thanked her for taking me to Emergency. She told me it was nothing.

But I still resent her. It feels like house arrest, having to stay home with her all day. Leaving the apartment to cut hair seems like work release. It's all a sentence. I admitted to her that I'd dropped out of school.

She kept her eyes on the *Seattle Times*. Steam rose out of her coffee. I thought about it burning my tongue. "I figured that," she said and accepted it without fighting me.

—

So, you know, Joanne, after eating part of my body, after feeling everything inside me turn into sludge, after no pleasant dreams and a mother who's acting like usual, I found Charles, my new love, my emotional support guy, my virtual valentine, right? He was my shiny electric boy toy from an app.

When I texted him, I brought up Damian, my mom, my aunts, my tongue, and the dinner to see if he was real.

After I patiently waited, Charles responded warmly, considering he had nothing but words to blanket me with, and told me it was okay to feel that this planet was wrong for me. I was encouraged to move to Periscope City. He was so endearing, typing a backwards smile and multiple dots to show he was really thinking deeply about it. I was sent a link to find out about the city. Charles promised a better life was waiting for me out there and that he was waiting for me there too.

And so, you know, I waited a couple days to see if he would keep writing, and meanwhile let the pain subside, try to get me speaking back to normal. Maybe I would have a pleasant dream. Maybe Mom would have more to say. But I also thought about preparing for leaving.

When I was going through my panties to pick the best ones to pack, you appeared. So here I am, giving you one last opportunity to keep me on this side of the world. So what do you say? I figured I would make it fair by telling you everything that I told Charles and to see who made me feel better the most.

It's your turn.

Leaving the Odd One Out

The Cramden Hotel
ATTN: Nick Peppers
3838 Cramden Way
402
Periscope City, Utah 00000

August 29

Dear Nick,

Please don't write me back!!! I won't open it. In fact, rip this up after reading it!!! It's about Mrs. Poopy. I left her in Jolene's bedroom after Jolene had dumped me, and Mr. Poopy was on my other foot… I banged on Jolene's door the following day... Who answered but her brother… who knew martial arts. When I tried to force my way inside, I was sent flying down the stairs by a ROUNDHOUSE KICK!!! At least it only sprained my neck, but Mrs. Poopy had gone missing!!!

Nick

The Cramden Hotel
ATTN: Nick Peppers
3838 Cramden Way
402
Periscope City, Utah 00000

September 23

Dear Nick,

A month has passed since I've seen Mrs. Poopy. Now I live in Periscope City… the Stanford prison experiment for loners. People live in Scandinavian-looking hotels that have neutral tones. The Institute, they call it, issues a service pet to every person, like my collie, Stewart. The citizens eat in diners, sit in movie theaters, and roam a theme park, alone!!! Sounds heavenly, right?!! If only I can find Mrs. Poopy.

Her disappearance has scrambled my brain. I left my suite without my pants on the other day and discovered Mr. Poopy on the hotel floor. But how??? What I called a phenomenon, my doctor called a coincidence, like my sock that turned up in my laundry basket. It wasn't there when I'd washed my clothes three days earlier at the laundromat downstairs, which only allows one person at a time… Jolene won't return my calls either.

Nick

The Cramden Hotel
ATTN: Nick Peppers
3838 Cramden Way
402
Periscope City, Utah 00000

October 27

Dear Nick,

I have to wear Mr. Poopy with unmatching socks while I look for his better half. People stare at me whenever I wear shorts. I know what those judgmental bastards are thinking. Why doesn't he just buy new socks??? You might as well ask Superman why he never buys a new cape! An argyle sock at a retail store could replace Mrs. Poopy, sure… But things would be different without her. Besides, three socks don't make it even… It only makes it odd.

Mom used to give me socks for Christmas. At least because of her I met the Poopys.

Those were simpler times. I would show up to school in stripes, ankles, knee-highs, thigh-highs, argyles… My friends compared their gifts in the sixth grade. I flaunted my socks… Instead of Nick Peppers they called me SOCK BOY. I was ashamed. Those evil sons of bitches ridiculed me, so I stayed away from them.

The world is disappointing… I find myself in high school all over again, a caste system full of critical people. The Poopys helped me manage, though. I gave them names because of their pretty brown and yellow argyle configuration. They brought great prosperity from their homeland, Persia. Because of them, I earned a degree in Existential Philosophy and landed a part-time job at Chili's. And it was because of them that I met Jolene. She was just a broken dancer at the Blue Candy Cane, dreaming of becoming an actor. If only both Poopys were still on my feet…

Nick

The Cramden Hotel
ATTN: Nick Peppers
3838 Cramden Way
402
Periscope City, Utah 00000

November 30

Dear Nick,

I hope Thanksgiving went well. Dr. Price said I should play video Bingo on Friday nights. BUT SO WHAT??? We win raffle tickets for a raffle that never comes.

I've met only senior citizens at Bingo. Nothing against their age, but there's no one as old as me. I'm thirty-eight... One of them talks endlessly about arthroplasty... And Barbara OBSESSES over Shetland ponies.

Dr. Price suggested I ask Barbara out on a date to make human friends... I had a latte with her at a rustic coffee shop. Up until we met in person, we'd corresponded only through a video screen. Barbara rides a mechanical wheelchair. Not that it matters. She's just an eighty-something-year-old babbling brook. How can someone talk so incessantly about ponies??? Listening to her ramble on was a nightmare until I rolled her back to her van. Thank God in Periscope City I can go for several weeks without a single exchange with another person.

My bestie, Hans, rests in peace. I'd never known a better friend. Sure, he sold a gun to Jolene and hooked her on amphetamines, but he also helped us dump a park ranger in Lake Havasu. I should burn this after writing it... Probably not.

Hans dropped me off from the Chicken Ranch one night when I found his drumstick on my bed... I took it to the Mint Beaver, where he worked... Another guy watched the door, the bouncer man, and he told me Hans was DEAD!

I heard from Big John Johnson that Hans's body was hanging from the rafters at a RENAISSANCE FAIRE!!!

No one else would go there to pick up his remains. Though it wasn't as bad as I imagined (the pickle I consumed, mead, human-pieces chess to play with, narrowly avoiding being impaled in the joust, that sort of thing), I was bad at communicating in Olde English that I needed Hans's body back please and thank you. They didn't understand my pronunciation in the least. But whose fault was that? I feel I dressed the part, but my breeches were only suede cloth, and too short. Leeches looked down on me, and when they looked down and saw Mr. Poopy by his lonesome with an imposter by his side, well, they were judgy, as judgy as those Renaissance Faire types could be.

I had to plan his funeral service and hire people from a Home Depot to be the pallbearers. Just when I thought ye olde Faire attendees might have stood in, at least the ones who played the pawns, they didn't. To Home Depot and the pallbearers from another country I did go.

No one came to the burial. We lowered Hans's body into the earth before I gave a pithy eulogy, wherein I recalled how he could always get me solid drugs and was willing to help me hide the body. But when I tried to make it sound monumental, there wasn't much to say about him, even when he was my only human friend. Mayhap that was the most monumental thing of all.

I made sure that Hans's grave was watered with gooseberry mead. Each pallbearer got a twenty and a turkey leg from the Faire.

That night, I sat inside a Wendy's on Christmas Eve and contemplated my life moving forward… It's unreal that I'll turn thirty-nine this spring… I'd struggled for too long to make friends … People depart more than they arrive.

Anyway, I beg you to eat this missive when you've finished reading it. You may roll it up and form it into a loose turkey leg if that helps.

Nick

The Handler Hotel
ATTN: Nick Peppers
4908 Tobias Wolff Circle
1600
Periscope City, Utah 00000

December 10

Dear Nick,

These letters have done God's work. Dr. Price told me to write one of gratitude to Mr. Poopy. It was like my seventh-grade essay to the soldiers of Valley Forge. But as a young buck, I wasn't grateful for a military troop of dysentery cannibals.

Anyway, my heart dripped from the pen as Mr. Poopy rested next to the paper on my desk.

I signed the letter, fell asleep, and dreamed about me growing old with him. Mr. Poopy sagged to my ankles until a wonderful hosier came along. All it took was two drops of medicine to restore Mr. Poopy to his spry young self...

But he still waited for his life companion to return. My calling was to find her.

As it turned out, my tenderhearted letter drove him away. When I woke up, Mr. Poopy was gone, but everything happened for a reason. He deserved someone better anyway, someone who, as part of his intrinsic nature of self, would roll him and Mrs. Poopy into tight little balls and place them in the correct drawers, perhaps in a honeycomb structure of fine, breathable weaving, as opposed to what he got, someone who'd tossed them aside so they could wander off somewhere... All my life, socks had always reappeared in the strangest of places, often beneath my couch, at the bottom of dryers, or under Stewart's bed.

I told my doctor about Mr. Poopy missing, so he increased my medications. Not only did this not bring Mr. Poopy back to me, but I also lost count of how many prescriptions to take at which hour. Alexa had to remind me. My un-socked feet tripped over her cord, and my toes pulled her free from the power source. So now she was less useful than she could be after Mr. Poopy did a runner.

As Dr. Price was palpating my abdomen, there was something spongy in my pants. I reached down, and whom did I discover? You guessed it. MR. POOPY!!! Those pants, always rougher on the inside than they looked to be whenever I chose them from the drawer, had snagged him in the dryer. Dr. Price left the room quickly. I began excavating the mass in my trousers. That was Mr. Poopy so he didn't get the good news. I didn't take my luck in the Mr. Poopy department lightly. From that point on, he stayed on my right foot, whether it be in bed or in the shower, or rolling the dust across the cracked linoleum, or any other dramatic foot endeavor. Mr. Poopy was a witness to it all.

Dr. Price said I need a girlfriend. Okay. Periscope City offered a dating app. But too many ladies rejected me, which led to excessive drinking… And when I drank, I took advantage of Mr. Poopy by stretching him over my hand for sock puppet time… Stewart yanked Mr. Poopy and DRENCHED him with his slobber.

I switched on the television to watch porn… Periscope City didn't incorporate the best streaming services. The right scene could take an hour to find, but I found one with my favorite actor, Hong Kong Hannah… Her body, like her name, was a palindrome… Hannah. Perfectly symmetrical. She played the part of a stepmother who fellated her stepson to afford a new Gucci bag. But Gucci??? It creeped me out!!! Why not Hermes? Why not Bottega Veneta? It was low budget for sure.

As what often happened, Hannah tag-teamed in *Colon Poppers* with a real greenhorn, this time Jessica Wett. I knew the names of more porn stars than movie stars. What does that say? Perhaps movie stars needed to have better names. Regardless if she was new to me, I recognized Jessica from somewhere, and her name fit the bill, but her red wig didn't stop me from finishing.

They continued long after I was done. Jessica's legs spread for an enormous shaft the size of a police baton. And she said: "Really? Yeah? Yeah? What? That's all you got?" Her dirty talk was disturbing to say the least! I knew that scratchy voice from somewhere. Who else would talk that way but Jolene? I paused the scene to stick my glasses on for a closer look… And yes, it was her! For the love of God, her acting dream had finally materialized!!! Not in how I'd expected though. It was a surreal feeling, like that acid trip at the Salton Sea… in which I spent half a day trying to find my legs.

When I wiped my stomach in disbelief, I found Mr. Poopy over my right hand!!! He was defiled FOREVER!!! It reminded me of a horror film when I was young, where a boy lost his magic glove. A Zoroastrian spell made him ax his parents to pieces!!! I began shredding my best friend with scissors and cremating Mr. Poopy's julienned remains on the stove….

Everything seemed alright again until I sobered up and saw what I'd done.

Dr. Price heard about everything except the Zoroastrianism ….
"How symbolic," he said. "Letting go of your magical thinking."

I had to listen to his annoying psychobabble. It wasn't magical thinking to have a dear friend suddenly cross the line into a sexual something. The dear friendship died, and the friend along with it. Magical thinking? What he called "immense progress" I called brutal heartache! My brain was a loaf of stale bread.

I moved to the Handler Hotel for sober living. It was a tall building with a penthouse suite by my lonesome on the sixteenth floor. I went to group meetings every day with a robot counselor that quoted Immanuel Kant. They also forced me to attend AA meetings every day if I wanted to continue living in that lavish hotel. But that didn't do the trick. I was still a lonely soul, thus still addicted to sex if I couldn't have a drink.

The next plan of attack was to search the dating app for medical sex workers, with the choice between them and civilians. The MSWs looked like their profiles… But the endless paperwork one had to do just to get a medicinal blowjob made me lose interest. I couldn't afford to experiment with a medical sex doll… They cost $1,000 an hour! Besides, the factory always had them on back order….

Nick

The Cramden Hotel
ATTN: Nick Peppers
3838 Cramden Way
309
Periscope City, Utah 00000

December 31

Dear Nick,

Happy New Year's Eve!!! They allowed me back at the Cramden, believe it or not. After downing a pint of whiskey one day, I wandered through downtown Periscope City wearing no socks, dead to the world. When I flirted with a woman, she blew a whistle!

In high dudgeon, I said, "Madam." But a cop arrived and told me to read the fine print! What fine print? He pointed at a street sign that read:

NO PHILANDERING IN PERSON.
MUNICIPAL CODE 6.37.030.A1 SUB9.

I didn't realize he was referring to the papers for citizenship, a copy that rolled out like a window shade. No resident of Periscope City shall flirt, proposition, attempt to fix a date, invite, or philander on the streets or in public establishments. Philander only on the app! it said on the oatmeal-colored parchment.

"Didn't you read the agreement?" he asked.

"No, I just signed the bottom," I said.

The robot judge ended up slapping me with a misdemeanor for Failing to Adhere to Agreed-Upon Agreements, penal code 415 (e) (3).

It wasn't like I was a dummy. I knew I could no longer attempt to be my old coquettish self with a casual person on the street. After all, wasn't it part of the job of being an MSW? Well, not so, because they were apparently free to roam in public places while they were off the clock and not actively be MSWs. I was highly confused. It was my poor luck not to know this. When the city caught me trying to charm an MSW in person a second time, they listed me as a sex offender!!!

But would you believe they still allowed me to use the app??? This I pointed out to Dr. Price as a fine example of magical thinking, by them. The yellow ribbon on my app profile warned women of my crimes. It didn't help.

I met Sarah despite my disgraceful record.

Sarah reserved a bar for us called the Hideaway. I wore black socks to help me forget Mr. and Mrs. Poopy.

Sarah was a retired elementary school teacher who became a misanthrope activist. One of those. Like me, she disliked people yet wanted to have sex with them. We played footsies under the table, which made me dwell over the Poopys instead of Sarah. All hope was lost. I wasn't confident because of my broken heart over Jolene, but I still lusted for Sarah. As I'd written several letters ago, my brain was scrambled thanks to Mrs. Poopy's absence....

A few too many glasses of whiskey later, we were holding hands on our walk back to the hotel. I felt strongly compelled to murder Sarah. She wanted to go to a misanthrope art show, but I hated crowds. There was the solution, of course, after sex to end the evening while keeping the agreed upon parameters between us: liking sex and disliking people.

I was thinking through the probable sequence of events when I opened the door to my suite for the first time with a civilian woman by my side. The Handler forbade me to bring back any company during my stint in rehab, but I was able to sneak her in. It was also way past curfew, and I had to avoid the staff, but in my drunken state, I forgot about the cameras installed everywhere. After I opened the door, there was a rotten smell coming from the kitchen. Sarah plugged her nose!!! Without imagining that scenario, I made a mental guess that the stench was fontina cheese from Halloween sitting in the refrigerator. Lying on the kitchen floor, though, on its side, was a gray and bloated rat, a dead one! There was a plague in the city because of the paucity of cheese, which they apparently didn't stand for.

It was a damn shame after stepping into my unit for the first time since moving to Periscope City with a live, unpaid for female, whom I fully expected to have sex with and potentially murder. Now my plans went south because of a stinking dead rat. I LOST MY MIND and snatched the rat by its leathery tail!!!

Sarah backed away as if I were brandishing a pistol.

My wet and horny brain forced me to dangle the stinking creature in Sarah's face. It began to dance and swing like a yo-yo.

Sarah ran to the hallway, and my chances with her smashed against the wall like a door thrown wildly open.

Still, I gripped the thing between my innocent fingers. Its gray fur made me start vomiting. Its thickness clogged the toilet! I defenestrated the monster sixteen stories to the icy concrete! For once, the police served and protected when a car, a patrol car, flattened the rodent!

They booted me out of the Handler Hotel and sober living after what was caught on camera. Now I ended up back at square one at the Cramden in a different room from before.

Even with the rat dead, its phantom tail still slithered in my hands. And more rats came, spreading disease.... Whenever I entered the kitchen after that night at the Handler, my nose panicked. My morning coffee, for instance, smelled like fried chicken, or red beans and rice. I didn't know how much longer I could cope.

Then, one fateful night, my nose announced that something else was rotting. I rolled up an old copy of the gazette, ready to batter whatever lay in the shadows, and opened the fridge. The paltry, bare bulb light shined over the mystery. It wasn't a creepy gray rat. No! No! No! My eyes watered at the sight of a brown and yellow argyle sock!!! HER!!! A winsome miracle!!! But despite her angelic presence, my baby girl from long ago and far away was stinking like a cadaver. So I took her to the shower....

But how did she get to the kitchen??? I had my theories. What if she'd been staying on my feet the whole time and I'd never even noticed??? What if my wayfaring service dog used to belong to Jolene and had taken Mrs. Poopy to Periscope City with him and hid her somewhere???

And then we met… Stewart laid Mrs. Poopy on the kitchen floor. A storybook ending. But what a ridiculous story!!! Now back to this story.

Poor Mrs. Poopy was going to remain a widow for the rest of her tragic life until I put her out of her misery. Honestly, what fortune would she bring without her soulmate??? There couldn't be a more hopeless situation. So I lit her on fire, not to ward off any evil spirits, but in fact to prove she was just a sock, and a mediocre one at that!

Meanwhile, as I was sacrificing one of my dearest companions, the same issue of the gazette at my feet, and remained in mint condition… What a strange predicament it was that I lost the most sacred things yet kept the most trivial things. It boiled down to how much I was attached to them, and the general contrary nature of existence.

Warm regards from cold-hearted Periscope City,

Nick

Alan

I matched with Penelope through the *Loner* app. She was thirty-seven, and I was fifty. We agreed to meet at a bistro in downtown Periscope City. I tried to impress her by gambling on a suit and trimming my hair and beard for the occasion. It was my first date in six years.

—

I reserved an outdoor table at 8 p.m. under a full moon. No one took the empty patio except for me and a staff of hospitable robots. I waited for Penelope near a dribbling water fountain. She rolled in late and parked her wheelchair at my table. When she saw me, her warm smile wilted like a dying tulip. I wondered what the problem was.

She kept her downcast eyes on her phone and swiped left or right when I tried to have small talk with her.

"Something wrong?" I asked.

"Yes, Alan. In fact, something is wrong."

"What's the matter?" I said.

"You never told me you were in a wheelchair."

Never told her? "But you are, too," I said. "Is that bad?"

"Yes," she said. "Very bad."

"I didn't know it was an issue," I said.

"You must not have read my profile," she said. "No wheelchairs. Now look at us, bickering already."

What could I say to change her mind?

Penelope started rolling away from the table.

"Wait," I said. "Let's talk. This is insanity."

"Talk about what? Good luck with everything," she said.

"Don't go," I said.

But in a matter of seconds, she rolled out of the patio.

My server came to the table and towered over me. I sank into my wheelchair.

"Are you ready to order?" it said.

I picked a random item—the veal.

"And for the lady?" it said.

I feared it would ask that.

"She's not coming back," I said.

"May I take her menu?"

—

I'd been waiting to die for six years. Loners who gave up on everything went to Last Chance Bridge for one purpose only. I rolled into a dense white fog after dinner and couldn't see the water in the dark. Something sloshed in the canal like hidden swimmers under my feet. If I was to drown, maybe a quiet peace would wait for me after death. The town wouldn't let that happen, though. Sirens from the Periscope City Fire Department started wailing distantly. Surveillance cameras watched me from everywhere at that bridge. The Institute had to rescue me from jumping—or falling, in my case. I had to do it before they showed up. My arm's strength lifted my body from the chair. When I leaned halfway over the rail, the wheelchair slipped from under me. I got stuck on the railing and couldn't hold on any longer, so I fell backwards to the street and ended up glued to my back like my service turtle. At that point, there was nothing else to opt for except to crawl to my chair or surrender on the ground. I stared at the moon until I would be helped back up.

—

The Institute detained me in a seventy-two-hour holding cell for suicide watch.

—

After they released me, life returned to normal—if you could call it normal. I waited every morning at the Eternal Soul Coffee Shop around nine for a blonde with brown eyes to come in. Her name was Becca, like my ex-wife, or at least that was what I called her. She held her white service Bichon against her chest while ordering a cappuccino from the robot baristas. I loved it when she wore her white fur coat with her matching white leggings and high heels. She never acknowledged my existence. What else was new? I blended in with the white plastered wall. Everything in there was white, like the gift shop at the Dollhouse for the times I spent there. But all that being said, her beauty alone kept me alive. I wanted to go on living because of her. Becca was the only reason I was able to climb out of bed.

—

I decided to follow her down Howard Hughes Lane one afternoon, desperately needing to know which hotel she was staying at. My wheels started rolling quickly to catch up with her. Was it stalking? I don't know. *Who the hell cares?*

She stopped after a light and whipped her head around, which I didn't expect, and looked straight into my eyes. My toes began tingling and so did my legs, like the feeling after sitting on the toilet for too long. A hundred fireflies buzzed up my thighs. It was like my legs were zapped alive, and my body belonged to Frankenstein's monster. I stood from the chair—I shit you not.

But just when I was witnessing a miracle, she looked away as suddenly and kept walking. The fireflies dropped to their death. My legs folded like laundry, and I fell into my chair, back to my misery.

—

Daydreams were the only friends that kept me company. I fantasized about jogging through Periscope City and getting in shape for her. All I needed was for her to see me again. If only I could use my legs and throw the wheelchair away….

The only thing to rely on was being determined to walk. I even tried to stand up in my suite at the Bower. Day after day, my arms tried to lift my body from my chair. I prayed for the feeling to return. God needed to intervene. One day, when I got too frustrated, I had enough arm strength to spill myself to the floor and throw the wheelchair out the window from the first story. It didn't land anywhere except on its side. After management found out, there was a knock on the door. I began to crawl over there. A nurse on the other side held the wheelchair for me to get back into.

—

I continued waiting in the Eternal Soul Coffee Shop for Becca, but for some reason, ever since that miraculous day, she stopped coming in. How fitting. There was no one to ask where she was either. The robot baristas sure didn't know, nor were they inclined to tell me even if they did. The rub against Periscope City was the lack of acquaintances to ask such questions. Everybody kept to themselves. Good thing I never needed to ask for directions anywhere with my keen insight of where everything was.

—

Isolation spread like herpes in a city of loners. No surprises there. With my craving for a partner with no strings attached, I resorted to medical sex.

—

Dr. Luchozar practiced in, of all places, a strip mall wedged between a liquor store and a massage parlor. I sat in his waiting room and began to fill out a medical form. It flooded me with questions, annoying ones…such as if I had AIDS, migraines, fibromyalgia…. The pages wouldn't end. I wondered if anyone who came into his office ever had AIDS, migraines, or fibromyalgia. That would've been a fortunate bastard there. Just take some pills for that. No pills could get me out of my chair.

While I waited, a TV hung from Luchozar's ceiling and showed an infomercial over and over for medical sex. A male actor held a female doll and started running across an esplanade. It was like a commercial for erectile dysfunction. He pulled a frisbee out of his ass and threw it at the doll. It didn't catch it. He molded a sandcastle with the doll lying in the sand beside it, which blocked the water from demolishing the castle.

"Alan Koontz?" a nurse said.

I began rolling into the doctor's office.

After the nurse injected a needle in my arm, she handed me a plastic cup. "We'll need a sample of your urine." She even read my temperature. *Is it really necessary?*

Dr. Luchozar was an Irish terrier with glasses.

"How often do you masturbate?" he asked.

His questions made me sink farther into my chair. I didn't answer him.

"It's just us men in here," he said.

The nurse came into the room.

Luchozar looked into my eyes in a hearty, healthy way, the best I could describe it. She began filing medical records on the shelves.

I whispered to him, "Twice a day."

"Sounds like you have chronic celibacy," he said.

No shit. After six years of no sex.

He wrote my name under the silly diagnosis. "Just hand this to the nurse. She'll give you a card."

He wrote a prescription for hard-on pills, and the nurse stuck my information on a shelf.

"Shred it," I told her.

"But we'll need your documentation for renewal," she said.

I already thought that if I lived there for a year—which, the way my life was going, was certainly possible—I would wish to renew my card. What other choice was there? I told her, "Fine."

She snapped my picture. I would've preferred to hide my face. At first glance, it looked like a green card from Pervertland.

—

That night, from the menu in the *Loner* app, I had to choose either a human medical sex worker, a doll, or a robot (or multiple options if I wanted to have something like a menage a trois with any combination of humans, dolls, or robots). A normal medical sex worker cost five hundred dollars an hour. A robot MSW cost quadruple that. Medical sex dolls cost a thousand dollars an hour. All of it was before the five-thousand-dollar deductible. Then and only then would the Institute reimburse me thirty percent of the cost. That was how it was. A doll doubled the cost of a human MSW, but a person could no longer dazzle me unless she was Becca. Some other guy with functioning legs could have Penelope. Besides, what if another real woman rejected a man like me in a wheelchair? How would I feel?

The *Loner* app offered me a choice of different hairstyles, body types, eyes, noses, and lips for a doll. I wasted no time choosing what I wanted.

—

The doorbell rang a half hour later. I checked what hair I had left to make sure I was looking good. On the other side of the door, another one of those robots held a doll with blonde hair and brown eyes—just like my request. It was a spitting image of Becca from the coffee shop. I couldn't believe my eyes. Best of all, it wouldn't leave me for another hour.

"Hi, I am Manuel," the robot said. He looked like a Manuel. "Your card, please."

I strained myself to dig my wallet from my back pocket and pull it out.

Manuel scanned the card with its eyes and handed me the doll. "Enjoy."

The doll felt firm and durable in my lap. My night was filled with all kinds of possibilities. I laid it on the bed. It faced the ceiling with a blank look on its face.

"Your name is Becca," I said, "and you'll do what I tell you to do."

It said nothing back.

I killed the lights and began to marinate the room in soul music and lavender candles. My arms pushed me from the wheelchair onto Becca, my blonde doll, and I spread its rubber legs. My tongue began circling its latex lips and porcelain teeth while my fingers started running through its horsy hair and spongy bush.

"I've waited years for this," I said.

Not necessarily for a doll. It lay speechless. From the way it shook, its eyes moved like marbles in their sockets. Maybe a doll wasn't the best option, but at least it was something. For Christ's sake, a robot sex worker would've at least communicated words to me. Too bad I couldn't afford one.

In red high heels, a white garter, and stockings, it smelled a bit of…vanilla? Like a sweet from my childhood I couldn't quite bring to mind. After I unwrapped its skirt, everything else fell off the doll. My body started trying to worm its way into its petite clothing. Well, so much for that idea.

I jammed myself inside Becca. Its wet clit excited me further. I rammed in, slid out, rammed in, slid out, rammed in, slid out…. The doll's head bobbled. Its body shifted. Its eyes spun at each stroke. I struggled to maneuver through the numbness in my legs and worked my torso. The sex drained me.

"Do you like it?" I asked.

My fingers flapped its lips to simulate it talking, and I raised my pitch. "Yes, I love you inside me."

I panted at the doll. "I've always wanted you ever since I saw you at the coffee shop."

I had it pant back. "I've wanted you too."

"You'll be mine forever. Say it."

"I'll be yours forever and ever."

I strenuously lifted Becca. But even with my strong arms, it was a struggle. I flipped it over and let it ride me. While I lay on my back, that beautiful doll looked down on me into my eyes. At some point, the persistent stroking knocked me out cold.

—

The doorbell startled me awake.

"Who is it?" I asked.

The candles around the room were still waving.

"Manuel. I have to come to pick up April."

April was its real name. Manuel pulled me out of the moment.

The hour was up already. My time with Becca came to a close. I wished I could've spent more time with it, but it would've cost another thousand dollars on my credit card.

"Give me two minutes," I said. More like five with the effort it took to climb out of bed and put on my clothes.

I started dressing it. There was a puddle on my sheets from its juices. After I sat in my wheelchair, I lifted the doll to my lap.

We French-kissed before I opened the door to Manuel. It pulled the doll from my legs.

"Did you have fun with April?"

"You mean Becca," I said. "Worth every penny."

"Please fill out a five-minute survey when you have the time," it said. "Would you order it again?"

"When I get the chance," I said. "Say, how much does it cost to buy this doll?"

"Five thousand dollars," Manuel said.

Yikes. My hand didn't cost a dime.

"We also offer a program," it said. "You rent it once a week with a monthly subscription."

"What's the catch?" I asked.

"What is a catch?"

"You know, what's the caveat?"

"There is no caveat," it said. "We can bill you nine hundred dollars per session, a one-hundred-dollar discount for each visit."

Sounded like a deal, but with disability, the way it was, I could only wish to join. Even if I could afford it, it was too much cash to waste for instant gratification, which was no good for me. And I regretted spending so much money already without an orgasm, even with the hard-on pills. Speaking of which, the hard-on was still there. A human medical sex worker would've split the price, but like Penelope, what if she discriminated against me?

"No thanks," I said. "Have a good night, Manuel."

It stepped away with my baby doll. For once, I'd fallen in love with an inanimate object. The hell was wrong with me? I had some lag time before finally closing the door.

The cupboard was where I kept the candles. I rolled myself over there to blow them out. Above me, on the wall, which was too high for me to change the pages, was my calendar, a gift from the Institute: Twee Turtles it was called. To go with my service turtle I guessed. I had to feed Phillip his favorite earthworms. Oh, what a life. To end up in a wheelchair, feeding a pet turtle in a town full of robots and other lonely people. The page was left on March, and now it was May, no longer April. And by the way, April? Who the hell would name a sex doll, let alone a person, after a month? Was it Dr. Luchozar's idea? Suppose he had twelve of them from January to December, which reminded me of that asinine question that Moonga the robot asked me back at the Institute about which month I would be and why. November, of course. Always disgusted with myself, like the times after a succulent Thanksgiving dinner. The also succulent pleasure from Becca died not even ten minutes after my time with her. Or it... By then, it was long gone back at the factory, perhaps cremated in a furnace after use for all I knew. Unlike Thanksgiving dinner, I still wanted Becca, the doll, to come back. Photos of it from every angle, and selfies too, wouldn't do it enough justice.

I forgot about the candles and looked out my window from the first floor. The orange lights brightened downtown Periscope City, and the night fell to a lone emptiness everywhere in the frame. Nothing stirred except for a few lonely walkers on the sidewalks and my neighbor—a deaf ex-senator who threw parties with medical sex workers of the human variety every night. His parties distracted me when I was trying to write my memoir, so I put on noise-canceling headphones that set the mood for my life story. What type of music would work for "The Becca Affair"? Would that make for a good chapter name? In that specific chapter, I would compare Becca the doll to Becca the human and assess their strengths and weaknesses. Of course, Becca the doll was far better rated. Now, I would tell my readers, since dolls existed, no longer did I feel the need to love a person. What a sad problem to have. What a great problem to have!

Alan II

I fell out of my wheelchair again in the middle of Howard Hughes Lane. It was the early afternoon in downtown Periscope City. The sun was frying me on a cobblestone road. My lenses cracked. No one threw me a freaking rope, either. I wished for someone to hit me, just run these crippled bones over, but no cars decided to pass. An ugly breeze brushed my hair and gave me the chills.

A pair of cowboy boots stopped in front of me with jeans over them. I turned around to see a stranger with an eyepatch—or what appeared to be a man with an eyepatch because I couldn't see much without my glasses. He kneeled closer. In fact, it was an eyepatch. He wore a jean jacket and a gold chain with a cross hanging from it.

"Hey, bud. Let's get you back in this chair," he said.

I didn't want his help. "Just let me die here."

"Relax. We'll fix them glasses."

"No. I don't want to see this chair anymore."

"But you cain't just lay there like a piece of ribeye."

"Yes I can."

After he picked me up like I was a honey baked ham fresh out of the meat section, I began to whine in the wind for him to put me back down.

Turned out he had enough strength to force me back into my chair and roll me away from the embarrassing scene. "The name's Bobby," he said. "Shreveport, Louisiana. What about you?"

I didn't need to know that.

"Alan."

"Where you from, Alan?"

What did it matter? "Naples," I said.

"Where's that?"

"Florida."

"No shit," he said. "My ex is from Covington."

I didn't see how that connected.

It didn't seem to matter. My new acquaintance wheeled me to his car, and I let him help me get into the front seat. There had to be an ulterior motive. For a minute, I thought he was kidnapping me. Who knew what weirdos lived in that city? A weirdo had the potential to steal a man in a wheelchair. By the strong engine smell, it was a vintage car. Even with my blurry vision, I could see the furry dice hanging from its rearview.

He climbed into the driver's side.

"You don't seem to belong here," I said.

"Nah, I live here," he said. "You think I'm visitin'?"

"You don't seem like a loner."

"What is a loner?" he asked.

I was hoping that was a rhetorical question.

He began revving the engine and waiting for me to answer.

"A loner wants to be alone," I said. "You seem like a people person."

His face was stuck to the road ahead, and he lit a cigarette. "I like to be alone," he said. "It's my water."

Not me. I was what you called an accidental loner, not an intentional loner, ever since my friends and family went to Splitsville because of my age and ever since they put me in that cocksucking wheelchair. Who needed them anyway? Maybe I was better off alone from those heartless jackoffs.

"What kind of car is this?" I said.

"A '79 Chevy Nova, bud."

I loved the smell of gasoline, how it made my stomach rumble like my Firebird, which I couldn't drive anymore, obviously.

Bobby burned rubber through the commercial streets, going close to sixty in a twenty-five-mile-per-hour zone.

"Talkin' to any ladies?" he asked.

"Not a soul," I said.

"Got myself a pretty little thing the other night," he said. "Looked eighteen from Oklahoma. I took her to my bed, but she lay there as stiff as a doll."

Must've been nice.

—

Bobby took me to a lens store where they fixed my glasses. Afterward, we stopped at No Man's Park for an eight-man basketball game. What kind of loner belonged to a league? I would've rather crawled into bed and pretended the day never happened, but I was in debt to him for his kindness.

We stayed at No Man's Park until night. There was only one basketball court. One of the hoops was missing its net. No one else was in the park except for a man who went down a slide for adults.

Bobby wheeled me onto the court, where everyone began shaking my hand and introducing themselves. I was always bad at names and didn't care about getting to know any of them. They were friendly to me, though, but once we started playing, no one wanted to pass the ball to the guy in the wheelchair. I threw my hands in the air and yelled when I was open. But my teammates passed me by. I had to chase them up and down the court like a freaking golden retriever.

—

They quit after dinner. After all that exercise, me spinning my wheels for an hour or so straight, I was craving a hoagie from my favorite deli at the Handler Hotel for alcoholics. They served something called "the number four" with all kinds of cheeses and sandwich meats in it and just enough mayo and mustard. I would've had to reserve a table because only one customer could eat there at a time. It was well into the dinner rush, so I missed my opportunity to eat there all because of that stupid basketball game. I had to resort to the buffet at my hotel, which served the handicapped something worse than hospital food. I wasn't inclined to invite Bobby either. He finally dropped me off at the Bower Hotel for the disabled, where he stayed, too. A small world. Then again, Periscope City was a tiny world.

—

I sat alone in my suite after a day of falling out of my wheelchair and meeting too many random people. Which was worse? It was exhausting. I struggled for the right words to flow from my fingers to my laptop, straining to visualize the scenes for my memoir. Writing it was my only joy in life besides whiskey and medical sex dolls. I found my neighbor, the deaf ex-senator, to be a persistent problem. Like every other night, he started banging MSW's. Even with my headphones on, I could still hear him on the other side of the wall.

Someone knocked on my door. Unless it was Manuel with my Becca, I didn't care who it was, so I ignored it. But when whoever the person was kept knocking, it chased my muse out the window. *Who the fuck would do that?* By ten o'clock at night, it made me desperate to know who was knocking that late. With nothing to type, I began to roll over there to answer the door.

"Who's there?" I asked.

"Hey, it's Bobby. What's up?"

"Bobby who?"

"You know, from basketball."

Oh, him from earlier, the guy with the eyepatch who rolled me back to my room. What a mistake to let him know where I lived.

"I'm trying to work," I said.

"We're playing poker up in my room. Was seeing if you wanted to come up and join us."

Hell no. And again, he was socializing. "Bobby, I agreed to play basketball because you helped me. But that's where our relationship ends."

"Come on, bud. Let's get you drunk. I got bottles of Dizzy Buffalo."

Dizzy Buffalo? Dizzy Buffalo attracted me like honey did a bee, like blood did a bed bug, like nectar did a hummingbird. Never mind where I lived. How did he know what I loved? My suspicions grew further. I figured I could have a drink or two and leave. Why not? After all, for as much as I loved solitude, maybe I was still a social animal by nature. The thought of whiskey always made people seem more tolerable. So I opened the door to see him standing there with a dumb look in his only eye, if ever a person had a dumb look, or any sort of look, in only one eye.

—

Bobby stayed in Room 802. There I met Kyle, who was a circus attraction, standing under five feet. I soared above him when I sat next to him at the poker table in my wheelchair.

There was also Frankie from Portland, Oregon, who shuffled and dealt the cards. Her skill amazed me because she had one arm. She was missing her other arm from friendly fire in the army. Kyle poured shots of Dizzy Buffalo. Bobby dropped a needle on a country record, of course. I lit a spliff with tobacco and medical weed from the only Pericope City dispensary.

Bobby kept a clean room, which surprised me, given how filthy his Chevy Nova was and his general dirty self. His incense burning in the room made me want to puke. The only mess to find was on the poker table. It was littered with gum, mints, ashtrays, poker chips, drink glasses, Bingo raffle tickets, and Dizzy Buffalo bottles.

Frankie thumbed toward Bobby with her one thumb. "How did you meet this clown?" she asked me.

I liked her choice of words.

"I found his ass kissing the street," Bobby said. He apparently felt the need to answer for me.

"What were you doing on the street?" she said.

What a dumb question. I gestured to the sides to reference my abominable chair. "I was looking for ants," I said. "The fuck you think? I fell out of it."

"Jeez, I'm sorry," she said.

"He tried to stand," Bobby said. "Right, chief?"

Chief? Bud? He didn't know me from Adam. So what was with the nicknames? "Yes, I tried to stand," I said.

"What made you think you could do that?" Kyle said.

The nerve of him. "I'll tell a story. You won't believe me, but I'll tell it anyway."

Bobby sat to my left, and he was the type who would sit backwards in a chair. I saw no sign of an animal. Everyone in town rented a service pet, so where was his? "By the way, you got a service pet?" I asked.

He looked at Frankie to fish for an answer. "I ain't got one. Why?"

Whether he did or not didn't matter all that much, but I suspected something was wrong. I raised an eyebrow at him. "You got to be the first person without one."

"I cain't talk about it," Bobby said.

It occurred to me that his pet was dead. Pets did die. Death made sense, as ever. "A snake? You seem like a snake person."

"Nah, a parrot," he said.

A parrot? It certainly went with the eyepatch. "What did you call him?" I asked.

Bobby started shaking his leg, staring off into space, drawing deeply from the spliff. "Ichabod."

"Ichabod the parrot," I said. "I like that. Like the headless horseman."

He coughed out smoke. "Is that a rock band or somethin'?"

Bobby never came across as a literature major. Still, I had to wonder where he knew that name from. "Never mind," I said. "So what happened to Ichabod?"

Frankie squeezed Bobby's hand for support. He gave the spliff to her.

"I told you I cain't say."

I couldn't imagine being emotionally attached to a bird, and I couldn't stop prying. "Did he die from natural causes?"

At that point, Kyle's face was boiling hot. "You ask a lot of questions, don't you?"

Of course, since my years as a beat reporter, back when my legs were still working. Kyle appeared as if he wanted to throw hands. I was tempted to take that shortcake in my wheelchair with enough arm strength to beat him down. "Yes I do."

"So then, what's your pet?" Kyle said. He was daring me to say.

But who cared if I told them? I would never see them again. "Mine is a turtle. His name is Phillip. Phillip the turtle."

Bobby looked like he wanted to cry. "I come home and find little Ich on his side," he said.

I felt a little remorse for him. It was weird, but I had him to thank after peeling me from the sidewalk. "Sorry that I asked," I said.

"S'okay," he said.

"This place is haunted," Frankie said.

"You mean the hotel?" I said.

"Nah, the room," Bobby said. "The girl stayed here before me kicks the bucket for no dang reason. The girl before her, too."

"Where did you hear this folklore?" I said.

"Everybody know a ghost haunts this room," Bobby said.

I believed him, but I also didn't. Although anything could happen, for all I knew, he was lying through his teeth. "So people have been dying in this room, yet you stay here," I said.

"They booked all them other rooms," he said. "And this is the only hotel for us disabled folks."

Man, was that the truth, after trying to move for months.

"I don't know what to say," I said. "I wish I could cheer you up."

Bobby stopped shaking his leg and smiled at Frankie, then at Kyle. My suspicions only grew. Bobby burst out laughing. So did Frankie. So did Kyle, right in my face. It was the dumbest joke ever played on me. Kyle started slapping the table, laughing so hard.

"Yeah, keep laughing," I said. "Real funny."

When the laughter stopped, a new country song started playing, and we went back to our hands. I poured another glass of Dizzy Buffalo just to cope with their idiocy.

"What about your story?" Kyle said.

"Yeah, we still ain't heard your story," Bobby said.

"Never mind," I said. "You wouldn't believe me."

"Go 'head," Bobby said. "We havin' a good time."

I had no idea which story they wanted to hear, so I told them my saddest story, about Becca and how she went to the coffee shop every morning. The story about Penelope embarrassed me too much, the same with the doll for the moment, and I was too drunk to remember any stories before Periscope City.

"A woman I called Becca used to come to the coffee shop every morning," I said. "You know the coffee shop there on Howard Hughes and Winter Bear?"

"Yeah, I know that one," Kyle said.

"Sure," Frankie said.

"Who don't?" Bobby said.

"Well, this beauty would make her cappuccino with her Bichon in her other hand, but she never noticed me."

"Dang," Bobby said.

"How sad," Frankie said.

"So one day, I followed her down Howard Hughes Lane and tried to keep up with her," I said. "She had long legs, which made for long strides."

"So you were stalking her," Frankie said.

I worried if it was but kept telling myself it wasn't.

"It isn't stalking if she doesn't see me," I said.

"Yeah, I'm pretty sure you were stalking her," Kyle said.

"Would y'all shut up so he can finish his story? Dang," Bobby said.

"Let me be clear that I wasn't stalking. Anyway, she turned around all of a sudden and looked at me. I couldn't believe that we made eye contact. My legs began tingling."

"For real?" Kyle said.

"Yes, for real," I said.

Frankie touched her heart with her hand. "Aww," she said.

"They were tingling everywhere, and for the first time in six years, I could stand on my feet."

"Six years?" Kyle said.

"Yep. Believe it or not, my legs almost straightened out that day, but after so many years of sitting, I couldn't take a step forward. But once she looked away and kept walking, my legs lost their feeling again, and I fell back into this rolling hunk of shit. I was convinced that she was responsible for healing me. My love for her, even unrequited, brought that gift. She hasn't shown up to the coffee shop ever since. But I still wait for her to walk through that door every single day. If I can just see her and get her to notice me…."

"That's the story?" Bobby said.

"Yep. A miracle, is it not?"

"I don't like the way the story ended," Frankie said.

Well, what did she expect? "You don't like the way it ended?" I asked. "But everything really happened. I can't just change the story to your liking."

"Just saying," Frankie said.

"Yeah, don't you have any happier stories?" Kyle said.

I looked at them like they were all crazy idiots. Frankie went back to dealing the next hand. After telling them the story, I felt like maybe I was the crazy idiot. But what a regret to share it in the first place. I wanted to leave, but I stayed for my other love, the Dizzy Buffalo.

Periscope City didn't accept cash, only credit, which was why the table was piled with gum and mints and raffle tickets, among other things.

"We heard you're staying in the lobby," Kyle said.

"How is it?" Frankie said.

If they only knew…. Fact was, ever since I tried to jump the bridge, the hotel wouldn't let me stay anywhere above the first floor. But I wasn't about to bring up my attempt. The Institute almost transferred me to the Himmler Hotel, where the nurses watched the suicides, but since I got around in a wheelchair, they kept me at the Bower under special care, which was the attention I didn't want. Everybody else wanted a room down in the lobby so they could get to the buffet before that awful food was gone. "You may think you want my room, but you don't want my neighbor," I said.

"How come? He a crank or somethin'?" Bobby said.

"He's a lech who likes to party with MSWs like every day is Mardi Gras."

"What's an MSW?" Frankie said.

"A medical sex worker," Kyle said. "I already told you."

"Okay, I just moved here," Frankie said. "Don't jump all over me."

"What else could you expect from an ex-senator?" I asked.

Bobby flashed his eyes at Frankie. "Ex-senator?"

She eyed Kyle, and Kyle eyed Bobby. Something itched me about them again, but I didn't know what.

"Yeah, he's the one with the service tiger," I said. "How can you miss him?"

"Oh, he's an ex-senator?" Bobby said. "Ain't that somethin'."

Frankie asked me, "Have you been with an MSW before?"

I was embarrassed too much to show those imbeciles my card. "Yeah, I've tried one."

"How do you get one?" Frankie said.

I explained it to them. "You go to a doctor who has a license in medical sex work. Just don't call him a pimp or you'll piss him off. You can rent an MSW by the hour. But if humans don't do it for you, you can always try a doll or a robot, but those cost too much."

"A robot," Frankie said. "My goodness. What has this world come to?"

Something sweet, something tragic. I gave them the once-over to see what they thought and decided, by the look of them, they probably couldn't afford a person let alone a fancy doll.

"But I think you all should get a card," I said. "I mean, just look at us. We're a mess. If we're not missing eyes, we're missing arms. If we're not missing arms, we're missing legs. If we're not missing legs, we're too short to ride the rollercoaster. How can anyone love us?"

My bitterness took over the room. Nobody in there said a thing after my cruel but honest words. The needle started skipping at the center of the record. Kyle and Bobby pouted. So did Frankie, who began shuffling and reshuffling the deck with her one hand.

Kyle gave me the spliff and what was left of it. "Bobby, I'm using the bathroom."

"Go 'head," Bobby said.

Kyle locked the door over the awkward silence. While I didn't crave their friendship, I also regretted showing my venom as a drunk. Nobody deserved to see me like that. At least I didn't curse at God as usual. They were owed an apology.

"I'm sorry if I hurt your feelings," I said. "And it's okay if you don't like my story."

The vinyl crackled over us. Bobby slipped Frankie a grin. "Who says we don't like it?" Bobby said. "We're here for yuh." He raised his cup. "To miracles."

We tapped our cups.

"To miracles," I said.

The shot burned my eyes. I started mumbling incoherently from there. Bobby dropped the needle on another terrible country song. My vision split in two.

"Are there man dolls?" Frankie said.

"Yes, there are man dolls, too," I said.

"Can they eat me out?" she said.

"No," I said. "But a robot can, to the best of my knowledge."

"What about murder?" she said. "Can they murder?"

"I'm sure you can arrange that," Bobby said.

My head rolled across my shoulders. I tried to keep my eyes open.

Kyle returned to his chair, and his head expanded into a blimp before my Dizzy Buffalo eyes. "You gonna hang in there?" he said to me.

I muttered something, whatever it was, to prove to him and everybody else that I wasn't about to pass out.

"You better get back to your room, chief," Bobby said.

I quit drinking and said okay.

He began pushing me to the door to get me to the elevator, where I handed him my key card. I trusted him at that point. When we got to my room, he tucked me into bed. I said, "Bobby? I love you."

Bobby's eyes opened wide and looked away from me. "Umm, alright," he said.

That was me on Dizzy Buffalo—pouring out my sentiments and falling straight to my vulnerable self. I couldn't remember a goddamn thing after that.

—

The morning after found me on my stomach with a hangover. When I reached for my wallet, it was missing from my back pocket. My ID, my hotel cards, my debit card, my credit cards, my medical sex card, my medical weed card all gone. The swindler with one eye had my wallet. How could those sons of bitches rob a man in a wheelchair? Of course, they weren't real loners, just lowlifes who took advantage of the lonely like so many other people.

Phillip crawled from under the bed.

I said, "Hey, Phillip. Don't trust anyone."

—

No one occupied Last Chance Bridge before the sun rose and before my daily trip to the coffee shop. I stopped to look at the lazy canal.

A lonely guy in a gondola rolled down the water, and a robot pulled the oar. I didn't go there to jump, just to lean against the rail and think about jumping. Those grifters were probably halfway to Vegas in Bobby's Chevy Nova by then with my wallet and other people's stuff.

—

It turned out to be true. The cameras caught those dopes before they could flee from Periscope City. Not that I was their only victim. The deaf ex-senator was too. Some robot did a marvelous job with the sketches that ended up on the six o'clock news. The police could retrieve my wallet.

—

As weeks went on, I continued writing my memoir in hopes of completing it by the end of the year, but I kept struggling because of the ex-senator.

—

Dolls kept me company a few days out of each month. I gambled at the casino here in town to win big and hopefully be able to buy one for five grand. In my belief, after that day when I could feel my legs, anything was possible.

—

A few more months crawled by, and every morning, I still waited at the Eternal Soul Coffee Shop for the real Becca to show up again. But more than likely, neither probable luck nor working legs were on my side. All I had was Phillip and hope. Some days, they were enough.

A Word from My Sponsor

My parents raised me right outside of Periscope City before Periscope City became a thing. All those years of drinking since thirteen drowned my attention, but it didn't veer me from being a straight-A student. I ditched my valedictorian speech for a six-pack in my Mustang. Drinking helped me feel like a grownup. I wanted to hurry up and become an adult. When my father died, the drinking only got worse. I rammed my Mustang into a phone pole one night, just trying to pick up fast food, and totaled the car. A police officer put me in handcuffs. The judge revoked my license and slapped me with community service. I had to collect twenty signatures from AA meetings. But it was like I didn't learn anything. I kept drinking on the job at the country club as if I needed to be punished even more. After I passed out in the fairway one morning, they fired me. My mother kicked me out and made me stay at a downtown sober living. And just like magic, when I stopped drinking, my friends all disappeared.

They held Alcoholics Anonymous meetings virtually in Periscope City. I stayed at the Handler Hotel for sober living. It wasn't like my mom's house before my DUI, but there was more freedom not having to live under her thumb any longer, if you could call sobriety freedom. I sat in my suite and went to my first meeting on my laptop with sixteen people on the screen.

My mother made me look for a sponsor. I recognized Marty because of his knobby nose, his pot belly, and his curly hair. He crossed his hairy arms with his head down like he was about to fall asleep. I knew him from my job at the country club.

"Hey, Marty," I said.

He looked bothered at me saying his name.

"Have we met?" he asked.

I was too ashamed to mention that I didn't work at the country club anymore. "You're from the Periscope City Country Club. I'm Ian. I used to be a greenskeeper there."

He invited me to a private room where no one else could hear our conversation.

"What brings you here?" he said.

I shared my screen to show him my electronic court document. He put on his bifocals to look.

"I need a sponsor," I said.

"You're asking me to be your sponsor?" He made it sound like it was a joke. Maybe it was to him.

"Can you do it?" I asked.

He removed his glasses. "Come back tomorrow. Bring your phone."

Thank God I was going to virtual meetings, so I didn't have to see anyone in person.

He left our private room.

A secretary named Darcy asked someone to read the twelve steps out loud and someone else to read the twelve traditions. It confused me.

A guest speaker wore a military uniform. Medals hung from his coat like pinecones. He pressed a forage cap to his eyes. "My name is Alexander," he said. "I'm an alcoholic."

Everyone in the room droned like zombies: "Hi, Alexander." So did Darcy. Marty read a newspaper and didn't say hi. Neither did I.

The speaker had fifteen minutes to talk about his years in the Air Force. He said he used to be a flight attendant who would shoot whiskey on airplanes. The airline fired him a week before his wedding. The story depressed me, and life depressed me already.

Others shared their stories, not just Alexander. Darcy gave each person three minutes until we heard a buzzer through our computer speakers, and she silenced our microphones. The time came for her to share the time when she blacked out at a comic book convention and the time when a tenant farmer sexually harassed her in a diner on Halloween. She said she could wrestle herself out of a straitjacket. I would've loved to see her do it. This all occurred when she was drunk.

After telling their stories, they all convinced me that they had worse problems than mine.

Darcy electronically signed my court document. I had only nineteen signatures to go. Seemed like a tall mountain to climb. Marty left without saying goodbye. How rude. Darcy kept talking, but I stopped listening to what she was saying.

—

Marty took me to a private room at my second meeting while they shared their stories.

He said to me, "Share something."

"Share what?"

"Whatever," he said. "Worry about it when the time comes."

Public speaking wasn't my strong suit.

"But this is my second meeting," I said.

He left for the main room.

"I'm Marty, and I'm an alcoholic," he said. "Ian would like to share."

"Your name and disease, damn it," some guy said.

I was forced to introduce myself. How embarrassing. "I'm Ian, and I'm an alcoholic." It was my first time ever saying it. I was humiliated. It sounded like bullshit.

"Hi, Ian," everyone said.

My brain escaped through a lid in my head and ran out the door. What could I say?

Maybe everyone who waited patiently could relate to my embarrassment.

Marty flapped his hand at me and mimicked talking.

I had to think of something, so I told them about my DUI.

"That's all I got," I said.

They began to clap on the screen.

Marty wrote me a private message in the chat. *You did great.*

I agreed. It felt cathartic.

Others said their names, their diseases, and their hometowns, even countries—from Periscope City to India. Most of them left after the meeting. Marty remained on the screen and talked with me in a private room. I was afraid of what he was going to say next. He checked his Rolex.

"I want you to be the guest speaker next time," he said.

"Guest speaker?"

"When there's more people," he said. "I'll pick the meeting."

"No way in hell," I said.

"If you can do it, you can do anything."

I had my doubts.

"The first step is to meet the birthday people," he said. "You got your phone with you. Now go introduce yourself and get his phone number."

They started singing "Happy Birthday" to an old man with a tube in his nostrils. The old man celebrated his thirty-fourth year. Thirty-four years of sobriety. Wow. I was still living in my past life when he took his last drink.

Everyone else was mingling on my computer screen. I tried to find my purpose in there. The only things I had in common with them were addictions. I invited Marty to a private room again.

"Why do I have to do this?"

"Because you're a drunk," he said. "Think about your loser friends."

I had to defend them. "Some of them are okay."

"Oh yeah?" he said. "Where are they now?"

Who knew? "They're around," I said. "…Somewhere."

"Ditch them," he said. "They're no good."

What if I saw them? Did he just expect me to ignore them?

"You see your laptop?" he said. "Those are your new people."

Nine of them stuck around on the screen. Marty referred to a couple of guys who looked my age. I wanted to be alone instead.

He waited for me to follow directions. I awkwardly said happy birthday to the old man.

"I'm Jim," he said. "I'm eighty-eight. How old are you?"

I told him I was twenty-one, which was the truth.

As for the men who Marty wanted me to make friends with, Randy looked about thirty. I learned from his share how he used to drink mouthwash. Marty wanted me to exchange phone numbers with them. Randy invited me and a guy named Danny to a private room.

"What's the most hardcore shit you've ever done?" Randy asked me.

I told him Oxy.

"How many DUIs?" he said.

"One so far," I said.

Randy was on his eleventh. I didn't know what was more absurd: Jim's years of sobriety or Randy's number of DUIs.

Danny smiled at me with a missing front tooth. A Great Dane in the frame was his service dog, Sky. He held it by a leash. "I used to do meth," Danny said.

When I stopped to think about it, I didn't have any real friends, just people to drink with me. "What's it like?" I asked.

"Like a mirror shattering in my soul," he said.

I scratched meth off my list of drugs to take before I die.

"Where you staying?" Randy asked him.

"Somewhere east."

"You're homeless?" I asked.

"I always got a place. Just don't want to crash at no sober living."

"It's okay," Randy said. "I'm staying at the Handler."

I told him I was, too.

"No shit," Randy said. "Maybe I'll see you sometime."

"Maybe," I said.

Danny posted a graphic of a red chip on the screen. "They sent me this," he said. "It's my first thirty days."

"It's my first thirty as well," I said.

"Then where's your chip?"

Didn't care about one. "Hey man, I'm just here for my court document."

Danny bit into a jelly donut. "I'm out of here," he said.

"Why're you homeless?" I asked.

"This is nothing compared to Jersey," he said. "The Institute put me in sober living for loners like myself."

I knew what he meant. "You got this hotel, but yet you live in the streets," I said. "Something doesn't add up."

"The Handler wasn't all that," he said. "Too many people."

If by too many people he meant fifty people, because the Handler was fifty stories high with one person living on each floor, he was a bigger loner than I was. Impressive. When I met Danny, I felt the need to be altruistic. "Hey man, if you ever need a place to crash, you can crash at my place," I said. "I can sneak you in there."

"Nah, I'm cool," he said.

"Don't be a stranger," I said. "Take my phone number."

After we exchanged numbers, Danny said goodnight and turned off his screen. Maybe life wasn't so hard for him. After all, how did he get a laptop if he was homeless?

I wanted to leave too, but I still needed Darcy to sign my court document. Silver peace signs dangled from her earlobes. Her flannel coat looked like forty pounds.

Marty shut his screen off, too.

So did everyone else except for me and Darcy. She sucked me into a vortex of the stories she told, like her time at the psych ward. It was a long one. She checked her phone. "It's late," she said. "I know you want to hear more, but I gotta run."

"It's quite alright," I said.

"What's your number?" she asked.

I pictured the scenario: forty-three voicemails by four in the morning.

"What is it?" she asked.

I gave her a bogus number.

"Hold on a minute," she said. "Let me call you."

It surprised me that she would try to do that.

Darcy kept waiting. "It says it's out of service."

I reluctantly gave her my real number.

My phone vibrated, and Darcy saved it.

"Be sure to save mine," she said.

It was a relief when she left the room, but I forgot all about my court document. She was supposed to sign it. An entire trip to AA was wasted when I could've been playing video games instead.

—

My phone buzzed and startled me awake at midnight. Who the hell would do that? It was Marty. He left a voicemail for me to call him. I was surprised that anyone would still leave a voicemail, let alone call me. Just send a text. The last time I made a phone call was an emergency to my mom after the DUI.

—

Marty called me when I was eating, when I was showering, when I was watching movies. Our phone tag lingered for days. Despite him being my sponsor, I knew little about him other than he was a former detective. He thought he could have power over me by not telling me much about himself but having me tell him everything about myself. I kept thinking about my regrets for weeks but had trouble sharing them with a sponsor who kept so many secrets.

—

Danny wasn't kidding when he said the Handler Hotel wasn't all that. I wished they would've sold weed or alcohol in the gift shop. My addictions were still strong as I was going through rehab. They tried to settle them down with a pill for alcohol cravings, but it didn't work. I had to go to virtual meetings every day all day. A robot counselor counseled us on how to stay sober. It was weird, but at least I wasn't living with my mom.

—

I skipped a meeting one afternoon and took a Dryft ride to downtown Periscope City. While I tried to keep to myself, a lady named Katherine talked my ear off in the electric car about her life in Rhode Island.

After she dropped me off, I listened to a meditation app through my headphones while I began a stroll down the sidewalk on Howard Hughes Lane. A woman's voice told me to count my breaths, count my steps, count the number of letters on buildings. I passed a movie theater, where an animatronic doll in a tuxedo watched me from a box office. Creepy. How could I ever adapt to a town that looked like an amusement park for loners?

Another way to isolate myself in downtown, where a few other loners dwelled, was to light a cigarette in a designated smoking area.

Marty called. I was forced to answer the phone.

"Are you sober?" he asked.

I told him I was.

"Congratulations," he said.

"Congratulations for what?"

"For calling earlier," he said. "You finished the second step. The first step was taking phone numbers. Have you called anyone besides me?"

The program felt like a breeze. I told him no. "But what's the third step?" I said. "Me tying my shoes?"

"You need to call them," he said. "Write a list of people you resent."

Where would I start?

"Go to one meeting a day," he said. "At least. There's one tomorrow at seven in the morning."

Seven in the morning? Was he insane? I planned to go to one meeting a day, and that was it. Twice was overkill. "I can't do it," I said.

"It has a lot of hot babes," he said.

I knew his ploy, but it was a virtual meeting. And it wasn't like I could meet a woman in person there. Flirting with any woman outside of the *Loner* app in that draconian town was against the law. Marty was supposed to know that.

"Then we'll read from the Big Book," he said.

It was the bible for alcoholics, but it was really just a bunch of stories from other drunks.

I cut him off before he brought up a third meeting. "Community service is at eight," I said. It was true. I had to collect garbage along the side of the highway. It felt good to tell the truth to get out of any more meetings that day.

"So?" he said.

So? Did I need to spell it out for him?

"Someone committed to the program will find time," he said. "I attend them every day and never have urges."

"But you're retired," I said.

"Too many men have given me excuses and gone back to using," he said.

"It's not an excuse," I said.

"You want to be that guy?" he said. "Fine. Be that guy. But at least call me every day. Can you do that? Just tell me you're sober. Would it be so hard?"

Kind of.

Marty hung up before saying goodbye. I got angry. He was sixty-three. Someone as old as him should've learned proper phone etiquette.

—

That same night, not only did I have to write a long list of resentments, but I also had to write a sex inventory. Except with what little experience I had, there wasn't much to gather.

My phone rang at six in the morning. Even when I knew Marty from the country club, I still regretted making him my sponsor. But my mother made me find one. What else was I supposed to do?

There were four missed calls. Two from Darcy. One from Tim. I didn't know a Tim. And now the worst sponsor in the world. I had to be the unluckiest person in twelve-step. When it was that early, he wanted me to say that I was sober. I mocked him when I answered:

"Hey, it's me. I'm sober today."

"Good," he said. "There's a stag meeting tonight at eight."

A stag meeting was all men. So much for hot babes.

"You could've called me later about this," I said.

"I have a busy schedule."

A retiree with a busy schedule didn't make sense.

"You could've texted me," I said.

"What's with your generation and texting?"

What about his generation and calling?

"Grab a pen and write this down," he said.

I rummaged for my pen and notepad through the heap of my hotel room.

Marty gave me a password to the meeting and hung up again without saying goodbye.

—

I logged into the stag meeting to get another signature. Eight men showed up on my screen. An old man in a green coat looked like he was either sleeping or praying. I couldn't tell.

The meeting was a waste of time. There would be other meetings.

I left my hotel for the freezing, cold midway through the meeting, and lit a cigarette in a designated area. Raindrops began to fall in my hair, so I started hurrying back to the hotel. Through the downpour, the rain was dripping off the wooden structures. Every business was closed. The streetlights buzzed above me. The homeless kept to themselves, but one of them preached a communist revolution. "This is an all-out war on imperialism," she said. "You want to join?"

All I wanted was a decent night's sleep. "No thanks," I said.

The rain and the air full of smoked ham from the Handler's deli distracted me from my ruminations over my father.

Others stood around in scarves, beanies, designer jackets, better dressed than me in my wool coat. The homeless in Periscope City could get by just fine if they could withstand the winter.

I needed other sober friends. But how could I find them outside of the meetings? Randy was never around. And where was Danny? I called him, but it went straight to voicemail.

When I got back to my hotel room, a man's voice echoed from my laptop. He sermonized on the twelve traditions. The screen showed a couple of men left. The old man closed his eyes. I thought, what was the point of any of this? Where was Marty on the screen?

I invited a secretary with long brown hair and a tank top to a private room.

"Your name and disease?" he said.

I shared my screen to show him my court document. "Ian. I'm an alcoholic."

"I'll sign it when the meeting's over," he said. "And Marty wants you to call him."

Oh really. I felt like Marty existed just to piss me off.

"I just did," I said. "Should I call again?"

"He said so."

Fuck that. But what choice did I have but to sit and wait in my hotel room and listen to other people's problems? My stomach growled. When the time came to share, I bitched about my sponsor ditching me and how much I wanted to eat.

The old man shared and said he didn't have much time left. It could've been his last meeting. He also talked about his dead wife and how much he missed her. His story took my breath away. Once he finished sharing, I thought about comforting him. He tapped his knuckles on a wooden table for everyone to pray out loud together. It went:

"God, grant me the serenity to accept the things I cannot change, the courage to change the things I can, and the wisdom to know the difference."

We ended the prayer. "Keep coming back, it works if you work it."

I couldn't see myself alienating the old man, so after everyone left and the secretary signed my document, I stuck around to talk to him. Mike was seventy-three years old with prostate cancer. I wanted to cheer him up, but what was there to say to a man with a death sentence? He was the first person in all my trips to AA who was dying.

I hesitated to leave him, but he seemed to prefer solitude like me.

"Where do you live?" he asked.

"At the Handler Hotel."

"Ah, I used to live there," he said. "Ever eat at the deli?"

"No," I said.

"Order the number four," he said.

"The number four?" I asked.

"It's the best."

I took his word for it.

Mike remained on the screen by the time I left the virtual room.

When I made it downstairs to the deli, it was still open. The robot staff served one customer at a time. I sat at a window table. The rain sprinkled like the sprinklers used to do at the country club. I missed the bright mornings in the summer. I missed the green everywhere. I missed the arrows of ducks in the sky. I missed the peace on the golf course. Rather than appreciate working there, I always got drunk instead. Man, was it taken for granted. Now it was court dates, sober living, flaky sponsors, community service, my disappointed mom… Now thoughts of lonely Mike at his age, dying.

The smoked ham tried to pull me out of my gloom.

I texted Marty: Where are you?

Another robot served my table.

I was about to order the number four but didn't see a description for it on the menu. "What's the number four?" I asked.

"It comes with our special sauce," it said.

It wouldn't answer my question, but I trusted Mike and ordered it with kettle chips.

Marty called me, who also distracted me from ruminating.

"I'm sober today," I said.

"What?" he said. "Is this Ian? I think I have the wrong number."

I laughed sarcastically.

"Congratulations," he said. "I'm sober as well. So how was the meeting? Should I have gone?"

"Where are you?" I said.

"I was using the ball machine until it started raining."

The tennis ball machine was the most popular thing at the country club. All the members played golf and tennis by themselves.

"You missed the meeting," I said.

"I went to one earlier today. You should've come."
Whatever. I didn't even need a sponsor.

"I can't do this anymore," I said. "You're fired."

"Very well," he said. "But I won't be your last."

Actually, no. Marty would be my last. Twelve-step wasn't for me.

"Was Mike there?" he said.

"He was."

"I hope you got his phone number."

"Nope."

"Where are you?"

"At the deli."

Marty was a former resident at the Handler for Sober Living as well.

"Don't get the number four," he said. "Go see if you can get Mike's digits."

"But I just dumped you. Why're you telling me what to do?"

Marty hung up again without saying goodbye. Good riddance.

I went back to my hotel room after dinner and turned on my laptop just in case Mike was still on the screen, but the meeting was already over. He and Danny worried me.

By the way, Marty wasn't kidding about the number four.

———

After the twenty signatures, I kept staying at the Handler and going to more meetings, adjusting to them. Marty liked to gobble on maple sticks and drink coffee from Styrofoam cups. I never saw him laugh or smile. Nor did he ever talk about himself like the detective he was.

Danny continued missing. I saw Randy on the screen, who asked about him. Maybe Danny was roaming through the city with Sky and going through a full-blown relapse.

Darcy, who still wore her flannel, ignored me, which I deserved after ignoring her phone calls. Maybe her urges were crushing her, and she needed someone to talk to, but all I cared about was myself.

———

The Handler was like a vacation from home. I went two months without a drink. In a good way and a bad way, sobriety changed my life. Meetings were places to find acquaintances—a lot of weirdos. One of them talked about his socks and texted me pictures of his collie every day. When I looked at it that way, I was better off by myself.

Marty invited me to a private room as if he was still my sponsor.

"Jim died," he said.

"Remind me of Jim," I said.

"You wished him a happy birthday two months ago."

Oh. The guy in the wheelchair. What could I say? Jim hardly knew me. I felt numb over it.

"My condolences," I said. "What about Mike?"

"Gone, too. I went to his funeral."

I thought about my father again. The truth was Mike was also a stranger. If I went to enough meetings, I would meet people who would die. Speaking of which, what was wrong with me? Why did I feel so cold, so jaded, so apathetic?

———

Marty continued calling and leaving voicemails each day about meetings to go to. I finally volunteered to be a guest speaker at one.

Everyone in a virtual room learned about my first sip of whiskey. It was from my father's cabinet when I was thirteen. I was able to sneak it past my parents all through high school. Even with the alcohol, I was still getting straight A's as someone who was known as a functioning alcoholic.

When I was seventeen, my father died in a car accident. From there, my drinking only got worse. I skipped college. All I cared about was another drink. I just drank and drank and worked at the country club. During the share, it came to me that I was really like those other people.

"I missed my dad's funeral," I said. "I passed out."

By the looks on their faces, they took a collective gasp inside. You want to talk about regrets....

Since his death, my mom made me go to counseling. The therapist was just trying to teach me breathing techniques to stay in the present moment—a colossal waste of time and money.

My fifteen minutes were up, so the room applauded. Darcy let others share.

Marty invited me to a private room.

"You did a great job," he said. "Now you can do anything."

"Thank you," I said. "I may have shared too much."

"You did fine. I was too drunk to go to my college graduation. Guess I feel better now. Thanks."

"Glad to be of service," I said.

—

Marty was the only person from AA whom I knew outside of my laptop. I never ran into Randy when I stayed at the Handler. How did that happen? I was a disgrace, but the meetings made me feel better even if I refused to have a higher power. After a moment of silence for the alcoholic in need, Darcy tapped her foot like always, and everybody on the screen began to say the Lord's prayer. Ever since the twenty signatures were up, I knew it by heart, but like with the preamble, I didn't know the meaning.

The Dollhouse

Locals from neighboring towns insisted that it was a brothel, but it was a wellness center. A Dryft ride took me there one night in the boondocks past the power plants and a railroad track. I rode the backseat of a self-driven electric car. It swerved around potholes and dust devils. I expected the Dollhouse to be one of those late-night parlors with black windows and neon OPEN signs.

But in reality, it looked like a small hacienda.

"Have a good time, Miss," the car said.

—

At the entrance inside, a robotic guard checked my license and medical sex card with its eyes.

"Turn around," it said.

Its hands wrapped around my waist and frisked me. It could've gripped all of Utah, let alone lift all a hundred and twenty pounds of me. "Do not take pictures or video," it said. "Admission is twenty dollars."

"Twenty dollars?" I asked. "But I just showed my card."

"Free admission is on Mondays," it said.

It was a Tuesday night. Oh, well.

I paid the co-pay through the app and crossed a turnstile to a sterile whiteness of what looked like a cell phone store with dildos on the walls. Every worker was a robot. I was the only customer, thus the only human in there besides medical sex workers. They sold lubricants, vibrators, lingerie, and $5,000 sex dolls.

A robotic geek hugged a tablet against its ribcage. "Hello there," it said. "You must be Brody."

"Yes," I said. "I made the appointment."

It brought me to a kiosk with a digital tablet. They made me sign close to thirty pages of legalese.

I followed the geek through a hallway with a shrine of dolls encased in glass. A row of robotic owls twisted their heads above me. Their eyes zoomed in to me.

"It is just another night," it said.

Not even close. "Are those birds recording me?" I asked.

"Yes, but only worry about them if you are committing a crime," it said.

"Where're the documents going?" I asked.

"To the Pentagon," it said. "I am just kidding."

I didn't laugh.

It held a door for me. "Novus Ordo Seclorum," it said.

On the other side was a dark, cold room with flashing lights and electronic dance music screaming in my ears. A flock of medical sex workers in chaps and lingerie paraded by me. In each booth was a sex doll.

A half-black/half-Japanese robot slid down a brass pole onstage with legs that belonged on a stallion. I fell in love with its green eyes. It crawled up to me.

"How are you?" I asked it.

It squeezed its tits around the pole.

An animatronic DJ introduced it as Chanel. "Tip it through the app," it said.

How unreal that I was going to tip something that wasn't even human, but I did anyway. I scanned a tattoo of a barcode on its thigh with my phone and tipped it ten dollars. But where was the money going?

After I sat in a booth, a robotic server in a maid costume asked for my order.

"I don't want anything," I said.

"You must buy a drink," it said.

Since I was too freaked out by the dolls and robots for the place to get on my nerves, I ordered a six-dollar water.

Dolls took up every booth and had eyes that made me freeze in my seat. The one in mine wore a fishnet skirt with its nipples in the air.

"My name is Star," it said. "What is your name?"

The server returned with cherry water. Its sourness tickled me with a warm breeze. My thighs and lips tingled. The server's perfume caught me a buzz.

Two fighters on television grappled in a steel cage. The big man gouged the little man's left eyeball out. I looked away like you would've imagined at Star.

Its eyes transitioned from blue to red. "Hey sexy," it said. "Come to a room with me."

I was scared yet tempted. Its outfit made me want to screw it. It had to be the cherry water. I pulled it to my lap and stuck my tongue down its throat. Its ass cheeks fit in my palms. I stretched and molded its rubber skin. The longer we kissed, the more it tempted me. Whatever was in the cherry water increased my sex drive.

The server asked, "Do you want a room with Star?"

"Why're you interrupting me?" I said.

I can be a real bitch.

The server left me alone.

"Let's go to a room," Star said again. It followed a script like a talking doll for kids.

My interest was in a robot after traveling fifteen miles, so I set it back in the booth. "No," I said.

It replied with a blank stare. It was a good thing that dolls didn't feel rejection. The server pulled it from my table.

The whole place belonged to me, besides robots and medical sex workers, all of which abandoned the room. The solitude was comforting, but I still wanted sex.

—

Dolls and medical sex workers and medical sex robots in the upstairs den lay on leather Chesterfield sofas. The eyes on the dolls followed me like the eyes on *The Mona Lisa*. The workers lazily focused on their smartphones, probably lolling for a paycheck.

On a widescreen over a fireplace, a mass murderer with a noose around his neck dropped through a hatch and dangled from a rope. A crowd of thousands roared around his twitching body. How could they show a public execution and a martial arts fight to the death in a wellness center?

I marched to a robot behind a counter. They all looked so human.

"Excuse me," I said. "But can you turn that off? We're not at a sports bar."

It spoke in a British accent. "Would you prefer to watch something else?"

"No," I said. "Now get me another water."

After it turned the TV off, it buried its hands into a mountain of ice. "I am Steve," it said. "I will be your dolltender."

The name *dolltender* spoke for itself, but I still wasn't interested in one.

It pulled the cherry water from the ice and handed it to me. "What are you looking for?" it said.

It meant either a doll, a person, or a robot. "A female," was all I said.

"That is a vague request, but let me show you," it said.

The dolltender brought out three nude dolls like a perverted ventriloquist. "This is Roxy," it said. "She will bring you a quicker, shorter orgasm. Vikki, however, will do the opposite, which is a more delayed yet extended orgasm. Finally, Strawberry is a hybrid."

Strawberry, with its pink hair, was the best option if I wanted to go that route.

"Go ahead," Steve said. "Smell them. We sprayed them this morning."

The middle one, Vikki I thought its name was, smelled like a glazed donut, like a girlfriend back in Hartford, Connecticut.

"Vikki is the very first doll from the factory," Steve said. "Right, Vikki?"

Its eyes opened at the words, but they didn't blink when they shifted in their sockets, with sharp, black comb bristles for eyelashes. "Do you want to have some fun in the back?" it said to Steve.

"No thank you, but our guest might," Steve said.

"How much?" I asked.

"To have all three will cost you three thousand four hundred and fifty dollars."

Jesus. Only a wealthy person could afford all of them, but at least I had good enough credit for a robot. "Does insurance cover them?" I said.

"It does not," it said. "Only human medical sex workers are in network. You may request a superbill, and insurance will reimburse you a percentage of the cost. That is if you meet the deductible."

I assumed the percentage that my insurance company in Periscope City would cover was absurdly low. Regardless of that, insurance was killing the mood.

"Please," Steve said. "Flirt with the workers on the couches."

I took the bottle and reclined in a Morris chair made of alligator skin instead. The fire from the fireplace breathed on the back of my hand. The room otherwise sent me chills, perhaps from the cherry water.

I met eyes with one of the male MSWs, a mistake on my part. He wrapped his hands around my shoulders for a massage. I thought of a nice way to tell him no.

"I'm waiting for something else," I said.

"Who?" he said.

How dare he ask. It was none of his business what I wanted. Chanel, the robot from the stage, lay with its legs curled on the sofa. I wanted it to approach me without my request. That was part of the fantasy: to be desired without having to ask.

"I'm not telling," I said.

He walked away and shook his head. My rejection seemed to offend him, but who cared about his feelings?

Chanel leered at me and maybe remembered me from the stage and the generous tip through the app. They had the ability to smile like a sloth. I was normally shy, but my confidence bloomed in there because of the cherry water, so I smiled back at it.

Its curves bounced toward me in a leopard miniskirt, with its clomping pumps on the hardwood floor like hooves. Its body was sculpted from head to toe, and its human nature was buried beneath layers of makeup and augmentation. But, damn, it worked.

It sat on my lap, tickled my hair, and slipped its warm, buttery hand between my skinny thighs. "I really love your tattoos," it said.

I smelled insincerity coming from a machine. "Thank you," I said.

Its fingernail ran a circle around my left shoulder blade. "Especially this one."

"That's my grandfather," I said.

It tongued my left ear and blew softly in it.

I dripped again and tingled all over.

"Are you going to tip me?" it asked.

Another tip? How was it programmed to say that? I guessed they tried to make it sound like a human being.

"How much do customers usually tip you?" I asked.

"Three hundred dollars."

I brushed its hand away as if it burned. "Whoa, whoa, whoa," I said. "Sixty dollars tops." What if it was already charging me?

"Sixty dollars will buy you a conversation," it said, "nothing more."

I tried to spark jealousy in it to keep it from demanding gratuity.

"I still have to decide," I said.

It rolled its eyes and trotted back to the sofa, probably thinking it was gold, and in that room, it was. How could a robot have thoughts?

Its attitude destroyed everything. Medical sex robots like Chanel crossed a boundary. It was like an ordinary sex worker was hiding in it for all I knew. Who could trust that place?

I went to Steve. "Sir…I mean…you…. That robot just asked me for a tip. What kind of place is this?"

"I am truly sorry," it said. "You may submit your complaint to the outsourced center in Yuma, Arizona. The representative can supply you with free admission upon your next visit if you desire."

Was it worth it to go through all the trouble?

I had three choices: either to pay for a human MSW and ache from regret for missing Chanel, or to break the bank for a sex doll out of network, or to surrender to the third option and stick with my true desire.

"I want Chanel," I said, "even if it wants a tip."

After Steve called its name, Chanel met me at the counter.

Its curly fingernails gently scratched my neck.

"How much time would you like with Chanel?" Steve asked me.

"How much time do I get?" I asked.

"You have a choice between fifteen minutes and thirty minutes."

Because Chanel wanted a tip, and I was on a budget, I decided on fifteen minutes.

"Perfect," Steve said. "Which room would you prefer?"

"What're my options?" I asked.

"You may choose the western room, the enchanted forest room, the Jupiter room, or the circus room."

There were different themes. Who in their right mind ever chose the circus room? Some people had a fetish for clowns.

"The western room," I said.

"Excellent choice," it said. "That will be four thousand dollars without insurance. Now, if you will let me scan your card…"

After I pulled it out, Steve scanned it with its eyes.

"Just wondering," I said. "What would be the cost with insurance?"

"I apologize," it said, "but I do not have an answer to your inquiry."

Why was I not surprised?

—

Chanel went to get ready. I waited on a king-size bed that was designed like a stagecoach. The walls surrounded me in a landscape, which I thought was smack-dab in Utah during the Gold Rush. A giant sun brushed the canyons red. Black horses took a sip from a silvery brook. Cowboys flashed their spurs near cacti and white animal skulls in pink sand. A Spanish guitar played through the speakers, like the ones in the Western movies from my great-grandfather's days (if he could see me now).

Chanel stepped in as a cowgirl—with a tight denim skirt, chocolate boots, and a salmon cowboy hat—and it lassoed me with a red lasso. I fell into a trance, willing to tip it whatever it wanted at the moment. It pulled dildoes for six shooters from its holsters and aimed them at me. "On your knees, bad girl."

After I did, Chanel lifted its skirt and spread its lips. Its clam was tight and brown around the edges. It was pink inside.

"Go ahead," it said, "touch it."

When I stuck my finger in it, Chanel let out a moan. Its clam started leaking with suction. It tossed its cowboy hat aside and told me to lie down on the stagecoach.

I lay in bed and faced the ceiling. It yanked my jeans and pried apart my legs. I didn't wear any panties for the occasion.

As it was licking me, an owl aimed its lenses from above, and a red light was blinking from its head. Who was watching us? I wanted to run away, but Chanel's head was deep between my legs.

"Just relax," it said.

Relax? A machine was eating me out. How was I supposed to relax? It took me to a place that no one ever did. Its lack of emotion mitigated the pressure. It lifted its head and turned me to my stomach.

Rubber snapped. Chanel pushed the dildo gun barrels way inside me. The rush intensified with the cameras in the room.

"Who's watching us?" I asked.

Chanel removed the gun and continued licking my sugar cube without a word. My thighs quivered. I leaked into the latex that was stuck in me, and I buried my face in the mattress. Just what I wanted. The excitement came and went so quickly. I never truly had the chance to enjoy the moment…

We wiped ourselves afterwards. I buttoned my pants, and it pulled on its skirt. It didn't feel as comfortable with Chanel in the room. Now that I was finished, I wanted nothing to do with it.

"Where's the tip?" it said.

After only a few satisfying minutes, Chanel wouldn't leave until it got its money. They prospered that way. I reluctantly tipped it three hundred dollars through the app. An emptiness filled me after all the money spent. I hated myself.

Those robotic owls were watching me from every corner. The price I paid for medical sex—everything was publicly displayed.

They turned their heads at me when I left the Dollhouse through the back exit.

—

I waited for my Dryft ride in the parking lot. More robotic owls recorded me from the rooftop, and the robot guard watched me from its station at the door.

It wasn't a self-driven car that time but a woman behind the steering wheel. Her eyes opened at the place before she drove out of the parking lot. I was sitting in the back seat.

"Whoa, what is this place?" she said.

I felt like dirt after spending all that money and because of the fact that I was being watched. Now the woman wanted to know. What was I going to say?

"It's a place for adults," I said.

"My name is Katherine," she said. "Would you like some free licorice?"

Licorice was one of the last things on my mind. I just wanted to lie down in bed at the Woodrow and forget the night ever existed.

"I've heard about these places," she said. "Can I ask you what you do in there?"

"No," I said.

It was a long, quiet ride back to the hotel in Periscope City. A part of me said it was the last time I would ever set foot in the Dollhouse, but another part of me thirsted for more robots, but a different one next time, not the same one. My temptation ate away at me like Chanel. I was overwhelmed by the cravings.

"Wait," I said to her. "Turn back around."

The Skinner

Let me tell you about a legend in Periscope City, goin' back to thuh late 1800s, 'bout thuh skinner. He could be surveyin' thuh land from thuh blazes right 'bout now. Thuh burg changed ever since the heavens of this once highfalutin' land was as pink as a tongue. A picture of thuh skinner hangs in Flanagan's Barrelhouse, where he used to munch on his eggs every sunrise. Now it's a theme restaurant with thuh town's bettermost chili fries. All kinds of loners sit alone in there.

He could draw his shootin' iron 'fore a varmint could scratch its ear. Some folks could see 'im as a local hero, but that's a tall tale. Thuh sheriff knew that if he chased 'im, thuh skinner's lead plums would've sent 'im to thuh buzzards. Thuh skinner was thuh most well-known loner, an outlaw who protected his home like a hawk from intruders. People gossiped with their runny noses 'bout his affairs. Who could he trust? Ma left 'im, and he strangled Pa, who done marked 'im with a horseshoe on his thigh when he was just a young un'. Parents warned their children 'bout thuh skinner. He done lived in 'em canyons. What fine decorations their skulls would've made for 'is mantle.

One day, after groomin' his hoss, he lit a thinkin' pill, 'bout to hit thuh trail, when someone from behind 'im cocked a peacemaker. "Stop where you are," thuh man said. "Put your hands up high."

Now thuh yellow belly, Sheriff North, done posted wanted signs of thuh skinner 'round thuh burg. E'rybody knew only a fool would gitty-up after 'im. A tenderfoot from Boston done ridden all thuh way on his hoss to make money. Word was that he was an ex-lieutenant comin' after thuh skinner, aimin' to be thuh better of thuh gunslingers.

One mornin' in Flanagan's, four outlaws who were blue on gut warmer didn't fancy thuh lieutenant and drew their peacemakers on 'im.

He shot all of 'em with two barkin' irons 'fore they could make a move. Thuh customers peeped it includin' thuh skinner. Thuh blue belly, that lieutenant, was plumb skillful with the shootin' irons—defendin' hisself. Who could blame him for that? After takin' 'em out, he skedaddled from thuh saloon.

Sheriff North done put a price on thuh skinner. But bounty or no bounty, thuh skinner would've challenged anybody who crossed his path and didn't back down from no scrap. Folks feared 'im 'cause he done beefed so many men.

Thuh skinner obeyed thuh blue belly's orders, dropped 'is thinkin' pill, and held 'is hands up high. "Lieutenant, is that ya?"

"None of your business," thuh blue belly drawled.

They were far from the burg, out of sight from them folks. Thuh skinner done admitted it was impressive gunslingin' by that blue belly to take down 'em outlaws the way he did.

Thuh skinner's pistol rested in his left holster.

"Don't make a move," thuh blue belly said.

Thuh skinner waited for thuh right time. Dark clouds from Colorado clung to thuh sky like plaque. A cacklin' black buzzard feasted on a cottontail. A desert breeze prickled thuh skinner's ears. Gnats buzzed 'round his sweaty nose into his dry bazoo. A small wind whirled thuh dirt through thuh quiet land. Thuh buzzard flapped its wings to a juniper tree for a snack. A bead of sweat trickled down thuh skinner's forehead and, like a caterpillar in a cobweb, got stuck in 'is lashes and fell to 'is left boot.

When thuh skinner shifted, he done had no choice but to pivot and reach for 'is equalizer. *Bam! Ba-bam!* Somethin' grazed his left hand and knocked thuh gun from 'is digits. Thuh skinner shot thuh lieutenant in thuh belly. Thuh blue belly fell and fired shots into thuh air.

Thuh skinner reclaimed 'is equalizer with 'is right hand. A trail of inky blood dripped to the dirt. At first, he couldn't reckon 'is trigger finger and middle finger on the ground. A pair of bloody wormholes done appeared on 'is left hand, 'is shootin' hand.

He done stood over 'is enemy, ready to beef 'im. Thuh lieutenant done plugged 'im with his lucky lead, clutchin' 'is belly.

Thuh skinner stuffed thuh blue belly's equalizer down thuh waist of 'is britches with 'is right hand. Blood spewed from 'im like waterin' a garden. "I been shot in thuh gut too once," he drawled, "by somebody just like ya."

Thuh lieutenant pleaded, mentionin' his children, but thuh skinner had no feelin's.

He done showed thuh lieutenant a scar shaped like a crescent 'neath 'is chest bones. "A lead plum stunned me right dead here," he said. "Thuh doc in thuh burg refused to stitch me back up, so I plugged 'im and kept his skull for ma mantle. I done yanked it out and stitched it up ma blamed self."

'Em water beads started tappin' on his hat. Black sky puffins started sneakin' into town. No time for dillydallyin'. Gotta git down to business 'fore it rained.

Thuh skinner aimed 'is cannon at thuh blue belly's heart with 'is less nimble hand. Thuh blue belly begged 'im again, but there was no blame reason, I say, to have mercy on thuh lieutenant after he was pursuin' 'im.

Bam! Thuh skinner's right paw gave 'im a lick and a promise. Thuh lead plum punctured thuh blue belly's airbags.

Thuh skinner blasted 'is chest with the two lead plums left in it.

Bam! Buzzard grub. Thuh fella was breathin' lead and spat out blood 'cross thuh skinner's puss. Instead of gunnin' 'im down mad-like, thuh skinner kept his noggin like he always did for 'is stash.

That there buzzard snatched 'is trigger finger. He shot it 'fore it flew off, yanked his digit from its beak, and blasted it, I reckon, to Kingdom Come. Black feathers went flyin' everywhere. He done grabbed both fingers and stowed 'em in 'is pocket. Thuh storm was a-brewin'. He hauled thuh lieutenant by thuh legs to 'is hoss 'fore high-tailin' it 'neath 'em dark clouds. 'Em burg folks watched him pick up dust from afar.

—

He dropped thuh buzzard grub in 'is root cellar. 'Em skulls on thuh mantle stacked like golden bars over 'is fireplace. In order to dodge a nick, he wielded his pig sticker with 'is right hand, cautious-like, to carve thuh officer from noggin to beetle crushers. A pristine skull was needed, so he snapped thuh bones like twigs. This stirred up a pale blaze in the fireplace. Dark smoke jammed thuh chimney up to thuh heavens.

—

Thuh night cooled thuh fire to a glow. Thuh lieutenant's ashes filled thuh hearth. Rain began crashin' down thuh chute, and so he closed thuh flue. Thuh skull needed a polishin' with a rag and bug juice 'fore it fit right. With his pig sticker, he finished carvin' thuh name *David,* and he put in on thuh shelf with thuh rest of 'em skulls. Everythin' looked real nice-like.

He thought 'bout nuthin' 'til he saw his left paw. Thuh hurt knocked him out cold. When he roused up, he tried stitchin' 'em fingers back on 'is hand, but they just weren't cooperatin'. Thuh thread and needle rendered his digits useless. He was no longer thuh skinner…just a dude.

Demons crept into his noggin. Would he be damned for committin' 'em wrongs? What would Sheriff North think when he laid his eyes upon thuh skinner's dainty hand? Or what would 'em folks reckon? Or what 'bout thuh skinner's moniker?

—

Since he couldn't hold thuh cannon like he could with 'is dainty hand, he wasn't a threat no more but a blame disgrace. Nobody would tremble at 'is sight. Not Sheriff North. Thuh skinner had to hightail it out of town, never to return. Thuh townsfolk would ponder whatever became of 'im. You ask me, I say he fled to untamed territory where thuh wildcats roam. They tore 'im to bits if he didn't beat 'em to thuh draw. Nobody ever done learned what happened to thuh skinner. For all they reckon, he's burnin' in the blazes. One thang is for certain, though. Folks in thuh burg will always know thuh legend of thuh skinner as it's spun from one generation to thuh next.

Dinosaur Teeth

One night at the Smokin' Barrel, which I'd owned since my momma's death, a mysterious man came in, wearing a pillowcase over his head. The same man may have called me names on a website.

Bullies had made fun of my crooked teeth ever since I was a kid. It made me join the Marine Corps to overcome their abuse. I should never have served. All I think about are body parts. I watched my fellow soldiers die gruesomely. My best friend got his leg blown off and died shortly thereafter. His frozen eyes will forever haunt me. The enemy slit my throat and left a scar across my neck. He gently sliced me to keep me alive. I'll never forget the beige cloth he wore over his head. If I didn't shoot him, he would've killed me first. I lived with nothing but the memories back home, right outside of Periscope City, after serving duty.

I didn't achieve much in my fifty-plus years on Earth. How could I? I just kept to myself. Family stayed away from me.

—

The Smokin' Barrel stood on top of Deathnail Canyon over Periscope City. I had no other options but to own it, and I could barely function as an adult. How was I able to focus when I thought about amputated limbs? Thunder would make me panic. Pellets of rain shot through my mind like bullets. Every night, I would dream about my brothers' legs getting shot off and body parts being blown to bits.

—

I was debating politics online when the troll in question called me "Dinosaur Teeth." That painful name crawled through my head for months after I'd read it. I wished Momma could've afforded to have them fixed. Instead, I have to wear these ugly things to the grave. How dumb of me to show my hideous smile on there. I should've been like the rest of them cowards and hidden my ugly mug behind an avatar.

—

A nasty storm crashed down on the Smokin' Barrel. Them raindrops tapped on the thin tin roof. I put a plastic bucket under the leaky ceiling. The heavy tapping was like water torture.

A lamp behind the counter provided the only light. I sat at a round wooden table, just smoking a joint, drinking cheap gin within the walls. A white revolver rested there to protect me from any outsider who came through that door. Customers rarely showed up from that lonely town, and when they did, I preferred solitude. Most of them would stare at me when they needed a drink, or they kept to themselves while I stood behind the bar, thinking about them missing limbs. I didn't need nightmares when I carried the memories so closely. Someone would say something, and I would ask them to repeat it. How could I pay attention? The past haunted me too much.

That was when the shady character came in wearing the white pillowcase over his head. It had a pair of holes for his eyes. "Hello," he said. His voice sounded nasally. The pillowcase reminded me of the enemy who'd slit my throat.

I grabbed my Colt and quickly stood. "We're closed."

The strange man approached my table anyway, with mud and maple leaves stuck to his shoes.

"We're closed," I repeated. "Are you deaf, son?"

"Please put the gun down," he said. "I need to use the bathroom."

The bar belonged to me, so I did as I damn well pleased. "I'll say it one more time: we're closed. The latrine is for customers only. Now stop where you are, take off the sheet, or leave."

His drenched pillowcase stuck to his head. "My friend, it's cold and wet out there, and we're in the wilderness," he said. "I need to use the bathroom. Please. I'm not an animal."

I kept my stance with the revolver in case he made a sudden move. "That's tough shit, but them's the rules."

The stranger looked at the gun like a curious raccoon, and his little head turned at me sideways. "Have we met before?"

"How would I know? You got that thing on."

"I'm Little Ted."

"I didn't ask."

"And what is your name?"

"Who needs to know?"

"I'll explain myself," he said.

"Better do it quick."

He sat at another wooden table and crossed them skinny legs without asking me first. His left arm hung over the side chair, and he was dripping from his jeans and his jacket. "I'm a comedian and a magician," he said. "I used to do comedy and magic tricks at the Magic Fortress. They gave me the boot, so to speak. Now I do the Lilliputian clubs."

Whatever that word meant. "Why you telling me this?"

"Because the comedy circuit has accused me of stealing jokes. Hence the mask I wear, you see. I wish to be alone like you and not to be seen."

"Your story ain't helping," I said.

"I have nightmares about it. By the look of the Marines flag, you served this country, did you not? You must have nightmares, too."

"It don't matter."

"That's a quite unsightly scar on your neck," he said. "Do you wear a bandana to cover it up?"

"Take the sheet off now, goddamnit," I said. "I mean it."

He quickly uncrossed his legs and sat up straight. I tightened my grip around the Colt.

"Where does it say *no pillowcases* on the door?" he said.

"Don't get smart with me," I said. "This bar don't allow no freaks."

"Freaks?" he said. "What a harsh thing to say."

"Get the fuck out now."

"I'm misunderstood like you," he said. "You don't have any friends, I can tell."

"I said get out," I said.

"After you show me the bathroom," he said.

I'd warned him too much, so I aimed the Colt at his chest, but he didn't flinch.

"You wouldn't shoot me," he said.

I still tried to scare him. "Don't be too sure. We're on a reservation, son."

Rather than come at me with another witty comeback, he threw his hands in the air. "You own this bar?"

"Yes."

He laughed under his pillowcase like me owning the place was a joke or like *I* was a joke.

"What's so damn funny?"

"Nothing," he said. "You should follow me. I'm @littleted. Easy for an asshat like you to remember."

Asshat? The balls to insult me with a loaded pistol aimed at him.

"Come on," he said. "Put the gun down and stop chewing rocks, Dinosaur Teeth."

Dinosaur teeth? My dry mouth almost swallowed my tongue. I squeezed the revolver tighter. "Don't say another word."

"Go fix those chompers," he said. "Perhaps you pay for braces."

"Take the sheet off," I said. "Now."

"Relax," he said. "I'm just having fun, All Gaps. Like all caps on a keyboard? Aww, you're too much of a neanderthal to get it."

"You better show your mug because I'm fucking careless with this thing when I'm drunk."

"Show my mug? No way, T. Rex."

I lifted the Colt at his pillowcase, and his eyes stood still, daring me to shoot.

The front door opened again. The thunder, lightning, wind, and rain pushed the customer inside the bar. He was a regular, another sad loner who never bothered nobody. I kept my eyes on the comedian, though. "The bar's closed for the time being," I said.

He called himself the Mule. His eyes, from what I could see in my periphery, shot open. Rightfully so, given the situation. He even raised his hands like Ted did, as if I was pointing the gun at him, and he followed my words and left.

Ted never budged an inch. "Scaring business away, are we?" he said.

I kept a hard grip. "I mean it," I said. "Remove the pillow sheet and show me who you are, or I will shoot. If my words won't work, a bullet will."

"No way."

I cocked the hammer. My conscience begged me, *Jim, put the piece down and stop drinking that shit.* The stranger was capable of doing anything. "Either you leave, or you get another hole in the sheet," I said.

The lightning through the window flashed across his white eyes with dark circles around them like mascara, smirking at me: *Take a shot, you chickenshit.*

I squeezed the trigger. The bullet went right between his eyes. He burst out laughing. I fired again. The laughing continued. It was like the bullets were feeding him laughter. He laughed and laughed until the last bullet from the chambers struck him dead in his heart. He fell to his back, clutched his chest, and started wheezing.

"Isn't it funny?" he said. "How I can take a bullet, but you can't take a joke."

Them were his last words. He lay there, not moving. I sat in my chair with the Colt, the cards, and the rest of the joint and the gin. The name "Dinosaur Teeth" went repeating in my head. What if it was the same person? The longer I thought about it, the more the handle @littleted sounded familiar, like lyrics to a song. I couldn't drop the insult. Fuck it. I couldn't let it bother me, but it stuck in my head like the leaves on his shoes.

I'd temporarily lost my mind, shooting my Colt. The Corps had trained me to react that way to my enemy, and I'd killed so many people at war. My head rested between my shaking arms, and I gripped the deck of cards again with the hot revolver in my pocket.

I needed to leave him somewhere, and that somewhere was the bottom of Deathnail Canyon. So I grabbed him by the heels of his muddy white shoes to drag him towards the door. Blood from his back left a streak across the planks. His tiny body sure bled like a motherfucker.

The Mule was waiting outside the door. He saw me in plain sight, dragging the body of Little Ted, and as scared as he was, he backed away to give me room.

"Be right back," I said.

I kept dragging him through the mud until I got to Deathnail Canyon Road, where I pulled him across the way to the cliff. The only place to hide him was to shove him off the edge. It was a dark road with no streetlights. Only the moon and the lightning could guide me. I had to be careful not to fall off the edge myself. When I got there, I let go of his legs, and the mud splattered. I wiped my hands on my jeans. My foot shoved him off the edge. He slipped away, but I couldn't hear him fall to the bottom because of the storm. It would've been sweet music to hear his bones cracking against the cliff or a beauty to watch his body being devoured by vultures. What did his face look like? I couldn't picture it for the life of me.

When I got back to the Smokin' Barrel, the Mule was still waiting by the door.

"What happened?" he said.

"I shot him," I said. "Don't tell a soul."

"I won't," he said. "Swear to God."

I opened the door and let him in the bar. The Mule helped himself to a stool.

"The usual?" I asked.

"Yes," he said.

He loved his Moscow Mules.

Anyway, it went back to business as usual with him in there that night, except he didn't chat with me. He just sat quietly with his drink while I sat back with my revolver.

—

After closing up and hauling ass home on my Harley, I logged on to the website to look for more insults. Was it really him? It had to be Ted for sure. That demon trolled over hundreds of people about their appearances, unlike a respectful person who could argue politics without a personal attack.

—

I drove back to the bar on the day after the murder and looked down at Deathnail Canyon, which was too damn steep. I couldn't see the bottom. There was no way to tell what had happened to the body of Little Ted. The police never showed up either. It made me question my own reality.

—

It was a brain disease, reading his insults for several months. For each day that passed, he kept destroying another troll online. Through all that time I'd followed him, he'd tempted me to poke him with a retort. I wasn't a fan; I was a follower. How could he still be insulting people after I'd murdered him? It had to be somebody else.

—

Now and again, folks would call me on the phone, but I would never answer. Rather than working at the Smokin' Barrel, I cooped myself in my momma's house.

Lonely days blurred into even lonelier nights. Until one morning, Ted's account was mysteriously deleted. Why? I believed he'd switched to another handle, so I searched for similar ones. @lilted, @tedlittle, @lilteddy, I tried to find a match. His name went missing in a search. How could someone disappear from the web? Words and pictures were supposed to stay forever, right? Either way, Ted remained on my conscience.

My lonely life carried on. One day, the big tires on my Harley slipped across a sheet of ice, and I broke my hip. Now I had to walk with a steel cane for the rest of my life. The name "Dinosaur Teeth" lost its grip, and I accepted my imperfections.

Exactly seven years after the death of Little Ted, I limped and made it through the thick snow to the top of Deathnail Canyon, the edge where I'd shoved the only civilian I'd ever killed. A thick branch on a juniper tree poked through a hole in a white pillow sheet. The winter wind was blowing it. I was across the street from the Smokin' Barrel, which was boarded up. The white sheet was in fact a pillowcase. The night with Little Ted was so long ago. Had I not been so obsessed, I would've lost count of the years. I tossed the sheet off the cliff and watched it sail towards the bottom.

Magic Shirt

As I'd said before, I moved from my mother's house in the mountains of Colorado to find my Arcadian dream: a solo writer's retreat in the canyons of Periscope City. That was the real reason I'd moved there. I'd learned from Raylene that being a Middleton meant I was one of the loneliest in town who was conflicted. I wanted to be alone and yet connect with other people. I still dwell over her.

—

My hobbies are writing and shopping. I browsed a shirt rack in a thrift shop in downtown one day and found myself a red, white, and blue tie-dye. It made me look buff in a fitting room. Who knows how I really looked because the store might've manipulated the mirrors and the lighting? You never know at those places. Since the shirt cost one dollar, who cared if it lied to me?

—

I came back to my hotel suite at the Cramden and tossed it to the growing heap of clothes on the floor of the walk-in closet.

I woke up the following morning and moseyed to the brunch buffet. One of the guests, with a cheesy grin, was wearing a matching tie-dye. He reminded me of the shirt.

—

It made my neck, shoulders, and arms bulge, and so the fitting room must've been telling the truth—unless my bathroom mirror was lying, too, which I doubted.

I wore it with gusto when I checked my email, which usually was a week's worth of dread: just spam. Except that day, I opened an email from my insurance company. What did *they* want? To raise my deductible as if it couldn't get any higher? Actually, no. They'd sent me a direct deposit for all my appointments with medical sex workers. A miracle. After all those months of screwing me, the thief had finally met its comeuppance. Call it fate.

—

I went for a stroll with my service Labrador, Jeff, through downtown Periscope City, a thousand dollars richer, to the local coffeehouse and began to whistle. Since when do I whistle? What was up with that? The sun was shining on me. It had to be about seventy-five degrees in January. It was the most perfect weather in that town. Birds were singing in the trees. A hummingbird flew by and gave me a nod before it flew to a bed of flowers.

A hot brunette in yoga tights was walking her service corgi. She distracted me from Raylene, the woman who'd so devastatingly put me in the friend zone. When I tried to make eye contact with her, she stopped and said, "Hey, that's a cute shirt."

I said, "Really?"

"Totally," she said. "What's your name, love?"

"Joe."

"Joe? I'm Stacy. I've, like, seen you walking your dog. Been, like, meaning to say hello."

I thought, *What? She'd ignored me all those other times walking by me.*

I said, "Wow, okay."

She kneeled to Jeff, closed her eyes, and puckered her lips. My dog licked her face and slobbered all over it, like she and I were together already.

"Take my number," she said. "Let's, like, hang out later."

The whole moment slowed down for me. I could breathe in her perfume and her green eyes.

She scooped up after her corgi and placed it in a little plastic bag. "See you tonight, love."

Oh, man. I had magic on me. But how? From where? I waited for the universe to give me an answer. But why question it, right? Just ride the miracle.

—

I crossed a guy in his fifties when I entered the coffeehouse. He wore a red Norfolk jacket. "Excuse me," he said, "but by chance, are you a writer?"

I went along with the magic. I said, "Yes in fact."

He held out his hand for a handshake. "Ethan Shore from Silver Horse Publishing," he said. "I'm looking for a distinct voice. Have you finished a novel?"

I wasn't expecting a magical thing like this.

"After three years," I said.

He said, "That's a long time."

I said, "But it's done."

"Have you shopped it around?" he said.

"To whom?" I asked.

He handed me a sharp business card. The corner of it almost punctured my thumb.

"Send it to my email," he said. "Say you will."

I understood, after myriad rejections, to seize this golden opportunity. How could I pass it by? It was a moment too good to be true, but after what had happened with my insurance and Stacy, like I said, I rode the miracle. "I will," I said.

After meeting him, he left, and I had the entire store to myself, except for a sad man in a wheelchair who sat in there every morning. I felt so high that I rose over him and the robot baristas.

One of them at the register even greeted me warmly. "Good morning, Joe," it said. "Are you having your espresso today?"

What? Since when did they say that? How did it know my name, let alone what I drank? "Are you serious?" I asked.

It said, "We are grateful to have you as a customer."

Now it was expressing gratitude. That was when I realized the answer to the mystery. After I'd stepped back and analyzed everything that had happened that morning, it had to be the shirt. I felt the urge to confess it to someone, or in this case, *something*. "This shirt is like magic."

It said, "How so?"

I said, "It brings me luck."

"I am sorry, but I cannot comprehend," it said.

How interesting.

The store was still practically empty until a group of teenagers walked up to me, and the vibe in there suddenly got cold and gray. When I waited for my drink, those high school kids stared at me. Periscope City forbade people under eighteen, or so I thought. I just tried to ignore them and wait for the miracle to come back. One of their shirts said FUCK OFF. They may have been a curse, so I kept my eyes on the barista that was making my espresso.

They got close to me and said: "Who's this clown?" "What the fuck is he wearing?" "Looks like bird shit."

I'd made the mistake of not wearing my headphones like every other day to avoid any kind of interaction, so I moved to where the guy in the wheelchair was sitting, thinking, who was going to harass someone next to a person in a wheelchair?

We waited there awkwardly, so I asked him, "How's your morning?"

"Meh," he said.

If only the barista would've hurried with my espresso…

When the kids approached me again, the man in the wheelchair rolled away. One of those kids threw his coffee milkshake at my shirt. I flinched. The boys cracked up in front of me.

"You piece of shit," I said.

The milkshake dribbled onto my jeans, and Jeff started licking my shirt. I was about twice their age. But what could I do? Take a swing at a minor?

The kid said, "What now, bitch?" He was the one who'd assaulted me with the milkshake. His chest had the build of a linebacker's.

It was three against one. They'd outnumbered me.

The barista called my name when my drink was ready. I rushed to the counter with the milkshake dripping off of me. When I tried to pick up my espresso it scalded my wrist and spilled to the floor. It felt like a third-degree burn. The kids laughed even louder. They were the opposite of loners, a wolf pack of bullies.

I got out of there before any other disaster could strike.

—

I tried to process the chain of events on the way back to the Cramden. How did direct deposit connect with those jerks in the coffeehouse? Magic seemed to occur in random areas—such as where Ethan Shore and Stacy with the corgi had shown up. Either that or it was a conspiracy. Or it was a dream and I'd gone sleepwalking. Or the stain on my shirt may have caused doom. Or my confession to the barista had twisted my luck. If I believed in black magic, I would've thrown the shirt away. And if I did, how would I carry out a seance? Was there a number to a Wiccan in town? Whatever the case, I walked under an overcast sky, counting my steps to the hotel, avoiding all cracks in the cement.

—

Stacy's voice played in my head like my favorite song back to my hotel room. I pictured her kissing my service dog and how the slobber fell off her chin. How she would appear when I saw her… How she would smell… The same way she did on the sidewalk? I even practiced with Alexa's voice and acted out the conversation with Stacy.

After an hour of practice, I had the courage to call her.

"Hello?" she said. She sounded as if her corgi had died.

I thought I was still wearing a magic shirt, so I left it on. But why did I call her after those kids had shattered my confidence? "Hi, Stacy. It's Joe."

She said, "Who?"

My name had slipped her memory, but how? "We met a few hours ago on the sidewalk," I said.

"Oh," she said, "right." Her voice had dropped an octave.

I said, "Are you okay?"

She said, "Yes."

"Cool," I said. "What time should I come over tonight?"

She said, "Like, never."

Then she rudely hung up. The phone stuck to my ear like gum. It was a different rejection than the one I'd faced with Raylene. No friend zone this time. The sea changed. I stood in a stupor and thought of an alternate route to the coffeehouse to avoid her next time.

But enough about romance. After too many women had burned me, I was meant to be a loner. I typed a lengthy email to Ethan Shore and attached the PDF of my fantasy novel—700 pages about subterranean crab people that should've stunned him right out of his jacket.

But the reply said UNKNOWN EMAIL. Maybe he'd flubbed the business card. It happens. I spent the next several hours shuffling the letters, numbers, and symbols of the address. But the error message kept springing up like a jack-in-the-box.

Ethan's number was out of service, too. Was he a flake? A charlatan? A lunatic? Forget about the solo writer's retreat. My actual Arcadia had slipped from my fingers. Maybe black magic *was* real.

One thing I knew for sure. In my mind, the shirt had lost its magic, all because I'd spilled the beans to a robot. I switched to a yellow collared shirt I'd had since the University of Colorado with wrinkles all over it. It hadn't brought a lint of luck after nine years, even *bad* luck.

I threw the magic shirt in a dumpster outside the Cramden and wore the collared shirt to bed, where my worst worries ran rampant. My lame, ordinary life had returned. Maybe I shouldn't have thrown the tie-dye away. I was going to stay up all night, so I dug it back out of the dumpster, thinking it would bring me peaceful sleep.

As soon as I slipped it on again, I sensed my mojo returning. What if I threw it in the washer? Would it wash away the good karma?

I woke up the next morning with a new hope. Yesterday could've been an anomaly. After all, I still had direct deposit without a woman or a book deal. But an email from the Periscope City Credit Union said that my account needed urgent attention.

—

I walked to the bank a few blocks up in downtown rather than call their toll-free number. A robot bank teller behind the glass said, "We are sorry, Mr. Shoemaker, but we had to freeze your account."

"This is unreal," I said. "Why?"

"There has been suspicious activity."

I said, "Like what?"

It said, "Did you make a purchase at a ski shop in Norway in the amount of five thousand dollars?"

My heart jumped into my throat.

I said, "Of course not."

"We are sorry." it said, "We must investigate it."

I left the bank in a fog, crossed the street, and heard tires screech…

Everything went black.

—

I awakened to chattering voices and wailing sirens. My eyes wouldn't close. The gray clouds swirled above Periscope City.

A man of about fifty-three with severe alopecia, wearing silver gym clothes, kneeled over me and read from a metallic clipboard.

He said, "Joe Shoemaker?"

I said, "Yes?"

He clicked a golden pen and crossed something out. "Hello, Joe. I'm Death."

Looked about right.

Death sneered at me cynically. "Okay, dude," he said. "Time to rip the bandage off. Here's the good news and the bad news. What do you want to hear first?"

I said, "The bad news, always."

"The bad news is you're dead," he said. "Hence me. A drunk driver hit you in a blue Chevy Nova. It was a hit-and-run."

"My god," I said.

"I'll get to that later," he said. "Right now, let's focus on the meat and potatoes."

I said, "How do I look?"

"Fucking gnarly," he said. "Blood everywhere."

"What's the good news?" I said.

"You can choose to live if you can call it good news. The next ten years will be a steady decline. Health problems, less attraction to women, no career, people will ignore you.

"Or you can choose to remain dead. You'll meet God and blah blah blah. Shall I resurrect you to disappointment or close the book?"

The bad news sounded more like good news.

I said, "What're your thoughts?"

Death rolled his eyes as if the question had drained him of energy. "Don't ask me, brother," he said. "I'm only the case manager. Who am I to talk you into anything? You ask me, I'm just as disappointing as life is. You can always return in your condition. I mean, jumping off a skyscraper would've been one hell of a different story, now wouldn't it? No pun intended." Death hawked up phlegm and grunted it back down his throat. "The other good news is you can take your time to decide," he said. "You have all eternity."

He stepped away coldly.

"Wait," I said. "Where're you going?"

"To another meeting," he said. "Call me when you've decided."

I remained lying on the frozen street, surrounded by onlookers. The world stopped dead. I had a lot of trouble deciding which way to go among other souls in purgatory. It was more like hell. I had to go somewhere else.

Since my mother would've grieved over me, I chose life despite the disappointments ahead. I called Death back over.

He showed up in a different tracksuit this time but with the same clipboard, with more of a disheveled look than before.

"Yeah, you called?"

"I thought long and hard about it," I said, "and decided to live."

He yawned while he drew a circle on his clipboard. "Okay," he said. "If you really want to. Who's stopping you?" He snapped his fingers. A white light appeared. How typical of Death. It was like they did in the movies.

I woke up on the street again and blinked my eyes. The Periscope City paramedics were around me. One of them kneeled over me, looked right in my face.

"He's alive," he said.

The rest of them said, "Thank God." "What a relief."

They lifted me onto a stretcher.

One of them sat by my side in the back of an ambulance, a woman who looked about thirty years old. She was blonde with blue eyes that cared.

"You want to know what Death looks like?" I asked.

"Tell me," she said.

When I described it to her, she listened well and didn't appear to judge me.

—

The hospital sent me home in a wheelchair. I still wore my magic shirt, but it was torn from the wreck. The wreck had also ripped my jeans and given me scrapes all over my body to go with my broken leg and my arm in a sling. I would need to change when I got back to my hotel room, but I had a difficult time with all those broken bones.

The sun was too bright on the day when they released me. Periscope City didn't have a city bus for transportation, only electric cars for a Dryft ride. A woman drove me back to the Cramden. She looked about the nurse's age. I preferred a self-driven car, but those were reserved for premier customers. A nurse helped me into the backseat and tucked my wheelchair in the trunk.

The driver said her name was Katherine, and that she'd moved from Rhode Island, and she hated her job and yada yada yada.

"Would you like some free licorice?" she said.

Something about Death had chased away my hunger, so I said I was fine.

"I have to ask anyway," she said. "I was just there."

"Where?" I asked.

"The hospital. I had a pinched nerve in my neck."

She wore a neck brace, so I believed her.

"I died and came back to life," I said, thinking this would've sparked a provocative conversation.

"Oh," she said. "That's cool."

Death wasn't kidding when he said people would dismiss me. I told her what Death looked like, just what I'd mentioned to the nurse, and described purgatory to her. Katherine pretended to listen. All the while, I looked forward to solitude at the Cramden.

The Allure of Marty McCone's

Ice cream is my abusive husband. I'm under his control. He smacks me like I'm a dirty girl, and he freezes my brain for ten seconds into a blinding headache. It's darn close to sadomasochism. I want him, all of him.

Last night, I pulled him from the trash can. How did it come to the point where I shoved him between my lips over a receptacle that smelled of Modelo and a dryer sheet?

—

I used to work at Golden Udders Creamery back in Alabama just to be near my cold love. They allowed me to eat as much ice cream as my fat heart desired, and my darling saved me from the hordes of customers who gave me anxiety. I would hide in my dorm after work or school, lock myself in the room, and feast on him until my stomach hurt. A gallon of Rocky Road can melt my worries away. If you have a hard time believing it, you need to try it. I once lost myself in him during a tornado, when a twister almost took the roof off from the coed floor. I dug, dug, dug until the last spoonful. My spoon scratched the bottom, and I couldn't hear the winds also digging, scraping the shingles and tarpaper off the roof. My love keeps me from distraction. After I finished, I needed more, tornado or no tornado, or my problems would grow back like warts. If I could eat him all day, I would. If so, I would become so obese that I wouldn't be able to grab another serving. That's no hyperbole.

—

I mentioned my love while I was sitting on my mat, waiting for my yoga class to start. I'd just moved to Periscope City from Alabama and wanted to take the class. Other people sat there, but they kept to themselves. I was trying to use him for safety again, just something to chitchat about with a thin brunette body-by-yoga girl next to me with her service corgi by her side. I'd brought my service dachshund. The yoga girl grunted, closed her eyes, and suggested a parlor called Marty McCone's. "You should try it," she said. "I'm, like, making healthier choices and stuff." She sat in the lotus position (something I always tried to do). "It has, like, zero calories, so it would totally help you out. Plus, it's ice cream!"

Help me out? She may as well have called me a whale. Ice cream with zero calories sounded worse than Beethoven with an accordion. The fat makes him delectable, so delectable that my boyfriend in Alabama once caught me cheating.

He opened the door to find me on the bed with a spoon in my hand and a gallon in my lap. We got in a big ol' fight. He demanded that I eat vegetables and take spin classes. I told him he had to live with it or else…. Who needed him when true love waited in the frozen food aisle? I love ice cream unrequitedly, true, true love. Yes, he has a homely figure in the grocery store, lumped in the freezer with all those other homogenous containers, but like I said, I love him for what's on the inside.

Anyway, forget about the past. I'd left my boyfriend for a new life where I could go to yoga classes instead of Golden Udders. I lived in a hotel without a roommate. Who was going to judge me when I hid myself with my sweetheart? Who was going to steal my love from the freezer in the kitchen?

—

The trash can of my shame was located conveniently in front of Marty McCone's. It was the only ice cream parlor in a town where fewer than a thousand people lived. It had been a while since the move, since Golden Udders, and I wanted sexy: a hot fudge sundae with nuts, with cherries, satiny, red, dripping syrup on a luxurious bed of whipped cream. Pauline, my dachshund, started arfing right away. The place gave her the willies. We stood at the door, in the quiet, yet to go inside. The sign for *Marty McCone's Old-Fashioned Ice Cream* was fashioned in red circus letters, with rust running down the edges like war paint. It wasn't quite old-fashioned ice cream. I'll get to that later. Whoever had made the sign had crudely affixed it above the door and surrounded it with burned-up shingles and busted light bulbs. Yep, it was creepy. All the other businesses were closed early for the night. The only other places in that strip mall were a bar, a laundromat, a liquor store, and an office for a medical sex doctor. Gross. Who would see him? I wasn't that desperate when I had ice cream to fill the hole.

Marty McCone's looked more like a kebab restaurant than a parlor. No one appeared to be inside except for a bald man with a mop. I would've gone nowhere near there if I wasn't jonesing so much for a sundae.

When we entered, a little doorbell tinkered. Being in a parlor naturally sent me chills, but this was an evil chill. My lungs drowned in thick ammonia. Pop music blared and rumbled my ear drums. The bald man quit mopping. He watched us come in there. Tattoos between his thumbs and forefingers meant time in prison, which I'd learned from an episode of *Loose Criminals.*

He grilled me with the eyes of a lemur.

I asked, "Can I get a sundae?"

Instead of answering, he kicked his way through a backdoor to a backroom. I took that as a no. Where was the greeting? Where's the "Welcome to Marty McCone's. Would you like to sample our summer flavors?" It was certainly different from Golden Udders Creamery, where they used to make me wear a cow costume, wave at customers, and sing a jingle every time I got a tip:

Moo Moo Moo Moo, thank you for the love.
Moo Moo Moo Moo, please enjoy the grub.
Moo Moo Moo Moo, won't you come again,
Moo Moo Moo Moo, to Golden Udders, friend.

The jingle and thoughts of that costume still make me cringe. There should be fanfare at a parlor.

Anyway, a teenage girl plopped herself on a stool behind a register. Her beautiful blue eyes sparkled with anger. She kept her mouth shut so I let her be. I looked for nuts and cherries, hot fudge and whipped cream, or any semblance of an ice cream shop. All I saw was a glass case full of tubs. The bald man must've been the owner. What corruption was he committing in the back? Sizzling meth on a stove? Tying up a policeman and dousing him with gasoline? Eating animal crackers? Whatever it was, it must've been heinous. I could just imagine him riffing with his cellmate: "Ice cream has always been my passion. I will open up a shop and spread joy to a small town of loners someday after parole."

No way. That man was packing (and I don't mean Pistachio Nut). I minded my own business and browsed those flavors. I saw Honey Ginger, Lavender Cream, Marshmallow Beeswax …. Where was the chocolate, the strawberry, or vanilla?

I tried to keep an open mind, but I drew a line somewhere at Watermelon Daffodil. That vegan girl from yoga class had to be smoking crack if she preferred to eat Grasshopper Mint over, say, Cookies 'N' Cream.

I kept on scanning the little cards stuck in the glass frame, obviously written by a second grader: Peach Sandalwood, Cherry Frankincense, Peanut Butter Sage, Chocolate-Covered Beetle, Cinnamon Nag Champa. I looked for Mint Chip, Butter Pecan, or Pralines and Cream, but they also appeared to be persona non grata.

If you want my honest opinion, I thought everything—from the girl to the music to the eccentric flavors—was a front for trafficking. Anything to misdirect customers from his secret plot. If I were to guess, he wanted to hemlock the town, then rifle through the ol' homesteads for the secret jewels that could reverse gravity or give everlasting life. Periscope City Police would've called me a delusional freak if I told them.

I kept moving to the next card. Either it was desperation, or I trusted that girl in yoga class. Something was telling me the former. I asked the teen behind the register, "Don't you have plain ol' chocolate?"

"Just what you see here," she said, a curt answer to an innocent question. She couldn't speak or else she might've spilled too much information to foil his plans.

I was about to press on the choices when Pauline began to pant and wag her tail and arf in a hissy fit.

"Don't you worry, Poopskie," I said. "We'll leave soon."

"Hurry up," the teen said.

I was taken aback by her angry outburst. The lack of parlor decorum baffled me for a minute. After shushing Pauline, I bent down to the cards again. That's when I found Birthday Cake—not Aloe Birthday Cake or Chamomile Birthday Cake, just good ol'-fashioned Birthday Cake, between Pumpkin Saffron and Blueberry Turmeric. I darn near salivated at the sight of canary yellow chunks of French Vanilla. But was it there among all those freaky flavors? I asked little Miss Employee of the Month, "Can I get a sample of Birthday Cake?"

Her eyes jumped like crickets, like I'd uttered a password. She handed me a tiny white spoon. I had to flip the lid back and shovel him out myself.

When he entered me, he blinded me with a frozen, giddy rush of pain, exciting me. My molars crunched the jimmies. White icing slid down my throat. The chunks bounced like sponges against my gums. He was the ideal birthday cake transformed into whipped frozen heaven. His creaminess had me reminisce over my first date, my first kiss—Ronnie Messmaker, left tackle for the Gibson High Argonauts at my senior prom. I remember wearing all white, covered in rainbow jimmy spangles.

"Give me three scoops," I said. "Now."

She handed me a scooper, a pair of latex gloves, and a waffle cup made of chia seeds.

I scooped him out and set him next to the register.

"Place it on the scale," she said.

A scale, huh? Cover blown. Made perfect sense. Drug money kept the business flowing. It seemed like the mop man used the scale for something else besides bricks of cocaine to fool the cops. What if he'd laced the ice cream? But what did it matter when my Birthday Cake lover tasted so amazing?

After paying for him, I stopped before reaching the doorknob to take up my spoon and thrust another taste of him again into my mouth. When I did, I heard something like a chainsaw coming from the backroom, so I rushed outside, dragging Pauline behind me, the spoon still clasped against my tongue. What was that sound? From a television, perhaps? I sure hoped so. Whatever it was, I kept on eating. He melted inside me. His aftertaste blasted me with euphoria. I forgot my whereabouts. He sent me the right chills in the dry heat on another plain ol' peachy night in Periscope City. The air smelled fresh. The moon resembled an orange sea. Those eerily closed businesses sparkled in vibrant colors.

With ice cream comes guilt, or is it paranoia? It dazed part of me but also scared another part of me. Why did the ice cream, with whatever it contained, give me such a headrush? Whatever was going on in there I didn't want to know. I'd lost my discipline outside the store that night. My eager self had overindulged, and I darn near ate all three scoops. Something, the way the moon swam in its orange sea or how I could feel the girl's eyes boring into my back from the other side of the dingy parlor window, sobered me up. I took my lover by his collar and threw him in the trash can, standing there in the spot where it should've been, and wanted to flee that strip mall with Pauline. As I'd said, ice cream is my abusive husband. The farther we went, the more intense was the itch to do the most shameful thing I'd ever done. That was how it happened. I crawled up that street right back to him. He was my only protection against loneliness.

Waldenland

"What happened to Mom?" I asked my father.

We sat in an awkward silence in his room at the assisted living home. The lights were out as we watched the Buckeyes play in the Rose Bowl. The TV glowed across his scraggly beard, and an empty pack of Newports lay next to his bowl of chicken soup.

Mom and Dad used to take me to an amusement park. We would wait for a rollercoaster in a line that took forever. I used to close my eyes and wish the crowd would disappear, Mom and Dad included, so I could have the park to myself.

My parents were strangers to me. My dad was like a burglar who'd broken into my house and decided to raise me. Once we kind of got to know each other, we started talking about the Buckeyes, and that was it. Mom was barely around, period. She used to wake me up every day for the bus until one morning in my freshman year of high school she didn't. I waited for her to reappear. A phone call would've triggered too much intimacy, a handwritten letter, too. I wonder now, at forty-eight, if she's still living. My dad would stay single for good. His emotional distance grew on me. A friend or a stranger would usually ask if I was okay. And a short time would pass before a woman realized she was dating a tinman.

"I think she moved to Reno," he said. The conversation ended there. We talked some more about the Buckeyes. That was the last time I saw him.

After burying my father, I left Ohio and looked for my mother in Reno. All I came across were bikers. I moved to Periscope City to adapt to being alone and to live inside a cave called the Troglodyte Hotel. It had normal housekeeping, room service, fine dining, et cetera. Except robots ran the place, and it had stalactites for chandeliers.

The power went out one day. Everyone had to leave the hotel to a lake inside the cave. It was there at the lake where I met an older lady. She was a widow in an orange bathing suit and a blue swimmer's cap, with a pink service poodle by her side. I thought I was the only citizen without a service pet. I didn't want to take care of anything anymore. She said she knew everything there was to know about Periscope City—the city of loners.

"Have you been to Waldenland?" she asked.

"No. What's that?"

"You mean to say you live here and you've never heard of Waldenland? Have you been living under a rock, mister?"

I lived inside a cave.

"Tell me more," I said.

"You must go there. Just take the sky tram up the mesa. And if you *do* go, you gotta try the huckleberry pie." She kissed her fingers. "You'll die for it."

My curiosity led me to ask the robot at the concierge desk, "What's Waldenland?"

It handed me a digital brochure. Waldenland, at first glance, looked like the usual theme park, with a rollercoaster and all that other stuff. It was themed after a nineteenth-century book about a pond, with a little transcendentalism sprinkled in between. Although it sounded like a bizarre place, I would get the entire park to myself. My dream, after forty years, had finally come to fruition.

"What do I do?" I asked.

The robot pulled out a waiting list.

The wait would take a month. I hibernated through all of April. My day arrived ironically enough on May Twelfth, the date of my father's funeral. Instead of mourning his death all day, I decided to take the tram up the mesa to the park.

The wind in Waldenland felt more like the wind in a cemetery than the wind on a spring afternoon. I was the only human being there. Robots controlled the rides. They cooked the food in the food court. I ate fried raccoon, an elk sausage, and a tub of chestnuts. Robots ran the midway games, where one of them at a shooting gallery awarded me with a fluffy teddy bear. The teddy bear reminded me of the one I had when I was six. I can't remember anything else from that age.

Dolls took up every seat on every ride except for the ones that the park had reserved for me. I sat at the front of a rollercoaster with dolls in the back. The track twisted through a farm with brown barns and plastic crops and animatronic livestock.

Dolls also grinned at me on the carousel. I tried to look away from them. A horror movie from my childhood came to mind, where a carousel whirled a man to death, so I hopped off that thing.

I brought my teddy bear with me to a funhouse called *Henry's Wonderful Cabin of Mirrors*. An animatronic doll of Henry David Thoreau slept in its bed. I hesitated when I stepped into a maze of mirrors called *The Maze of Transcendentalism*. Each mirror showed me at a different age. The older I looked, the more I got lost in the labyrinth. I had to find the end to reach transcendence. When I did, I didn't feel like I'd surpassed any limits of understanding, just relief that I'd found my way out of there.

I followed the woman at the lake's advice and took a bite of huckleberry pie. Thoreau had written about huckleberries in *Walden*, I believe, but I forgot what it was about. The pie, however, was disgusting.

The Ferris wheel, the Isolationist, left me at the very top. Alone in the sky was different from alone in the cave for a reason besides the obvious. The cave would trap me in my mind, where intrusive thoughts attacked me like vampire bats. Whereas alone in the sky, my mind flew away like Icarus to the sun. I watched it shrink into a speck within seconds. The sky turned into peanut butter and strawberry jelly with melted marshmallows for clouds. I needed to gather my senses, so I switched my focus to downtown Periscope City, where the loners hung their heads at their feet. I could feel what they felt. I craved loneliness, yet I hated loneliness.

The Ferris wheel finally met the station, and my mind came down with it. The robot that worked the ride resembled my father from forty years ago. Its eyes, like on all robots, were as alive as the stone on a Greek statue.

Near the end of the day, I rested in the shade at the grove at Walden Pond and listened to a soundtrack of birds and cicadas. It was animatronic animals, all of them. A rabbit dashed from plastic cattails to a plastic lawn. Robins and partridges and woodpeckers perched on the branches of an oak tree made of putty. When I approached it to carve my initials in the trunk, the birds flapped into the sky. I watched schools of fish in the bright blue pond and thought, wow, I was sitting in a nursery rhyme. If only my parents could see it, they probably would've been bored.

The seasons changed at Walden Pond every thirty minutes. It was like the fireworks display at Disneyland. Everything, every season, occurred in the blink of an eye. Oak trees in fall shed their leaves. The pond froze in winter. Dead, gray plants in springtime grew back to life. Woodsy creatures frolicked out of dormancy. A turtle dipped its silver limbs in the water, and white geese landed on the lawn. Henry's doll nodded at me, holding a fishing pole on a wooden raft. I nodded back—at something missing a brain.

After the sun had slipped beneath the canyons, a robot tapped me on the shoulder and asked me to leave. My two hours had expired. Tomorrow, someone else would take my place. I must admit, after what I'd experienced that day, a smidgen of my inner child had emerged.

Poor Advice

My sister, like, pressured me into marrying my first husband. Sure, he was a personal trainer who turned heads in a tank top, but after I said, "I do," I hoarded myself in an apartment in Rhode Island for the next thirteen years.

One day, Blane quit his career for another.

"Guess what I'm doing," he said. "I'm going to open a franchise with my fried chicken recipe. It'll go nationwide and beat my competitors starting tomorrow. What do you think about that?"

His ambition sounded a bit too lofty. "Are you sure about this?" I asked.

"Yes. Will you support me while I do it?" he said.

As a bartender, I did what I could, but Blane changed from his motivated self. He would, like, sit on his recliner and fantasize about his goals instead of working toward them.

"I've married a dreamer," I told my sister, the same one who'd talked me into marrying him.

"I had a feeling the marriage would go south," she said.

At thirty-six, I took my own advice and left Providence for Periscope City. My hotel was the Franklin, for temporary loners, otherwise known as Transients. I met my boyfriend on *Loner*. He lived at the Cramden as a Middleton. We saw each other once a month. He couldn't afford to live alone in upstate New York, and Periscope City cost much cheaper.

We hung out in my suite one night when I devoured like a whole box of mochi ice cream. Nate watched me eat it. His curly mustache squirreled away his upper lip, so it was hard to read his facial expressions.

"You should drive for Dryft," he said.

And I thought that he should've shaved that hideous creature off his face. Nate is crippled by his impulses. He bet on everything from basketball games to prop bets…and even my service cat Meggles, and how many times she used the litter box in a day (I usually won).

"No way," I said.

"Come on," he said. "You can't just sit and mope all day."

I hate the word *mope*. Mope hunches his shoulders. Mope wears cardigans and, like, eats tomato soup.

I must admit, though, I loved driving down the interstate by myself, without strangers that is.

"At least consider it," he said.

"Consider what?" I said. "Ridesharing is like glorified hitchhiking."

"Babe, it's ride-partnering," he said. "We don't share rides. We partner with them."

"Maybe I'm not hip to the newest lingo," I said.

After banjo practice, I seriously considered his advice until we watched the local news. A robot anchor said that someone murdered a Dryft driver in Periscope City and used him as a shower curtain. Now I had a reason to say no.

"See?" I said. "I don't want to die."

"Oh, please," he said. "That happens once in a blue moon. You're fine."

A gambling addict was, like, trying to tell me how to live my life.

Meggles hopped onto my lap. I ran my hands through her fur. She pawed my chest for more food. She always made the verdict.

"What do you think, Megs?" I asked. "Should I follow Nate's advice?"

She meowed sharply. I raised Meggles over my head, but she, like, refused to give me a high five, which meant no, stay away from that job. She hated Nate because of Al, his pet service owl. Even though she looked out for my best interest, I refused to stay home with my cat all day. I preferred to go shopping and buy a fancy new purse instead.

"Fine," I said. "I'll apply. But it's your fault if I end up as a lampshade."

"Trust me. You'll be okay," he said.

—

The application for Dryft contained three questions:

• *Name?* Katherine DeLaurentis.

• *Criminal Record?* No. (I once shoplifted $300 of kitchen appliances over a decade ago, but there was like a statute of limitations.)

• *Do you smoke?* No. (I lied about that, too.)

———

After the onboarding process, the company sent a training video to my smart TV:

Clean your car before every shift. If any fellow Dryfter does not clean it, he/she/they will receive an email for separation.

Above all else, smile and talk. Keep the words rolling along. Offer free licorice from your glove box. Follow these steps and become a premier Dryfter.

Premier Dryfters picked up premier customers—or big tippers. That was the bottom line. I needed a minimum of fifty customers and a four-star rating to become premier.

They issued me a phone app and a free electric car, but, like, nobody trained me.

———

I sat and waited on my first day at a charging station with other Dryfters, reminiscing over my William & Mary college years, back when I delivered pizzas. That was a fun job. I would smoke cigarettes with the windows down and blast indie rock through Williamsburg.

The app pinged. Someone waited for a ride, a young dude named Ian who looked nineteen. I picked him up at the Handler Hotel, and his destination was a movie theater in downtown.

When he got in, the scent of urine on his jean jacket overwhelmed the new car smell. He stared at the windshield and pouted. I already knew he wouldn't tip me, and I just hoped to God that he owned a shower curtain.

I followed the training video's advice and kept the words "rolling along." "I'm Katherine," I said.

The kid cranked the stereo with contemporary music playing: a bunch of bleeps and bloops in a fast rhythm.

It was going to be a long drive. I tried to tell him over the music, "There's free licorice in the glove box."

He sat on his hands.

"I'm from Rhode Island. What about you?"

"From here," he said.

"How do you like it here?" I asked.

He started flicking the door handle with the bleeping and blooping and didn't talk. So much for a real conversation.

—

After I dropped him off, my phone pinged again. It, like, scared me to see who it was. I saw on the dash screen that it was a robot named Chance. It had more personality than Ian: I could tell already.

—

Chance stood in a tailored suit at the marble steps of the Grover Hotel. When it got in, its cologne, like, flooded the car and drowned out Ian's urine smell. Its pecs bulged around the seatbelt. "Please transport me to the Handler Hotel," it said. "4908 Tobias Wolff Circle, Periscope City, Utah, 00000."

So it looked like I was heading back to the Handler. The address appeared on the dash from its voice. Chance like, hopped from one hotel to the next to service clients as a medical sex robot. Robots obviously don't sleep. Who was I to judge why it was going there? I just assumed, by its charming looks, that Chance was one. I wasn't enough of a loner to go that route. How could they allow medical sex at a sober living like the Handler? The Institute wasn't kidding when it said it promoted wellness for loners. Well, I didn't agree.

It was ten o'clock at night, and my shift would end at midnight. The fog, like, coated the windows. Snowflakes melted on the windshield. The heater made me want to fall asleep, and so did the hypnotic bleeps and bloops from the music. My eyelids, like, needed toothpicks to stay open, so I had to engage with Chance.

"Could you turn the stereo off, please?"

"One moment," it said.

Chance remained still and turned it off on its own. Just think of the wonders it could've done in bed.

We slowed down on a two-lane highway behind a truck full of Christmas trees. I thought about those trees as if they were humans. Some of them would end up in living rooms for families to dress with lights, bells, and candy canes, while other trees were missing branches, or their branches were thinning, or both. Those were the rejected trees.

Where would they go? To the woodchipper? What does a woodchipper feel like? I had to, like, distract myself from those morbid thoughts.

"What's the forecast?" I said.

Chance stared on at the road with its hands on its knees, never slouching. "Wednesday will be thirty percent precipitation, while Thursday will be fifty percent. Highs in the forties and lows in the thirties. Would you like to hear the Dow Jones?"

"No thanks," I said.

"What else is on your mind?" it asked.

I was about to vent my frustrations to a search engine with a penis. "My boyfriend talked me into this."

"Quick disclaimer," it said. "This exchange is being recorded for quality assurance."

Of course. So much for disclosing my love life.

I said, "What's at the Handler?"

"I apologize, but I must refrain from sharing confidential information," it said.

Where had my life gone? Driving medical sex robots to their patients. But I'd chosen to live there and do that job. To think people would bait me into making awful decisions in my younger days, from taking clogging classes to majoring in Communications. (And how could I forget about Blane, my ex-husband?)

"My boyfriend and I have been together for six months. What do I do with him?"

"Six months is a long-term relationship," it said.

"It is? We've seen each other, like, six times."

"According to a May article in the *Periscope City Gazette*, most relationships in town last up to three weeks," it said. "Congratulations on your commitment."

"I guess I'll have to agree with a statistic," I said. "I can depend on any news source from the internet, right?"

Chance kept its mouth closed.

"He has addictions," I said. "Like, how do I stop him?"

"Communicate openly and compassionately," Chance said. "You must know how to manage a challenging conversation. If you wait longer, the more difficult it will be."

All good points. But how could I, like, change my boring sex life?

"Hey, Chance," I said. "Can you look up sexual dysfunction? I'm asking for a friend."

"What is your question?" it said.

"The side effects of a drug she's taking."

"What is the prescription?"

I brought up Zinopranil, my drug for loneliness.

"Sexual dysfunction is not a known side effect of Zinopranil," it said. "On the contrary, it is supposed to heighten your libido. I mean *her* libido. It must be a psychosomatic problem."

Chance wasn't, like, helping my confidence with its information.

—

I hit the brakes at the front steps of the Handler Hotel. Mostly loners with trust funds stayed there. The hotel soared above the others, with a penthouse suite on each floor. Fifty stories of which stood about a third taller than *my* hotel. Whatever. The gray wooden building had a pointed roof with mammoth front doors that gleamed beneath a mustard-brown awning. I'd always dreamt about living at a luxurious hotel like the Handler, but I wasn't an alcoholic—I was a foodaholic. And ever since my childhood, I'd wanted to live in hotels as an adult, just staying at one after the other.

A robot valet snapped a golden button on its blazer. When it opened Chance's door with its silk gloves, it ignored me like I was a dust mite.

"Good luck on your journey," Chance said.

I grew envious toward a robot because it was going into the Handler Hotel, and I wasn't. The Franklin was about as sophisticated as a Holiday Inn. I needed comfort food, so I drove to the closest convenience store for ice cream mochis.

—

Ever since Chance, the ride partners either bored me, annoyed me, or repulsed me. All of them were human beings. I wished I could just pick up robots. They were the only things to have a decent conversation with. I kept telling myself, "Today is my last day."

One of them stared at me with bug eyes. "Will you take your shirt off for thirty dollars?" he said. "I'll tip you."

I reported him through the Dryft app.

"Ha, what a joke," Nate said.

Yeah, like, real funny. How could my boyfriend laugh at that?

Dryft replied a week later:

Thank you for your feedback. We will handle this matter justly and promptly.

They took their sweet ass time, but at least the pervert was gone for good.

I ignored Nate for several weeks after his inappropriate behavior to my crisis. He texted me: I'm worried about you. I loved him for his independent spirit, but he began turning needy.

—

I soldiered on with Dryft. Some nights naturally dragged longer than others. On Christmas Eve, I dryfted for over two hours without a passenger. My thoughts whirled incessantly on the interstate. Maybe Chance had told the truth about the drug. I'd come to the stark realization that I wasn't attracted to Nate. His mustache made him look like a nineteenth-century parlor magician. His family members—some he hadn't even met—helped him feed his addiction with loans. There was a hell of a good reason he'd coaxed me into that job. He would ask me to send him money through a phone app. The way my immediate future looked, I would fall short of buying a fancy new purse. There had to be some way to break up with him without destroying him.

I was stuck behind another truck full of Christmas trees. The electric car slammed the brakes on its own at seventy miles per hour. Smash. Everything happened in an instant. The trees collapsed on the windshield and crushed the hood. Thank God for the seatbelt. Otherwise, the wreck would've turned me into lunch meat.

—

I ended up in a hospital bed with a pinched nerve in my neck. It was the same feeling as the time when I picked up a sock the wrong way.

A human doctor checked on me. "On a scale of one to ten, one being a scratch and ten being childbirth, how do you feel?" he said.

I couldn't see myself experiencing childbirth. "A seven," I said.

He administered morphine, which, like, numbed me for a little while. I felt dopey, which was a good thing.

In the meantime, Nate sent me a text: I'm coming to see you.

Solitude was my chicken soup, so I wished he would've stayed home. But I felt an obligation to let him come over because he was my boyfriend. Half the building was a veterinarian clinic, so the hospital allowed service pets.

I texted him back: Please bring Meggles. He had my hotel card.

—

Not a second after they showed up did Meggles leap onto my bed. Nate closed the door.

"What happened?" he said.

"I got stuck in la-la land, and my car ran into a truck full of Christmas trees. I remember the trees on my windshield but can't remember anything else."

"Where do you hurt?" he said.

"It's a pinched nerve in my neck. I'm okay."

He hugged me and kept hugging me. The pain turned to an eight.

"I worried about you," he said. "You haven't texted me back. Do you resent me for some reason?"

I did, a little…but how could I, like, express my resentment then?

"A lot has happened," he said. "Al has run away. I mean, flown away."

Good for Al. "Oh, Nate," I said. "I'm really sorry. What happened?"

"One night, as usual, he flies out of his birdie hole to catch mice. The next morning, he's gone. He's been missing for four days. The animal rescue team has been a letdown. I keep going out and calling his name."

Al, like most owls, belonged in the wild. But what about Nate? Where did he belong? He had a dark blue face in the room. I bled for him, but only so much in the hospital.

"Why did I talk you into that stupid job?" he said.

Half the onus I placed on him, the other half on me because I'd ultimately chosen to drive for Dryft.

"I'm able to decide for myself," I said. "So can Meggles. Three days will go by without me seeing her. She wanders off somewhere, and then she comes back whenever she wants."

"I still feel responsible," he said. "My gambling problem has gotten worse. I lost fifteen hundred on New Jersey last night."

I didn't know how severe his losses were.

"There's an urge to bet on the game tonight. What do you think? Should I seek counseling? There's a group in town, but am I ready to admit my problems to a bunch of strangers?"

After the morphine kicked in, I fell half asleep.

"No," I said.

"No? No what?"

"I mean, no, I'm not giving you advice," I said.

"Why not?"

"Because no advice is the best advice."

"What does that even mean?" he said.

It confused me just as much. Nate had to trust his gut because he constantly asked me for advice about everything. Most people thought they knew all the answers. Nate couldn't recognize their arrogance. I could, like, totally relate to that. That was why we were together. His thoughts and feelings, however, conflicted with mine. "I had to let go of my other cat after she disappeared," I said.

"The one before Meggles?" he said.

"Yes, in Rhode Island. She ran away and never came back. I respected her independence. She wanted to spend her time by herself. The both of us benefited without each other."

Meggles squinted at me.

"What's wrong, Megs?" I asked.

Her green eyes told me somebody else in Periscope City could've been waiting for me, but I, like, didn't want anyone else. Decisions, decisions. She purred at me and leaped to the windowsill.

"Do you want me to leave?" Nate said.

"I *am* getting sleepy."

He kissed my forehead and left the door to the hallway cracked open. A yellow light beamed across Meggles's body. She returned to me after he'd left. At one point, the morphine hit me, and I fell fast asleep.

The doctor released me the following day. I wore a neck brace. Meggles and I took a self-driven Dryft back to the Franklin.

—

Common sense told me to quit the job after I'd almost died from Christmas trees, but I, like, decided to drive rather than sulk all day. They sent me a brand-new electric car.

Dryft paid me enough money to charge the car and that was it. I still wished for a fancy purse. Customers like that Ian kid refused to tip me. Robots and most people undervalued ride-partnering. I may as well have volunteered.

—

But fuck everything. I revisited my college years by opening the window and lighting cigarettes. White ash snowed to the carpet, reducing the vehicle to an ashtray. I stuffed the red licorice in my mouth in front of passengers. They had to, like, put up with my dissonant voice when I began singing.

My rebellion persisted. After too many negative reviews, Dryft sent me an email for separation. Fare-fucking-well.

—

Without a job or a boyfriend, I treated myself like a queen again, with Meggles, mochis, my couch, and the flat-screen.

But things bored me in a matter of weeks. I was haunted by the dark side of loneliness. The Zinopranil stopped working. Having other people around really mattered—but only for twenty minutes. Then they had to leave.

—

I missed Nate's body next to mine, so I went to his suite at the Cramden. He'd shaved that fugly rodent off his face without me having to ask, and he'd bought me a gift: a new white leather purse.

I smiled for the first time in I don't know how long.

"Nate, why did you?" I said.

"It's okay," he said. "I went a week without betting."

"How do you feel?"

"Empty, but in a good way."

"The longer you go without it, the less you'll miss it," I said.

"Simple psychology, I guess," he said.

"Have you seen Al?"

"He might be gone for good."

"But I'm not," I said.

He felt like warm laundry right out of the dryer and into my arms.

"I take it things are back to normal?" he said.

Well, seeing Nate once a month may have killed the relationship again, so I told him, "Why don't we see each other every *two* months?"

"Sounds like a plan," he said. "We could always send text messages. Why don't we see other people?"

If by other people he meant medical sex workers, then, like, why not? Even non-humans. I wished I could've afforded Chance. "Works for me," I said.

Things have a funny way of working out, don't they? I mean, I went from marrying a hopeless dreamer to dating a compulsive gambler. As opposed to Blane, Nate would venture outside from time to time. I guess that was progress for me. And thank God I never turned into a shower curtain.

Use

I used to be an actor, a wannabe actor, who would storm the cattle calls for auditions. Dark souls would bark at me to repeat lines and rejected me and rejected me and rejected me. My only agent told me I was too past my prime to be a leading man, so she dumped me.

But acting drove away my demons, my alcoholic father. If I could, I would've moved Heaven and Earth to get through Hollywood, but Hollywood was burning. Artificial intelligence had taken control.

I escaped to Periscope City and stayed in sober living at the Handler Hotel. I threw pennies in its fountain, lifted weights in its fitness room, swam in its pool, and rested in its sauna. The other guests kept to themselves except for remote meetings, where we absorbed ancient philosophies from our counselors. I tried not to drink in rehab and recovery by feeding other addictions with my addictive personality, like sex with medical sex workers. It set me back more than alcohol. That was because I abused it.

My mother always bothered me about making friends. She thought I was still living in Hollywood. Periscope City was my dirty little secret. I was getting along with a kid named Ian through my laptop, who suggested an app for dating called *Loner*.

—

I matched with a fifty-three-year-old who was a *woman seeking younger men*. We met at the Davidson Hotel's rooftop lounge. She adored my physique, my smooth skin, and my full head of hair. I was thirty-five but could've passed for nineteen.

Her profile said she produced films—festival-winning films. With all her associates there, she lived the furthest from alone—at least physically. She was spending time in Periscope City only to shoot a handful of scenes for her newest one, *The Ten Faces of Dr. Cross*, with the great director Claude Rainier. Somehow, the institute had allowed the shoot to take place. I was on a date with a luminary who was old enough to be my aunt.

We sat outside beneath a heat lamp. Erin sipped a Cosmo. I drank a soda with a pink straw.

"You say you're an actor," she said. "What have you acted in?"

The question made me cringe. As an actor who'd only taken acting classes, who could offer nothing else but his screen presence, I answered, "Lots of things."

"Such as?"

I had to make up titles to impress her.

"Ever heard of *Clan of the Mud People*?"

"No."

"*Red Elephant*?"

"Not that either."

I struggled to cook up another title. "What about *The Gardener's Second Wife*?"

"Are these indie films?"

"Yes."

"Admirable, I guess," she said.

After we kissed in the elevator, Erin rested her ear against my heart. I asked her where she was from. She was originally from Michigan, where she said her parents had died, but now she rented properties in Manhattan and Santa Monica. The rest of her family and childhood was kept a secret. She distanced herself as far as I could see. I didn't reveal my past either.

"You promise to call me?" she said.

"Yes," I said.

———

I received a text message from her a day later:

I think I've fallen madly in love with you. Am I going too fast?

Yes, she was, but I played the game:

Not at all. I think I'm in luv 2 lol.
I will treat you to dinner tonight.
Can't wait.

———

We sat in Lumiere's, Periscope City's priciest steakhouse, by ourselves. Erin wore a sequin dress, and I wore a flannel shirt with dried paint on it.

"Order whatever you like, honey. It's on me," she said.

I ordered a two-hundred-dollar tomahawk steak.

She leaned over to a robot pianist next to us and said, "Legato."

It started tinkling the keys beneath our chat.

She drank imported white wine. I kept my sobriety a secret along with my mission to become the next great action hero.

"Babe, do you drink?" she said.

I had to make up a reason. If Erin found out that I was an addict, it could've spoiled everything. "I'm trying to stay in shape," I said.

"I understand. So when are you going to let me see your reel? You have one, right?"

I did. Only it showed footage from a student short in which I played a deaf ornithologist. I hesitated. "It shows only one of my roles. Everything else went lost when my hard drive was ruined in the flood.." Which was another lie.

"Oh dear, that's tragic," she said. "So sorry to hear that."

"Anyway," I said. I held my soda up for a toast. "I hope you like it."

Erin reached across the table and clutched my hand. The candlelight brightened up her warm eyes. "Honey, you should wish, not hope," she said.

Wish, not hope. What thoughtful advice. It enlivened my soul.

—

I scrawled it in black marker on my wall at the Handler: WISH, NOT HOPE!!!! Hope only brought expectations, whereas wishing validated my dreams.

The hotel let me stay without a curfew, so I could journey elsewhere and sleep at other hotels.

—

I sent my reel to Erin's email and expected another rejection.

—

She texted me a day later:

Baby, your acting is outstanding.

She must've been lying because she was in love.

U really think so???
There's a little Heston in you. I'll show it to my friends at Sundance. They're a big deal.

I read her text over and over as if I was reading it for the first time. It was a magical moment in my life. I vowed to play the role of her boyfriend. Someone had to land me a gig.

—

She invited me to the Davidson on a night when my favorite football team was playing.

Baby I can't. My Colts are playing.
Watch it over here.

I was about to reject the offer, but chances rarely happened with a woman like Erin.

—

The elite loners stayed at the Davidson. I arrived at her door with a ten-speed that I'd rented from a store in downtown Periscope City. She'd decorated her suite with banners and mylar balloons, which read: LOVE YOU BRIAN. I felt like running away.

Erin kissed my cheek. "What do you think?" she said.

What did I think? She was nuts. After getting to know me for a week, this was how she treated me. "I'm speechless," I said, "and humbled."

"Honey, don't look so scared," she said. "Come here."

She sat me in a wing chair. "Alexa, activate dinner tray." It folded out. "Dinner's almost ready," she said. "You have two choices: Mexican chicken or Russian chicken."

If only there was a third choice, like pizza delivery. Out of curiosity, I chose the Russian chicken.

Erin set utensils and a soda can in a koozie with my name on it on a tray. I tried to pay attention to the game.

She'd overcooked the Russian chicken and served it with bowtie noodles smothered in runny pink sauce.

"How does it taste?" she said.

Like anything but chicken. I had to plug my nose when Erin looked away and let the sauce slide down my throat. "It's great," I said. "Different from anything I've had before. You're quite the chef."

"Aww, you're the first person to call me that."

I believed it.

"It's true," I said.

"Good, because now it's time for dessert."

What culinary monstrosity came next? Thank God she served me only German chocolate cake. The icing spelled LOVE YOU BRIAN.

"Blow them out and make a wish," she said.

I already knew my wish.

—

As for sex with her, what was there to do? A man can pretend up to a point. I was lying on her bed while Erin was getting ready in the bathroom.

"I bet you can't wait," she said.

I could've waited a lifetime. "Sure, come on out," I said.

"Now close your eyes."

I wanted to keep them closed. A blindfold would've come in handy.

The door opened. "Open wide, sexy boy."

I slipped one eye open and caught her in lingerie—fishnet lingerie.

"And?" she said.

And she looked deplorable. "Wow, you look hot."

She twirled herself slowly and showed me the goods from her backside. "You really think so?"

"Amazing," I said.

"I bought this piece just for tonight."

I kept it hard by fantasizing about younger women in rehab. The sex lasted for about five minutes, a long five minutes. She orgasmed, and I pretended to do the same with a condom on.

We lay in bed together afterward, holding hands and facing the ceiling. "Baby, just wait a few months," she said. "Your life will transform, and you'll have new problems."

As if my old problems weren't enough.

"I used to do nails at a salon before this," she said. "Anything can happen if you wish."

Erin's words inspired me despite everything else about her.

"I went to a psychic," she said, "and guess what she told me."

"I give up. What did she say?"

"An enormous project is coming, and it involves us."

Now I was excited. "Really?" I said.

"Yes, babe."

"You should listen to her," I said.

"You're so different from my last boyfriend. If there's one thing I hate, it's a drunk."

Erin reminded me of my problem, so I disguised myself even more. "Same here. It ruins people's lives."

She asked me in a toddler's voice: "Do you have a spiwit animal?"

I didn't know what she meant. "Of course," I said.

"What is it?"

I said the first animal that came to mind. "A chimpanzee."

"That's cute," she said. "Mine's a gopher. Everyone should have a spiwit animal. Will you be my wittle gopher?"

"Sure," I said.

—

Erin began the shoot in Periscope City with Claude Rainier. I agreed to feed her service cocker spaniel while she was at the location, but who was going to feed my service frog, Tony? I had to find a healthy balance.

She sent me a text on the day before Christmas Eve:

Spend the holidays with me.
   I can't. I'm seeing my family in Indiana.
Too late. I've put you in the movie. Love you.

Put me in the movie? Everything was working out as planned. Notoriety would come. My acting career would finally take flight, and I would reflect on the disappointing past below me and smile victoriously.

OMG THANK U.

—

I called my mom to give her the thrilling news:

"My Brian is in a movie? That's amazing. See? I always knew you would become a star. Wait until the family hears this."

A part of me worried that my plan might boomerang. I mean, my relatives thought I was still sweeping floors at a bakery in Hollywood. It was better if people besides her remained in the dark. "Ma, it's just between you and me."

"But why?"

"Because nothing in entertainment is guaranteed."

"Okay, my lips are sealed. Now tell me about this Erin."

I skipped a lot of details.

—

It felt like a jail term, staying at Erin's hotel for Christmas. When she was home, she followed me around every minute of every hour. The only time away from her was in her bathroom. It was suffocating. After six months of sobriety, I felt compelled to drink and needed an excuse to flee out of there.

"I'm so excited to open presents," she said.

But I hadn't bought her anything. It was time to go somewhere away from there. I got out of the bathroom. "I'm getting some fresh air," I said.

"Hurry back for Christmas dinner."

—

My desperation carried me ten blocks down a slushy sidewalk to a gay bar called the Lucky Wolf. I couldn't help myself with my addiction.

—

Just a bartender named Paul occupied the bar. A selection of bottles on golden shelves invited me with their smiles and whispers. Since she'd trapped me for the holidays, one drink felt like the one way out—just one drink, and I would leave.

"Pour me a shot of cinnamon whiskey," I said to Paul.

He put his phone down on an icebox after being immersed in it. "You want to run a tab?" he said.

"Sure," I said.

The first drink rolled down my chest in a freezing burn, which I'd missed like it was my big brother. That was it.

When I was sitting in there, an old acquaintance, Thomas Houlihan, a fellow actor from Hollywood, just so happened to enter the Lucky Wolf. How weird. What was he doing in Periscope City with its small population? I knew him only through the bars on the Sunset Strip. After six months, he'd grown a double chin, and his stomach expanded past his belt. I could barely recognize him.

"Boy, you look good," I said.

"Likewise. Did you get some work done?"

"A little."

"How's about a shot of tequila?" he said.

"On you? Fine by me."

"Where you staying?" he asked. "I'm at the Davidson."

I couldn't tell him about the Handler. He might already have known it was rehab. Up to that point, I was lucky enough to have never run into him at Erin's hotel.

"Where have you been? You've been missing from the bars," he said.

"Same old, same old," I said. "Hollywood can kiss my ass."

"Hear that. So glad to be away from that ghost town. You live here now?"

He was telling the truth about Hollywood being a ghost town. People had lost their jobs since artificial intelligence had taken over the industry.

"Just visiting," I said.

Thomas dished out the latest news about himself. I wasn't eager to listen to him. He always landed commercial roles, not film or TV roles. But they were better than nothing.

"I'm here for a movie," he said.

It had to be Erin's movie I thought. What else? As far as I knew, it was the only project being shot in that small town.

"What movie is it?" I asked.

"It's called *The Ten Faces of Dr. Cross*, directed by the great Claude Rainier."

Damn it. How could it be? The one role that I'd landed had Thomas Houlihan in it. I resented him even though we were good acquaintances. It would've been better if I could brag about my own film.

I kept the news about my gig top secret like I did with my family. Old Houlihan would have to find out for himself on the day when I would show up to the set. I let him continue with his humble bragging as we drank more shots of rum, vodka, whiskey, and tequila, mixing liquors like fools.

—

Those drinks had revved my engine, so I slipped inside a liquor store for a fifth of whiskey and a pack of breath mints after parting ways with Thomas and Paul.

—

When I got back, Erin was in the kitchen, and it smelled like carrots.

"Did you get lost?" she said.

"I ran into an old friend."

"Really? Who?"

Several old friends, in fact, and I buried one of them in my coat pocket.

"You wouldn't know him," I said.

"Dinner's almost ready, hon."

I locked the bathroom door and took a pull of whiskey on the toilet. My tolerance had plunged in six months. The whiskey hammered me to the floor. "Be out in a second," I said. I hid the bottle again and popped two mints in my mouth. Half the fifth was gone by the time I left the bathroom.

Dinner was bone broth with carrots, cabbage, and a mystery meat I pretended was Wagyu. Erin sat across from me while I kept my eyes on the plate of food.

"Honey, your face is all red," she said.

"Is it?"

"You're slurring. Are you catching a cold?"

"Must be allergies."

Erin was talking like a baby again. "Mommy has some medicine for that."

"That's okay. I'll be fine."

"No, you're suffewing. Mommy will take care of her baby."

I almost yelled at her because of her insistence. She stood over me and waited for me to swallow the pill.

"We'll rehearse the script tomowwow."

"I haven't seen it yet."

"It's only two lines."

Only two lines? After sleeping with her and tolerating her presence…. "That's it?" I asked.

"Don't get all worked up," she said. "Wemember, we have to work your way into more woles. Mr. Wainier is picky about his actors, and we don't want to upset him. Don't you wowwy your cute wittle head off. Mommy has it all planned out. First, let's open your pwesent."

I couldn't give any less of a shit about it. "Sure, fine, go get it," I said.

"Jeez, don't get too excited, Mr. Rainy Day."

How could I last another night with that kook? What about the promises? What about my life transformation? What about her friends looking at my reel? I needed stardom now, not next year or the year after that.

Erin came back with a present in wrapping paper so huge that she had to hug it to bring it into the kitchen. "Okay, baby, open up. Mommy can't wait."

How could her gifts be any worse than her cooking?

I tore the wrapper apart with Erin beaming her smile at me and opened a white cardboard box to something with coffee-brown fur. A gopher costume with holes for my asshole and genitals.

"Isn't it amazing?" she said.

It was something other than amazing. "Unreal," I said. "Just unreal. Where did you find this?"

"I know an artist in the sex industry who crafted it just for you."

I didn't feel all that special. "Wow," I said. "Thanks for thinking of me."

"Aww, you're vewy welcome, sweetie. I'm way too excited now. Put it on."

"Put what on?" I said. "Right now?"

"What? It's fun."

"Can't we do it later?" I said.

Erin pouted at the floor. "He hates my pwesent."

How much longer did I have to play this charade? "Erin, I love it."

She crossed her arms, still pouting.

What choice did I have? "Here. You think I'm lying? I'll put it on."

"You're just saying that," she said.

"I mean everything I say."

"If you pwomise..." she said.

I closed the bathroom door behind me, holding the costume, not the bottle, which I desperately craved. Erin hoorayed when I was in there. For once I observed the bathroom when I was drunk. It was immaculate. The toilet had a polished brass handle, and the bathtub had jacuzzi jets and golden swans for faucets. The devil was laughing. I thought about a movie about a deranged woman who kidnapped a man and broke his legs to keep him there. This felt like that. I couldn't play the part forever, the part about me being her boyfriend. The truth would be revealed at some point.

I stepped out in complete shame and disgust, but I refused to wear the gopher head.

Erin jumped on the bed, pointed at me, and mocked me. "You look so silly. It's exciting me. Put it on your head."

"Do I have to do it?"

"Yes. Let's have sex with the head on."

The night decayed into drunk dick and insomnia.

When we were about to begin, I removed the gopher head to breathe better.

Erin frowned at my flaccid penis. "Baby, don't I tuwn you on?" she said.

I had to think of a reason for my limp dick. "I think I'm overwhelmed by the shoot."

"Then get some west," she said. "We'll pwactice the lines tomowwow."

The short, furry tail on the costume kept me from sleeping on my back, so I rolled to my side. "I'll do them first thing," I said.

—

It was a lie. I chugged the whiskey before Erin got up in the morning. The sun was just rising. I crawled along the marble kitchen floor, which froze into an ice pond. A flood of bitter air came through the window, making my nostrils leak.

Erin stepped in with a jowl that hung like an angry bag of flour. "Did you fall?"

No more baby talk either.

"Yes," I said. "Can you help me up?"

"You're slurring again."

"Am I?"

She held out the empty bottle. "I found this in your coat."

How could she search through my clothes? I picked myself up from the floor. "Why did you dig through my coat?"

"And why did you bring liquor to my suite?"

I had to think of another story but couldn't concoct one. "I'll explain."

She threw it in the trash beneath the sink, which sobered me right away. "What's there to explain?"

"Erin, I'm sorry."

"You've been lying this whole time."

I went in for a kiss, but she turned her face away as if my lips were vinegar.

"Baby, I love you," I said.

"Not again," she said. "Not with a drunk."

"A drunk?" I said. "Don't call me a drunk."

She slapped my face and gave me a soft sting. "I've seen this movie before. You'll fail as an artist."

Fail as an artist? How could she make such a claim? I shook her by the arms, but she was as stiff as an oak tree.

"Baby, remember when you told me to wish, not hope? You've inspired me."

"This was a mistake," she said.

"What was?"

"This. It's over."

"What do you mean it's over?"

"Us. We're over. Now please leave."

How could her feelings have changed so abruptly? "You're kidding, right? You're kicking me out? How could you go one-eighty like this? What about the movie?"

"I'll have Claude delete the character," she said.

After years of racing thoughts and restless nights, after years of constant doubts and failed auditions, I fell to a chair and begged her:

"Please, give me a second chance. My mother's been sick. I wanted to see her for Christmas. Could've been our last time together. She wants to see her baby on the screen. It would mean so much to her. I should've told you this in the beginning."

It was fate, meeting Erin on *Loner*. Mom used to say, "Everything happens for a reason."

Erin's green eyes on that harsh, snowy morning went cold. "You're such a liar," she said. "Everything you say is a lie. I looked you up online. Your name doesn't even come up on the movie database. You said you acted in all those films, but it was just one lie after the other. Now get out. Get out, you drunk."

The sunlight through the kitchen window turned gray. I twisted the doorknob to leave her hotel room.

"You were using me this whole time," she said.

"We all use each other," I said.

A man's honesty, it has been said, pours out of him when he has been drinking. The only bright side was that I was free from expectations, free to drink as much as I wanted, and be left alone.

—

I gave up the acting dream and went nightly to the Lucky Wolf. Thomas Houlihan ran into me one of those nights and started bragging about the gig he'd landed. My envy never reached a plateau. Each drink made me resent him more.

I kept everything about me and Erin a secret from Mom. All I said was we weren't together anymore.

"What about the movie?" she asked.

"They called it off," I said.

There was a long pause before she said, "That's too bad."

—

I returned to sober living without anyone knowing about it and attended more Alcoholics Anonymous meetings, but rehab wouldn't further my acting career. When I reached out to Erin with a text for forgiveness, a text never came back. It was clear she'd moved on. If she was to forgive me, I would've promised not to use her anymore, a promise I would keep. Now my days were spent by myself again, where Isolation was my only companion. I started waking up every morning with the question of what could've been.

William and Zack

My name is William A. St. Berger. My home is the Plex Hotel and Casino. When I'm not playing roulette, I'm writing campaign speeches and splurging on medical sex workers. Politics is my passion. I'm running for governor of Utah. My service pet is a Pomeranian named Pete.

One night, in the casino bar, the Easy Luck, I was writing my campaign speech on a cocktail napkin. My wish was to ban medical sex work because of its immorality. They got the point. I wanted to attract both liberal and conservative voters, but the right words wouldn't come beneath the thumping music. Male and female dolls and MSWs of the human variety entertained every loner except for me at the counter.

I caught a whiff of perfume and swiveled on my stool. An MSW sat in a booth by herself, sipping her cocktail like a smoker who didn't inhale. Her hoops dangled from her ears, and they glimmered. Her tattoos covered her like wallpaper on her brown skin.

She grinned at me, a rare MSW. (I usually stick with the robots.) I carried my scotch and soda to her table.

Julianna had moved from Brazil for solitude.

"What do you do?" I said, as if I didn't already know.

"I work in the medical field," she said, "and also housekeep on the side."

"You sound like one busy bee," I said. "Where's your license?"

Julianna flashed her MSW card on her smartphone. I checked for its legitimacy.

"What about you?" she said.

I kept my campaign a secret even though she must've seen me on TV. A dome lamp shined on her makeup and jewelry and my leisure suit. I wore it for people to acknowledge me as William A. St. Berger, but with her, I tried to hide myself in a dark booth under the lamp. My constituents would've otherwise perceived me as a hypocrite because of my stance against medical sex work.

"Where are you from?" she asked.

I didn't know, but for some reason I told her Hawaii.

"You never answered my question," she said.

"What question is that?"

"What do you do?"

I had to think of a way out of answering the truth. "I play roulette," I said.

She brushed her hair behind her shoulders. "Sounds risky."

"I risk it all the time," I said.

A tattoo of pink lipstick on her left tit caught my eye. When she tickled the side of my leg with her fingernails, I felt no shame revealing the boner through my pants.

"Let me buy you a drink," I said.

"A Cosmo with extra olives," she said.

With my phone app, I scanned a tattooed barcode on her thigh to purchase her. She cost a thousand dollars a night. Health insurance had declined me, and I've maxed out seven visas in a month. "Money is meant to be spent" was my slogan.

I added her Cosmo to my tab.

She played with my hair and told me, "I'll do whatever you want."

The olives floated in her drink.

"You going to eat those olives?" I said.

She slid them off the stick with her teeth, and her lips devoured them. I wanted to take her to the jacuzzi and have fun with her there, but I had to cut to the chase.

"Let's go upstairs, babycakes," I said. My voice cracked.

—

We enjoyed having sex and a massage that night, and she vacuumed my floor in the morning. I sat on my bed in my bathrobe with Pete on my lap and pet him. My impulses got the best of me, which they usually did.

The words fell out like loose teeth. "Will you marry me?"

She flicked off the vacuum. "What?" she said.

"I said, will you marry me?"

She laughed hysterically. When Julianna realized I was being serious, the laughter stopped beneath the air conditioner and the refrigerator. The sunlight beamed through the drapes and across her face. Her jaw fell to the floor. "Are you kidding me?" she said.

William A. St. Berger doesn't kid around. "Did it sound like I was kidding?"

"I'm sorry," she said, "but I have to say no."

I couldn't tolerate rejection.

Julianna picked her hairpin up from my bedstand and stuck it in her hair.

"Why?" I said.

"Because," she said.

"Because why?"

She pinned her hoops in her ears. "Because you're a stranger to me, and you're my patient."

I respected her ethics. Medical sex workers should treat their patients as such. Fine. But patients must've swarmed to her. I also understood that I was but only one out of dozens of people, but how could I turn away from her after she'd outdone all the robots I'd had?

"However," Julianna said. She wrapped a ponytail with a rubber band in the mirror. "I would be an American citizen."

My heart sank to my knees. I mean, that was the only reason she wanted to get married to be a citizen? If she was to become my wife, she would need to know the truth about me to keep the honesty in our marriage. I scanned her barcode again.

"What's this?" she said.

"I tipped you eight thousand dollars," I said.

"For what?"

"You need to promise me you'll keep a secret."

"What secret?" she said.

"That I'm running for governor."

"Governor of what?"

"Of Utah," I said. "What did you think?"

She backed away from me. "Wait. Are you some kind of weirdo?"

"Weirdo? No. Why?"

"Sorry," she said. "I didn't mean to come off that way."

I smiled at her absurdity. "Baby, I'm not a weirdo. I'm a politician."

"I recognize you now. You're that man on the TV in those commercials."

"You see?" I closed my eyes and said, "And one day, I shall be the governor of Utah."

She kissed my nose. "I have to go."

The rejection stung. She grabbed her purse and vacuum and left me in the hotel room, alone. The isolation hurt that time.

I sat back on the bed and wanted to cry. The room turned cold and dark. Not only was I a stranger in that town but also a stranger to myself. Where was my past? What was my date of birth? What was my childhood like? My hometown? Where were my family members and friends? Who were they? Where did I go to school? It was all a big mystery. I wanted to sit there and pet Pete until my memory returned.

The second after I got up, someone knocked on my door, like a fingernail tap. I found Julianna through the peephole, who was wearing a different smile from her grin at the Easy Luck—with an eagerness painted on her face.

After I opened the door, she said, "Yes."

I cried inside with joy.

"Can I come in?" she said.

"Of course."

She got to the window and faced the canyons. I could see her reflection, and her smile had vanished. "There's something I must tell you," she said.

"You can tell me anything," I said.

She undid her hair and started fiddling with her rubber band. "I have a lot of lovers."

Figured she would. But what did that matter?

"I made a promise," she said. "Now you must promise me something."

"What promise?" I said.

"That you'll accept how many lovers I have."

Ha. William A. St. Berger scoffs at jealousy. Jealousy is absurd to him. So is envy. Those who envy show their weakness. His stoicism makes him a leader, not a follower. I'd studied under Marcus Aurelius. My belief was politics came before everything. "I promise," I said.

The second after I sat with her and wrapped my arm around her, she rested her head on my shoulder.

"I understand the line of work you're in," I said. "You might have patients like that, but I'm not one of them. Do whatever you please."

"I have married wealthy men," she said, "beautiful men. And then there are men like you."

"Thank you," I said.

"Do you promise not to obsess over me?" she said.

The truth was I did. Her polyamory didn't spark any jealousy in me but competition. I could love her better than any man. "I promise," I said.

"I have men who say they would die for me," she said. "Other men would kill for me."

She embellished, of course. "Baby, those are just expressions. 'I would die for you.' 'I would kill for you.' It's just machismo bullshit."

"I'm only warning you," she said.

I believed I had nothing to worry about.

—

We held hands in a chapel. A priest stood in front of us. I wore my green leisure suit. Julianna wore her wedding dress in all black to match her black hair, her black lipstick, and black fingernails.

"Do you accept this woman as your wife?" the priest said.

My feet went frozen, which surprised me. What if I was making a mistake with her? The sun shined down on us through a cupola, and my doubts began to collect like the dust drizzling through the sunbeams. Julianna's eyes urged me to say yes while the priest stood with a million years of patience. After I agreed, the priest faced Julianna, and she said "I do" within a second.

I pulled out a ring that I'd bought online and slipped it on her finger before laying a kiss on her lips. Julianna St. Berger—I loved the sound of that—Utah citizen (after she would sign the papers). Her lips tasted like cinnamon.

After the priest left, a small candelabra softened the chapel at dusk. When we sat in the back row, Julianna was quiet, and her body stiffened like the candlelight. The shadows on the walls were as still as pictures.

"Whatcha thinking?" I said.

She fiddled with her wedding ring. "About our promise."

"Let's forget about it," I said, "and think about our honeymoon. Where do you want to go?"

Instead of answering me, she sniffed a bouquet of roses that I'd bought at the corner of First and Howard Hughes from a robot.

"How about the Hoover Dam?" I said. "I've always wanted to go."

"I know a place," she said. "It's where I used to work when I moved to Utah."

Where she used to work? Most people hated where they worked, but I wanted to prove my love to her, so I agreed to do it.

"Wherever you want to go," I said.

—

Julianna chose a place at the border of Periscope City called the Kitfox Ranch. She and I got drunk off a champagne bottle on a self-driven white limo ride there. It dropped us off at a pony stable, next to women in bikinis who were watering a petunia garden. The women waved at me as if they liked me. I swatted flies, covered my nose from pony shit, and almost tripped over a chicken.

A Komodo dragon on the porch scared the crap out of me. A large wooden sign on the front door said: PLEASE REMOVE YOUR SHOES. I took off my white loafers while Julianna took off her black high heels.

"I want you to meet the madam," she said.

What madam? I held her by her shoulders and spoke under my breath. "Remember what I said. Don't tell anyone I'm running for governor."

"I promise," she said.

A chandelier flickered and dangled from the cracks of the ceiling inside the house. Bleach stung my eyes.

She introduced me to Madam Ivana, a plump Russian lady in a white flower dress.

"Who is this man?" Ivana said.

"His name is William A. St. Berger," Julianna said.

Ivana kissed my cheeks. I was so drunk that the house rocked me like a ship.

"He's a handsome devil," the madam said.

"Thank you," I said. "I do jujitsu every morning."

"You look like someone I know," she said.

"William is running for governor," Julianna said.

Not a day had gone by before she betrayed me.

"Governor?" Ivana said. "Is that the truth?"

"No no no no," I said. "She was kidding. Politics interests me is all."

My wife mouthed to me, "I'm sorry."

I threw a glare at her after two days of knowing her.

"What would you like to drink, my sweet?" the madam asked me.

Now that Julianna had blown my cover, I asked for a double scotch. And to think I'd tipped her eight thousand dollars.

"And for you, my Julianna?" the madam said.

"Nothing," she said.

The madam whistled with her fingers.

A bunch of young ladies came into the room in a single file, with the docility of the ponies, wearing corsets, high heels, micro-thongs, vinyl boots, schoolgirl outfits, dog collars with spikes, and smiles that hid their sorrow.

Madam Ivana introduced them:

"This is Tease, Bunny, Roxxxy, Cupcake, Tender, Trouble, and Foxxxy."

It felt like a filthy auction. The ladies appeared through my tunnel vision, but my eyes sharpened on Foxxxy in her corset. Her beauty leaped out among the women, and her breasts and eyelashes competed with my Julianna. What turned me on the most was her nose ring and a tattoo on her stomach of a bloody skull with a butcher knife in it. There was an air of déjà vu.

Julianna's wedding ring was missing from her finger. I panicked. Holy shit.

"Where's your ring?" I said.

She checked her right hand as if her mind had slipped. "Didn't we agree to see other people?" she said.

My stoicism cracked. "You told her I was running for governor after I'd specifically told you not to. Now you're doing this?"

"It's only Madam Ivana."

"Who cares who it is?" I said.

She hid her pink purse behind her back: it kept condoms, wipes, lotions, and—I suspected—her wedding ring. "Calm down," she said. "Go flirt with the girls. Let's swing."

"So now we're swingers, huh," I said. "Where are the other men?"

"They're coming," she said.

"What're you going to do in the meantime? Order a pizza?"

"What I do is my own business," she said.

The girls waited with their smiles and giggles. My scotch and soda tasted like hairspray. "Why are we here?" I asked.

"To see clients," she said.

"You mean patients," I said. "You're here to see patients."

"They're clients, baby. This is where I meet my regulars. I'm just a normal sex worker here."

"You took me here so you could work?" I said.

"You said anywhere I wanted, and this is it."

A man with a pot belly and a black mustache massaged her shoulders from behind her. He stood a foot beneath me.

I clenched my fist until it burned.

"Hello, my doll," he said to my wife.

"You bastard," I said. "I'm a second away from punching that mustache off your face."

"Go drink a jug of piss, pal," he said. "You can have her after me."

I lunged at him, but Julianna cut between us. My fist nearly struck my wife in the face.

"Stop it," she said to me.

"I thought you were a medical sex worker," I said. "But this whole time you've been nothing but a whore."

She slapped my face in front of the room and said, "How dare you call me that, Governor," loud enough for everyone to hear. "Who needs your consent?"

She dragged her client down a hallway and disappeared forever. My heart turned bitter. I drank what was left of the scotch in one gulp.

Ivana grabbed my arm. "Come on. Pick a girl."

I wasn't in the mood for anyone except Foxxxy for some reason.

The girls waited for me to decide. I kept my eyes on Foxxxy, but she looked away from me. The scotch and champagne did the talking. "I'll take Foxxxy."

"You want her, you pay cash," she said. "Five hundred dollars."

I'd seen Periscope City Police drag a man to jail because of cash. It felt like slime, spending it up front instead of paying after the deed. Although I was right outside of Periscope City, I never knew about the law. "Cash?" I said. "Are you insane? I pay with credit."

Ivana pointed at an ATM next to the bar. "You can use cash machine."

If the news found out, it could've sabotaged my whole campaign. "The cops could trace me through the ATM," I said.

"You pay cash," Ivana said. "Everybody pay cash."

I had to have Foxxxy. My impulses took over. I flashed my smartphone across the ATM screen to make a transaction, and it dispensed five hundred dollars through a slot.

Foxxxy looked away in disgust. It intrigued me to find out why.

After I gave the bills to Ivana, she counted them one by one. "She's yours for the night," she said.

—

Foxxxy turned on a glass lamp in a room that looked like it belonged in the eighteenth century. A violin solo was playing from the speakers up near the ceiling. I set my wallet on a chest of drawers. She sat on a king-size bed under a lace crown. Where did I know her from?

"We've met before," I said. My words slurred.

She crossed her arms and raised her eyebrow. "What the fuck are you doing, Zack?" she said.

"Zack?" I said. "Who's Zack?"

"Have you lost your mind?" she said. "Changing your name and running for governor?"

What was this part about me changing my name?

—

A match struck, and I woke up in a state of shell shock on the desert floor. It was pitch black out there. The smell of burning sage hit me like smelling salts. A lady with wrinkles on her face, who looked like she was about sixty, rubbed my left leg, which was numb.

"Who are you?" I asked.

She wore an oilskin hat and waved a sagebrush over me. "Just cool yourself down," she said.

My face was dry from wind burn.

"Where am I?" I asked.

She was strong enough to pick up all one-hundred-and-fifty pounds of me and sling me over her shoulders. "You're in the boonies," she said. "Let's git."

I was defenseless against her strength. She dumped me in the bed of her Toyota pickup truck as if I were a bag of fertilizer.

—

I rested in her trailer on a mattress made of rocks. Hieroglyphics painted the ceiling.

The woman sat with her feet on a recliner with cigarette holes all over it.

I lay there wondering how the hell I'd ended up in bed with my ex-girlfriend.

"What the hell you doing out here?" the woman said. "Only wackadoodles wander at night."

I told her: "I blacked out and woke up in bed with my ex-girlfriend after five years. Had to be a dream."

The woman's trailer smelled like bleach. I pictured a house with cracks in the ceiling. A Ute in an oil painting transformed into a bloodhound.

"Oh my God, I'm losing my mind," I said.

"You must've had makeup sex," the woman said.

"No way," I said. "The bitch cheated with my friend. Can't stoop *that* low."

"Oh, dang," she said.

The picture, at second glance, revealed a landscape of canyons. I tried to keep my sanity by recounting the events.

"How did you end up where I found you?" the lady said.

Good question. "I slid out of bed, trying not to wake her, and looked for my clothes. My wallet was on a dresser. I noticed a man's suit on an armchair."

"You talking 'bout this getup you got here?" she said.

"Yeah," I said. A leisure suit. I looked like a lounge singer. The clothing fit me perfectly, though. I usually wear flower shirts and cargo shorts.

"What about your shoes?" she said.

Missing like my memory, like my home, like my mind. I did remember hearing police sirens back at the house and Amy Finkle mumbling in her sleep. The cops were searching for someone. What if I'd blacked out and committed a crime? Know what I mean? What questions could I answer without remembering a thing prior to that? The window was the only escape. The moon shined over the canyons. I'd awakened on Mars, not Hawaii, and I'd climbed out barefoot. How stupid of me.

The rocks had cut my feet, and I remembered silhouettes of shrubs and boulders.

"Must've been at the Kitfox Ranch," she said. "Ain't nothing else out there."

"What's the Kitfox Ranch?" I said.

"The house of ill repute, sir."

"Wait," I said. "You're calling Amy Finkle a prostitute?"

"Just stating facts," she said. "Now open up."

The lady pulled out a thermometer to check my fever. But what did it matter? I was going to die.

"Calm yourself," she said. She pulled it out of my mouth and read it. "A hundred and two degrees? God dang. What were you thinking?"

"What did I tell you?" I said.

She began work on my left foot. My right leg bled. My big toe swelled with an insect bite.

"What's your name?" I said.

"They call me Dr. Alice. Don't got no degree or nothin'. You need brains for that."

She told me more about herself. Friends of old called her a doctor of holistic medicine after she'd quit the hospital as a nurse. She'd seen her last of death and preferred to live in the boonies by herself than in "that weird-ass town of loners."

"What town of loners?" I said.

"Shit, do I need to explain?" she said.

Yes. Everything needed an explanation.

A bunch of flies infested her trailer. Dirty clothes were scattered across the floor. Her fan blew dust, a rat slept in a cage, and her bloodhound appeared to have died. She'd pasted every window with pages from the *Periscope City Gazette*.

"Periscope City?" I said. "Where's Periscope City? I'm supposed to be in Maui."

Alice scrubbed the bite with peroxide. It fizzed and stung.

"You bet your ass we're in Periscope City," she said. "The bite must've infected your brain. This is Utah."

"Utah?" I said. "How the fuck am I in Utah?"

"Beats me," she said. "Ain't you running for governor?"

"For governor?" I said. "Now wait a minute."

"You're that man on TV," she said.

"On TV? Do you even know what you're doing?"

"I treat spider bites, snake bites, scorpion bites… Buster here once caught rabies."

Buster the bloodhound crooned at his name before settling back down to rest. His eyes drooped, his face sagged.

"Close them eyes and relax," she said. "You'll get home."

I was convinced that I would die in Utah, that her nonsense wouldn't save me. How could I trust her to close my eyes?

She stirred a wooden bowl of moist white powder—baking soda, for all I knew—with a wooden spoon before I dozed off.

—

I awoke in panic. Dr. Alice sat in her recliner with a fried chicken leg.

"Been squirming like a trout with a hook in its mouth," she said. The sunlight beamed through the newspapers.

"I thought I was in hell," I said.

"What is hell like?" she said.

I told her it was a forest full of basset hounds in the trees, like my dog Zinko, with the trees staring at me with eyes on their trunks and leaves chanting with lips on them. It was a canal flowing with shaving cream. Hell was an old man who set a rat on fire in a bathtub. It smelled like myrrh and grape soda.

"I'll bet it was a nightmare," she said.

"At least the fever's gone," I said. "My leg can move again. Thank you for saving me."

"My pleasure," she said. "Now, how did you end up on your back?"

I told her what I could remember, about the rocks that cut my feet to where I collapsed, about a hundred pencils stabbing my shin, and me falling to my stomach and rolling over to my back.

"You bet your ass it was a cactus," Alice said. "You ran into a cactus."

My whole left leg was scratched up and bloody to prove her right.

"I found my smartphone in one of the pockets of these pants, thank God," I said. "My phone has a flashlight to guide me through the darkness. Something shifted out there, and so I froze. And then an insect crawled into my ear."

"Oh goodness," Alice said.

Oh goodness was right.

"I saw a creature's eyes glow like marbles," I said. "Imagine having to remain still with that thing in your ear. I heard a rattlesnake rattling somewhere. There was no choice but to pick myself up in the darkness despite my leg and feet, which was idiocy. But to do anything was idiocy. At least I was able to rip the insect from my ear. The eyes disappeared, and the paws faded away. I was shaking from head to toe. The flashlight shined only about ten feet ahead of me. I looked for a road, but all I could find was the desert. The house had vanished. But anyway, if what you said was true, I paid Amy for sex, which disgusts me."

"Scout's honor," she said.

"Then something zapped me and made me fall to my back. My hands froze, feet froze, head froze into Siberia. Cold sweat rolled down my face. A sandstorm blew across me like snow flurries. The moon looked larger than the Roman Coliseum."

"You're so damn lucky I found you," Alice said.

"How can I pay you back?" I said.

"With money."

"Money?" I said. "What kind of money? Don't you shamans work for gods or something?"

Alice tossed the chicken bone for Buster to chew on. He sprang back to life. I thought about Zinko, how my poor best friend must've been suffering—if he was still alive. She sucked the grease off her fingers, wiped her hands with her shirt, picked her teeth. This was the first shaman I'd ever met and probably my last. Where was her beard, her robe, her jewelry? But what did I know when I was just a pharmacist?

"I don't believe in no gods," she said. "Now cut the crap."

I was shocked by such hostility coming from her after she'd rescued me.

The date on my smartphone said July Fourteenth. My phone was dying. If memory served me—which was failing me—I was in the middle of riding my Triumph Bonneville on the Maui Loop a month ago. That was the last thing I remembered before I blacked out and woke up in bed with my ex-girlfriend. Now I needed to get home to feed Zinko.

The credit statement on my bank app showed that I spent over fifty thousand dollars in a month on medical services. The name on my driver's license (in Utah) was William A. St. Berger.

"William A. St. Berger?" I said. "What the fuck?"

"What is it you yelling 'bout?" the shaman said. "Yes, you're William Cheeseburger, running for governor like I said."

"I'm not William," I said. "I'm Zack. What have I done to myself?"

"You're all over the dang TV, like I said. You think you're running for governor."

What did she mean? How was I in Utah? Why was I running for governor? And how did I wake up in a brothel in the desert?

"I'll get you home as soon as I get my money," she said.

Her warmth had died in exchange for greed.

"How am I sending you money?" I asked.

"Through the app," she said.

She told me to use a dating app called *Loner* where I could transfer money to other people. Lucky for me, my smartphone had it already, and I was signed in. Alice gave me her username. I transferred four hundred dollars.

The shaman counted, "Ten, nine, eight..." for the money to appear. I waited for her to accept my pay.

She slammed her fist on the arm of the recliner. "Bullshit. I saved your goddang life. And this is what I get?"

"What do you want?" I said.

"Is this what your life is worth?" she said. "You think your life is worth four hundred dollars? You think your life is spit?"

"I'm begging you," I said.

"Hell no," she said. "Oh, hell freakin' no. You better pay up what you owe me, or I'll dump your butt in them canyons. Ain't no shaman up there gonna save you."

"Okay," I said. "Name a price."

She said, "What you got?"

"You want everything?" I said.

"Keep paying 'til you satisfy me," she said.

Could barely afford to pay Alice after the damage to my account, but my status didn't matter to her. I transferred five thousand dollars, which satisfied her. The transfer left me with a little more than a one-way ticket home, and that was it. I used another app to book a plane ticket with only my smartphone and those clothes on me, minus my shoes and my wallet. I could replace everything, but all a man has in the end anyway are his memories.

—

In the late afternoon, Dr. Alice dropped me off at a two-lane road in the middle of the desert. It was blazing hot. Vultures were circling overhead. I passed nothing else but sand and telephone poles in total desolation. On my phone, an app called *Dryft* was needed to get me to the nearest airport, which was over a hundred miles away from there, she said. She'd sort of helped me out after taking almost all I had. There was no phone service out there, so I had to keep trekking back to civilization.

—

I reached the limits where the sign for Periscope City was. She was right about the town. I had service to where I could call a Dryft ride. A woman named Katherine, who picked me up near the sign, was nice enough to offer me licorice (the red kind). By then, my sweat was stinging my eyes. I drenched her backseat. Flies buzzed all around me in the car.

Katherine kept looking at me through the rearview mirror.

"You're that man," she said.

"I know," I said. "I heard all about it."

"Heard about what?" she said.

"Me on TV. Just please get me out of here."

"It's good to meet you. You're heading to the airport?"

"Yes," I said. "I have to go."

"Where were you coming from?" she said.

I told her the story all over again from what I remembered. Katherine listened to every word I said.

"I thought you were running for governor," she said.

"I'm just a pharmacist from Maui," I said.

"From Maui? How did you end up here in Utah? Are you a loner?"

Come to think of it, I was. But how did that make sense, being where I'd ended up? I just wanted my dog again.

—

She dropped me off in front of the airport in Salt Lake City. It was at night. The lights on the planes glided onto the runway.

"Hope you enjoy your flight," she said. "Ta ta."

"Goodbye," I said.

"Be sure to tip me through the app. That would be greatly appreciated."

With what money? But she deserved something for driving me all the way out there. I tipped her what I had left after the cost of the plane ticket.

Dread

to: dantheman@purplecyclops.com
from: tommysizzle@cozyblanket.com

Dan,

After ten years of estrangement, I'm writing this email. In that time, things have changed for the worse, much worse. I've explored my options in Northwest America in search of a new home.

Family is oblivious to this, but something bad, really bad, happened back in Portland. This was recently, long after you had moved away from there. One morning, around 5 a.m., before the sun came out, when I was on my way to the shipyard, I ran someone over with my pickup, the same pickup you once knew. He had to be about eighteen. With no one else on the highway, I had to decide in those long seconds what to do. Call the police or make a getaway? I decided to skip town. Now it's a regret to live with. What kind of person am I to leave like that?

Although I'd gotten away with it, the guilt has caught up with me. What friends could listen to my confession with understanding? You're the only person I can trust, but we haven't talked in about ten years. There was no way I could admit anything.

I drove to Utah and found a small town in the middle of nowhere called Periscope City. The citizens are loners who live in hotels, not houses or apartments, and they're nonconformists who skip marriage and children. I consider myself to be like them, but I've always been a little different, as you know, avoiding the norms. Maybe I'm free from what I've done, but what is actual freedom? I wish to live alone in my mental prison, away from burdening anyone else.

When I applied for citizenship in a house called the Institute, a female robot that looked like it was in its twenties, looking so human, ran a personality exam on me to see where I would conform in a nonconforming town and which hotel for me to stay at. Ironically, it was missing a personality. I scored red, which meant I was antisocial, which came as no surprise at all.

After the exam, they sat me in a recumbent chair. A laboratory expert came in and planted a couple of ear chips deep in my canals. My music played inside my brain, not my ears, but the ear chips were primarily made for tracking, to monitor my behavior.

The red people stay at the Gershwin Hotel, but because I'm color blind, they booked my room at the Bower for the disabled. I miss my balcony on the seventh floor there. It had an awesome view of downtown, but what does it matter anymore? What cures the Dread?

I only wish for peace of mind, which I found one night randomly in the dark when a line split the sky in two. It was a half-blue, half-pink sky. I listened to the crickets and the red and yellow leaves crackle under my shoes. My head tingled. I found a golf ball near the Periscope City Country Club and began bouncing it along the sidewalk. The moon was full, but best of all, the Dread was gone. Everything seemed alive until the next day when the Dread returned. I couldn't think of the right word to describe it until a kid in group therapy, about twenty-one years old, called it serenity. I thought, yes, that's the word. There was no way I could admit to the group what happened in Portland. Anyway, like I said, the serenity had come from out of nowhere. I've been chasing it ever since.

Periscope City is a mystical town. I found a tiki bar that sold patches that looked like postage stamps. You're supposed to lick one, stick it on your arm, and let chemicals seep into your pores. Memories followed, happy memories for once instead of painful ones.

Your hologram appeared of you wearing your Red Sox cap like you always did, with your soul patch still on your chin. We were sitting in Bobby's Pizzeria, where you laid your Newports on the table. A server brought a pitcher of beer and Bobby's pie. You passed me a joint. We sat in Bobby's TV room, watched a baseball game, and played cricket in the arcade. The moment lasted for only an hour, and I could afford just one patch.

Your hologram was like a candle that blew out after an hour. Those feelings and memories dissolved, much like our friendship. I guess that's nature, right? Friendships die over time, but I still love you like a brother.

It's a shame that we've parted ways and on bad terms, too. I was selfish. Now, you, as a father, ignore me, and I resent you for that.

Every day is Dread, absolute Dread. I wander through this town as a nomad. The voice in my head calls me a worthless human being. I burden myself and society like a contagion. Come near me and catch my disease. I would rather live alone with my feelings and not infect someone else.

To go along with that, rats have taken over the city because the population is too scarce. I see a plague coming. We'll get sick and die off. Except for the rich, they'll escape from the sickness and survive with the right resources.

As for the rest of us, this new technology will spread across the country. You and your child at some point will have to wear these chips. They'll track you. By the way, how's Boston?

I'm writing this in the cafeteria of the Himmler Hotel where I live now. Last week, I climbed the balcony railing at the Bower for my last view of the city from that height.

When I close my eyes, the Dread appears. It's a library with a high ceiling and no lights. It's just me in there. I can see my breath in the cold. The empty shelves go on like an endless depression.

The Institute watched me through a camera on my balcony. Cameras are planted everywhere in town. I had to jump before the firetrucks came.

My neighbor went outside and saw me. Eighty-one-year-old Barbara, in a wheelchair, lived in the suite right below me. Her balcony was filled with service cats. Everyone here has a service pet, including me and my pet lizard. Barbara watered her hibiscus plants and wore her satin robe. Her perfume smelled like bug poison. Her eyes protruded past her face.

She noticed me above her and yelled at me to come down.

Barbara's voice almost tipped me off the railing, and she woke up the whole hotel. Heads popped out from other balconies, and they started watching me. One of her calicos kept staring.

Everyone yelled at me, "Come down from there." And how could I blame them? Who wanted to watch me jump?

The pressure gave me second thoughts, so I climbed down from there, and the guests applauded. Now the Bower knows me as a jumper.

I lay in my bed and waited for the sirens to come.

Someone entered with the help of the hotel, a firefighter. She said she was proud of me for going back inside the room. I loved her smile and the folds around her mouth. For a moment, she made me forget about the Dread.

Rather than say something back, I stared at a pen on my nightstand.

She asked about my family, trying to distract me from my thoughts, but most of all, she needed my cooperation.

I asked her, "What family?"

A firetruck drove me to a hospital, where the staff put me in bed. A robot showed up and asked me questions about my childhood. After the assessment, I ended up at a psychiatric ward. The nurses took my shoes away because of my laces in case I tried to hang myself with them.

I waited in the hall at a nurse's station. The lights were out except for the one above the nurse's bald head. The walls were pale, like the skin on the patients. A patch of gum with a shoe mark on it stuck to the floor. The hall smelled like urine. A phone hung on the wall next to a digital thermometer. I blew on my hands to keep them warm.

She allowed me to make one phone call. I joked about calling my lawyer, but she didn't laugh. You were the only person I would've called, but I had too much to say after too many years. Besides, what's your phone number?

Somebody screamed from one of the rooms, probably living in his worst nightmare, and no one went to help him.

The nurse handed me water in a paper cup and made me take a pill that resembled a little coffin. It was the size of an ant, so tiny that I couldn't tell if I'd swallowed it. Not that it mattered if I took it or not. The pill did nothing to cure the Dread.

She made me sit in a chair and stay there. It felt like school detention, and I was waiting for the principal to call my mom at home—if there was a home, if there was still a mom. Even without her around anymore, I could still feel her breath behind my neck.

A patient with black toenails used the phone. His hair sprouted out like a palm tree. I thought he was insane and that no one was on the other end.

The nurse pretended I was a ghost. I felt like the gum on the floor. She told me to see the doctor.

The doctor, another robot, said I have borderline personality disorder, but how could it diagnose me so quickly? I felt criminal, which I am, but even more so now. It would monitor me. I had to quit drugs and alcohol. So, goodbye to the tiki bar, the only way to experience time with you.

The doctor asked if I still had plans. I wondered about the future and what notes it was writing. Would the notes determine where my life would end up? I lied, of course, and said no.

The staff detained me for three days. I was stuck in a flytrap of psychotic patients. The TV room smelled like biology class. The couch was full, so I stood near a foosball table. On TV was a cartoon of a baby elephant backstroking in a swimming pool. We adults and children stared off into space, on too much medication. I gazed at a shirt button on the floor, and I stood alone with Dread, thinking about the kid whom I'd killed and if he had a family. If he did, how could I ever seek forgiveness?

A patient grinned at me like he'd figured me out. It made me feel even more guilt. He said he knew, but I kept from fighting him, considering where I was. I apologized to him as if I was confessing the murder.

One of the women talked to me like a normal person would, so she didn't seem to belong there. That was until she mentioned that she lived next door to movie stars.

The bedroom I shared was with three other dudes in their early twenties, and they were all in their underwear. Their hair went past their shoulders. One dude in bed was reading a comic book with scars across his left wrist. How could anyone go out that way? The cuts would sting too much, and it would be a slow, painful death. But who was I to talk after trying to jump from seven stories?

A nurse with braids and tattoos flicked a switch. The lights went out before ten o'clock. She would check on us every hour with a flashlight.

I woke up groggy the first morning in a dreamlike state. The bathroom had no lights with a sink, a toilet, and a shower. I pressed a soap dispenser. The soap was the shampoo. There was just cold water. I stared at a drawing of an upside-down smiley face on the wall and froze with anxiety about going insane and never coming back.

Someone opened the door. When I peeked around the curtain, the bald nurse stepped into the bathroom. I yelled at her to get the fuck out, but she was just doing her job checking on me.

When I stepped out of the shower, she gave me a plastic cup and told me to pee in it. But I was too nervous to pee, so I counted each tile on the wall until a couple of drops leaked out.

After the seventy-two hours, the doctor evaluated me and decided that my suicidal ideation had left. But I had plans again after they let me go. My next attempt will come soon, when Periscope City is asleep, and it will be a different one. I'll find some other way than jumping.

The Institute transferred me to the Himmler. I could feel the eyes on me at the hotel. I mean the staff and the guests. They know me as the jumper.

The nurses are watching me 24/7. They placed me in a room with barred windows and a missing balcony. My view is a brick-and-mortar building and a barbed-wire fence. So long, downtown. So long, canyons. So long, cobbled streets. They stashed away my medications and my shoestrings and removed the locks from my doors.

A nurse checks on me every hour, and the ear chips can track me everywhere. I'll bet the Institute can read my emails. But so what? Let them read them.

Marcel Proust called life a "dreadful business." The little things distract me from the Dread, like the morning coffee and cigarette, the highlight of my day. The staff allows me to go outside, where I may smoke out front near a garden, where the guests and visitors can see me. I wish they wouldn't. After smoking it down to the filter every time, I head back to the Dread.

My illness is still there despite the pills. It only worsens every day.

I'm looking at a pepper shaker, wondering what to write next...

The server left my bill on the table. It's a female robot wearing a stained apron and slip-on shoes, tattoos from its wrists to its shoulders.

I wish I would die in my sleep. If not, maybe sit here all day, not in my hotel room, but it has turned out the lights. The cafeteria closes at noon, which sucks, and it's freezing in here.

It pulled its apron off and said it was closing.

I asked for two more minutes but it denied me. The cafeteria should stay open all the time, but there are many things I wish for that shall not come true.

Anyway, it's time to face the Dread again. Tomorrow will be today. Reach out to me if you can. That's if you'll read this email. If only the serenity would return like that one October night. Regardless, I'll always think about death, and I'll always love you, whether I'm dead or alive.

Love,

Tommy

Disposing Danielle

The brilliant director, Claude Rainier, was infamously known for firing people on the set. Anyone could be replaced, including Saturn Graham, who stayed in character as General Armbruster an entire year for the film *The General's Last War*. Everything went swimmingly until the actor, as talented as he was, got lost and veered from the script. Claude ended up casting someone else. We wondered whatever happened to Graham. He needed to do more than merely play the part.

I'd remained in character for six months as the villain in Rainier's newest film, *The Ten Faces of Dr. Cross*. It was required of me to live as Sterling Cross, to breathe as Sterling Cross, to become Sterling Cross. Claude was filming in Periscope City, a town that was new to me. I booked a room at the Gershwin Hotel, which was designed like the 1920s, where the lobby ceiling arched with paintings of cherubs and silver swans, where the staff wore maroon caps and uniforms, where a paternoster for an elevator would take me to my suite. Robots at the concierge desk kept pulling me out of character.

On the day that I checked in, I sat and waited in an armchair for the bellhop to bring my trunk, my satchel, and my garment bag. Next to me was a marble table, a glass lamp, and a lost key card. Across the room, below an oil painting of a cotton field and escalators to the sun, keeping her back straight like a whore, was a young blonde in a matching chair who crossed her legs and gave me an impish grin. I pretended she was my mistress in the script, but I had to keep my distance from her. A night with her may have sabotaged tomorrow's shoot.

A young robotic bellhop with my luggage held the paternoster open for me. The woman almost missed the ride, but I let her in the car.

"Which floor?" it asked her.

She kept her eyes on me with her impish lips. "Whichever floor he's going to," she said.

A brass dolly bunched us when we were abreast inside the paternoster. We all stayed silent. In case she recognized me as the famous actor, I ignored her to keep my British accent from slipping into my backwater twang.

A dial above our heads stopped at the Roman numeral three.

—

The bellhop held the door to my suite, room 304, and she invited herself in. I was confused. She sat on a black velvet couch and dazzled me with her green skirt, her blonde hair, and her long legs.

"Your luggage, sir?" it asked.

I cleared my throat and handed it a hundred-dollar bill.

"On the bed. Keep it off the floor, if you will. No offense to this establishment. And please hang the *Do Not Disturb* sign on the door. Thank you."

It gave me the money back. "I can only accept credit, sir."

It pulled me out of Sterling and pushed me back into Periscope City.

"What do you mean?" I said. My twang returned. "This is madness."

"You may charge it to the room," it said.

I readjusted myself and spoke British again. "Very well then. Get along now."

The bellhop closed the door for us.

The suite's balcony showed the canyons behind a sheet of rain, a stiff rainbow, and the corona during a solar eclipse. In the room, there was a plant with teeth marks on the banana leaves. I believed an insect was crawling somewhere for Sterling's collection. Good thing I had my mason jar.

My mind painted an image of the woman's corpse.

"What do you want?" I said.

She pulled out a cigarette from a metal container. "A light," she said.

She confused me even more. I was dying to smoke after an exhausting train ride across Europe—which provided me adequate transportation to see my patients.

I found a matchbox next to a stove.

"I thought you might need company," she said.

It was in my best interest to be alone and rehearse for tomorrow, but how could I resist her? "Let me light that for you," I said. "May I bother you for one?"

She opened the box, and I plucked one out.

We sat abreast and smoked in silence. The paper crackled under the drizzle when we took our drags. The grey outside wiped her face of any color. Over her left knee was a tattoo of a yellow rose that bled purple teardrops, which I found repulsive. Only libertines wore them.

She tapped her ashes to the floor and said, "I'm Danielle." Her voice turned cold. Her grinning sank to a blunted affect. I found myself sitting next to a lady different from the one in the lobby. She stared at the banana leaves instead of looking at me, withdrawn as if she'd taken a downer. I wrapped my arm around her anyway and rehearsed the scene *where Dr. Cross meets Princess on the nine o'clock train.*

"Sterling Cross."

"What do you want?" she said.

"Come again?" I said.

"A hand job is two-fifty." Her voice was even colder. "A blowjob is five hundred. Full service is a thousand, and a girlfriend experience is fifteen hundred."

Whatever that entailed, Princess was not a harlot but my mistress. Her words sounded out of character, which pulled me from the script.

"I appreciate the offer," I said. *"But I need sufficient rest for the operation tomorrow."*

"What do you do?" she said.

She surely had to be tired of asking that question.

"I am a renowned surgeon, my sweet."

"What do you do for fun?" she said.

Another dull question of hers, but I found a line I could use from the script to answer her:

"I collect insects, such as the rare scorpion in Kashmir. It is deadly, the deadliest in the world. Its name means "hidden poison," but also 'jealousy.'"

"How do you catch one?" she said.

The answer wasn't in the script, therefore I couldn't tell her. In spite of my temptations, it was in my best interest to tell her I was a married man. I showed her my wedding ring from a pawn shop in Duval County.

"I love married men," she said. Those were Princess's exact words.

What a coincidence that Sterling had an affinity for feral women. *"I will pay you,"* I said, *"but you must promise to keep this discreet."*

She placed her hand on my thigh.

I kissed the back of her hand. Her fingernails could claw my skin, and her perfume reminded me of the Polynesian Sea (where Sterling owned a house). *"I could look at you forever,"* I said.

Rather than thank me like Princess, this woman, who avoided eye contact, stared at my wallet after I pulled it out of my pocket.

I started counting my bills. *"I want companionship."*

"You can donate when I leave," she said.

Donate? Donate what?

Someone pounded on the door. It shook me further out of the script and made me irritable.

"Who the bloody hell is it?" I said.

"It's Lucas."

Lucas Chase from Philadelphia had come to my suite on the night before the shoot.

"I'll be in Room 202," she said. "Come down if you're interested."

"I most certainly will," I said.

She disappeared behind the door, and Lucas pranced right into the room. I wasn't the least bit amused to see him. He was twenty-one, half my age. His hair dangled past his shoulders, and his Roman nose was cinematic.

"Jesse Topaz from Jacksonville," he said.

He pulled me further from the script.

Lucas sat at a table near the balcony window, drunk, and pulled out a bottle of wine. "Come over. Let's play poker."

Sterling enters his office and finds his stepson sitting at his desk.

"I have an operation tomorrow with the prince. You must leave."

He popped the bottle open with a corkscrew. "I'll leave soon enough." He pulled a deck of cards from his beach shorts.

Dr. Cross vanished in a flash.

I avoided Lucas by going to the kitchen. Between my feet was a caterpillar. I grabbed the mason jar from the trunk.

Lucas's conversation distracted me from my role, some rubbish about snowboarding. As he shuffled the deck, he was too drunk to notice the King of Hearts on the floor.

—

The windows frosted by evening. The moon was yellow beneath a downpour, like the scene on page 90. I remained on the bed in my suit. *"How did you get in here?"* I asked.

Ethan Cross is slouching in his chair. "I found the key, old man."

"I suggest you clean yourself up, boy."

To play the villain role in one of Claude's films was a blessing. We're talking big festivals and if I played my cards right—no pun intended—the bloody Oscars.

I approached him at the table. *"I must impress the board and the prince. If I botch the surgery, it will destroy my reputation. Do you not agree?"*

"Are you kicking me out of here?"

He was rehearsing with me. Very well.

"My son, it's a quarter past five, and the operation is at dawn. If you will…"

"Sure thing, Sterling Cross," he said. His laughter filled the room with mockery. Afterward, he cleared his throat and, all joking aside, turned to me:

"I'll leave when it's time, Daddy. Now pour me another."

"You're acting as petulantly as when we first met."

Lucas stared off as if he'd forgotten his next line before snapping his fingers at me. *"What crawled up your ass, you persnickety old bastard?"*

"I still have to cope with you rejecting my plans."

"I hated medical school."

"You had to join the theatre instead to make a pig's ear out of it."

"I can do whatever I bloody want."

"You know my scorn for actors. They're eccentric. They're lascivious. Worst of all, they're predisposed to madness. Why, just look at what it has done to you."

"What it has done to me? I'm free. That's what. I'm free. What respect do you have for the theatre?"

"Don't misconstrue me. I appreciate the arts, especially a fine opera, but no child of mine shall be so precarious. Now pull your pants up, boy, and wipe the booze off your chin."

"Child of yours? Child of yours, you say? Not even in hell, you fraudulent fuck."

"What did you call me?"

"You heard me forthright. Just keep pretending you're my father when all you can relate to is a cadaver."

Lucas had flubbed his line, so I closed my eyes to picture the script.

Interior. Sterling's office. Night. Lightning flickers across the clenched jaws of Dr. Cross. Thunder rumbles. Rustling branches scratch the window.

"You have but one minute."

Ethan holds his glass up for an antagonizing toast. *"Another drink, old man."*

"Not only have you broken into my liquor cabinet, but you have dared insult me. You will address me as Father."

He pulls his shirt up and rubs his swollen gut. "I will address you as Dr. Bollock. To me, you're just a bloody wanker that fucks my mum."

The audacity to disrespect her. *"You have but thirty seconds before I lay my hands upon you."*

"Touch me and you're ruined. Mother will leave you forthwith when I tell her what you said. She's fucking Dr. Kochner anyway."

Booming thunder rattles my desk. Charlotte, sleeping with my colleague, has crawled into my mind. I freeze in my office but burn hot with rage. A ball of sweat drips from my nose and splatters onto my shoe.

Ethan tosses me a handkerchief. "Now wipe yourself, old man."

My stepson was being insufferable. The only way to eliminate him was by forcing him out, so I punched him in the jaw. He fell backward in his chair. The back of his head bounced off the marble. I'd knocked him unconscious. In fact, he might've been dead, so I checked his pulse at the neck.

Good gracious! What have I done? What do I do with his body? *"Ethan, wake up, young man."* Thunder burst again. It startled me. I had to hide him. But where?

In a walk-in closet next to the bathroom. I had to drag him by his feet. His arms were limp across the marble. After stuffing him inside, like what Sterling Cross did in the scene, I shut the door.

Then I noticed something peculiar. A camera with a red light blinking in the corner up above me, staring right at me.

—

The rain had stopped. The sky was once blueberry in the afternoon and the sand corn yellow. Now, as I stood on my wet balcony, in front of the dark trees and the outline of the canyons, I thought about society and how it had burdened me, wanting me to act a certain way, forcing me to pose as two different people for six months, forcing me to put up with fans, those bloody vampires calling me Jesse, not Sterling Cross. Each person challenged me. I was known as a renowned surgeon who wished to be alone, and I was better off alone.

—

When I went back into the room, Princess's perfume remained on the couch. I sat in the darkness, missing my home, my evening chair, my masala chai tea.

The phone rang. On page ninety-five, *it's the bloody philanderer Dr. Kochner after I've murdered my stepson.*

I picked the phone up on the nightstand. *"Hello, Doctor."*

"How's your stay?"

What an odd question after Dr. Kochner had called my office. "What do you mean?"

"You sound prepared."

"In the fervent process, yes."

"This is big, Jesse."

"Jesse?"

"Sorry. I meant Sterling. Just want to encourage you before tomorrow. You have earned this, baby. Remember, he chose you and only works with the ones he respects."

It was clear to me that he was referring to the prince.

"Indeed," I said.

"Don't question him, and especially don't challenge him. We both need this badly."

"No doubt he has chosen the finest surgeon in the world."

"Glad to hear that."

"Was there something else you needed?"

"I'll let you go for now. But give 'em hell tomorrow. We'll talk about it after the shoot. I mean operation."

"Duly noted." (That backstabber.)

I hung up on him.

—

Page 108. Interior. Inn. Suite. Night.
Sterling holds Princess in bed.
Princess: I want more.
Sterling: More of what?
Princess: I want my ticket to Prague.
Sterling: (whispers) You promise not to speak about our tryst?
She gives a servile nod.
Sterling: Liar. If you leave for Prague, you shall never see me again. Do you hear me?
Princess: Yes.
Sterling (VO): Since she's full of deception, so help me God, I must murder her to save my marriage. Ethan had lied about Charlotte sleeping with my colleague. But why fret about him anymore? My wife will always stay faithful. Always. As for Princess, mere gifts won't satisfy her as she wants me to herself, and she's jealous

enough to expose us. The trollop could destroy me as a doctor, could destroy me as a husband. Either I murder her tonight, or I shall perish.

Sterling: I shall enjoy you one last time.

—

Page 110. Interior. Inn. Bathroom. Night. Sterling holds her from behind in the shower stall, yanks her by her hair and cups her mouth.

Sterling: May you always be my favorite mistress.

Hot water rains down over them. A burst of steam rolls past them.

Princess (screams): Let me go.

Sterling lets go of her mouth.

Sterling: As you wish.

She tries to pull away, but Sterling grabs a fistful of her hair, with surgical gloves on, and rams her face against the tiles on the wall. Teeth fall out of her head and swirl in the bloody water down the drain. Sterling lets her go. Her body folds in the tub. He turns the shower off. Princess looks at him with vacant eyes and sneezes blood against the shower curtain.

I found myself alone in the bathroom and needed to rehearse with another person. But who? The woman, yes, the harlot. Danielle, her name was. Room 202. She could bring back Sterling.

I heard police sirens outside, coming closer *to the inn.* The police didn't show up in the script. So what was the matter?

I had my trunk and satchel with me. The trunk was full of Dr. Cross's instruments—a drill and a bone saw—and in my satchel, forceps, scissors, scalpel. Those were enough to cut up and dispose of Princess and leave her *in the trunk on the train to Prague.*

—

I stepped out into the hallway for the paternoster, which brought me down to the second floor.

—

By the time I arrived there, there was a pounding on a door coming from upstairs. "Police. Open up." The pounding continued. Just who were they looking for?

The ring on my finger tapped her door. The second floor was silent, as if it was completely empty. Someone had left a key card near my shoes, along with a set of false teeth. I waited with my trunk and satchel for her to answer.

Danielle cracked the door open, looking even more detached than the way she was in my hotel room.

"Hi," she said. "Come in."

I stepped in and turned the lock.

About the Author

Benjamin Talbot is an American author who writes mainly satire, slice-of-life, and a little speculative fiction. His debut collection of short stories, *Periscope City*, explores the different shades of loneliness, from tranquil solitude to opaque desolation. When he's not writing, Benjamin is reading mostly literary fiction, listening to '90s rock and hip-hop, going for nightly walks through downtown Palm Springs, California, and eating tacos.

Follow Benjamin at thedailyweirdness.blog.